A QUEST FOR LOVE

Barbara Donlon Bradley

A QUEST FOR LOVE
Copyright © 2019 by Barbara Donlon Bradley

ISBN: 978-1-68046-742-0

Published by Satin Romance
An Imprint of Melange Books, LLC
White Bear Lake, MN 55110
www.satinromance.com

Published in the United States of America.

Cover Design by Caroline Andrus

CHAPTER ONE

An anguished cry filled the air as Arian dropped to her knees beside her father's bed. "No, Papa, don't leave me."

The doctors, who stood around the royal bed in the spacious medics' suite, watched father and daughter silently.

"Sa, it's okay." He gave her a watery smile. "We knew the risks."

The young woman dashed at the tears spilling down her cheeks at her father's endearment. She hated this room. It smelled of illness and death. "I can't do this without you."

"You must!" He grabbed her hand, and pulled her closer, his voice barely a whisper. She hoped it was too low for the security system to pick up. "You are the only hope now. Go to Drahar. Find Dresuer. Stop this madness."

She nodded her agreement, against her better judgment. Her gaze slid to the soft blue gauze curtains that hung from the ceiling, the only spot of color in this stark white room. How could she leave her father to die while she pursued this crazy quest?

The doctors started murmuring to themselves. Several moved toward her. "Princess, we must try again."

"No." Her violet eyes glittered with unshed tears. She stood to face them. "He has been through enough. Let him be."

"But…"

"I will not stand by while you subjugate him to your cures. They make him weaker, not stronger. Leave us now. I want to spend the last few moments of my father's life with him, alone."

Although several looked at her in shock, and she heard at least one sharp intake of breath, they did as she requested.

"Why must I do this now?" Her iridescent white gown rustled as she knelt back down beside her father.

"You know how much I love that necklace."

She brushed her fingers against the small round, polished crystal that rested against her skin. Arian had gotten it as a gift from Dresuer when she lost her mother. It allowed her to have a little privacy when she was surrounded by her ever-present guards and servants. Recently she had used it to keep the general from hearing what she and her father spoke about. Touching the globe in the right places she created a small shield that would allow them to speak freely.

"Why can't this wait for the proper time of mourning to pass?"

His hand, which used to be so strong and callused from hard work, softly patted hers. With each of his movements, light glinted off the small monitors attached to him. "Sa, if you stay here, your life will be in grave danger. If you don't leave immediately, you might not have another chance."

"And how will my absence be explained? The people will think I abandoned them, and General Varal will take control anyway." Tears started to slip down her cheeks again.

He shook his head slowly, as if it took a great deal of effort. Pain etched his face. "You are going to the mountains to follow the ancient Taree. Once you fulfill the burial rites, you'll have six lunas to complete your mission."

"Six lunas, Papa, what if I fail?"

His frail hand lifted her chin. "You can't fail, Sa. Too many lives depend on your success."

Arian stood rigidly on the platform near the craft that would take her to the mountains. The arid morning air penetrated the long traveling cloak that covered her clothing. She tugged on the soft felt hood concealing her face. Everything was packed, and neatly stacked in her hover craft.

The wails of the priests lamenting the loss of their king filled the air while they watched the urn being secured in the craft.

She watched them silently. Her nerves tight with fear. If the general had any inkling of what she hoped to do, he'd kill her instantly.

One of her young hand maidens led her Miran to the platform. The young woman knelt before presenting the leash to the new queen.

Taking the supple leather strap from the girl, Arian petted the Miran's thick fur, using soft clicks and whirrs to calm its aggressive nature. The large beast settled at her feet, slowly rubbing its massive head against her calf. Arian tried not to react when its long whiskers tickled her sandaled feet.

The soft fur on the Miran's long tail wrapped itself around her leg, sending a tingling sensation all the way up her back. She rubbed under her beast's chin in response.

"Everything is ready, my Queen," said one of her attendants.

She nodded. Following the protocol for mourning, she remained silent, kept her face hidden in the hot cloak, and climbed aboard her hovercraft. With a punch of a button, she sealed herself in, and engaged the autopilot to the mountain retreat. The engines thrummed softly as it left the platform and picked up speed.

Absently, she rubbed her chin against the Miran's neck. Everything sped by as the hovercraft flew across the land. "Orla, how am I going to fulfill this vow? I have never left the palace before today. What do I know of the galaxy?"

The Miran tilted its massive head and looked at her intently. A soft shimmer surrounded the animal. In just a few moments, instead of the massive feline, sat a beautifully sculpted, tawny skinned man. Deep turquoise eyes, framed with thick raven brows that flowed up to his hairline, watched her. Thick black hair that looked more like a mane, flowed into brown, then tawny gold, with the shoulder length ends white. Full sensuous lips curved in a smile, revealing straight white teeth. Arian could see the feline in him when he smiled. His human shape, just as

3

massive as the Miran form, displayed broad shoulders, thick arms, a lean waist, and long well-muscled legs.

Arian bolted out of her chair with a gasp of surprise. Her reaction to the rare times she witnessed Orla's shape-shifting. Although her heart beat a little faster, she recovered quickly, sinking back into the chair. "I'm sorry, Orla, but, but I have never gotten use to your metamorphosis."

"Do I frighten you, Mistress?"

"N-no, of course not." He shifted so rarely, she had witnessed it only twice before. Orla had been her pet since she was an infant. Dresuer gave her the Miran as a gift the dura they were betrothed. Her pet had shared a bed, and bathed with her, but never in his human form. Seeing him as a man made her stomach do weird little flips. "It's just, well, you're unclothed."

Orla smiled at her. Another slight shift in his aura and he wore the typical clothing of the warrior caste of her planet. A heavy flap of leather covered his loins, large metal bands encompassed each well-muscled bicep. "Is this better, Mistress?"

"A warrior, Orla? How will the off-worlders react once we leave this planet?"

A low growl rumbled in his throat. "We will be the off-worlders then, Mistress."

She nibbled on the soft pad of her index finger. "I know. Yet, I don't know what to expect. How am I supposed to act? What am I going to see?"

He gave her another smile. "Spoken like a true adventurer."

The heat of a blush rose up her throat and into her cheeks. "I am curious."

"That is natural, Mistress."

She nodded. First, they had to set up their camp in the ancient caves of the Taree. Once she contacted the temple to alert them of her safe arrival, no other contact would be made until she completed her time of mourning. "Father cleared the path for us to get off the planet. After that, we are on our own."

"Mistress, I mean no disrespect, but General Varal could have learned about your father's plan."

Arian sighed. "You're right of course. So how are we going to get off this planet?"

"I am your older brother, escorting you to your wedding on Drahar."

"But it is so simple!"

"Exactly. General Varal will be looking for something your father could have planned, or some elaborate cover-up. Who will question a brother and sister from a small farm on their way to a wedding?"

She leaped out of her chair and hugged him. "That is perfect."

Orla was glad he had set up everything the last time he had gone off on his own. He knew her father was ill and spent his last time traveling to set up several scenarios for them to use. Varal wouldn't find them easily.

What he didn't understand was why her father never explained who Dresuer was to her. It was a title, not a person. The man knew why he had been given to Arian as a cub after the betrothal. He had questioned his father and hers, trying to figure out why no one had told her the truth. Neither gave him an answer that satisfied him. All he knew was it was to protect her. Something he agreed with. She needed to be protected at all costs.

Arian found movement very difficult in her wedding attire. The large headdress with a veil to conceal her face was cumbersome and hot.

"Do I have to wear this now?" she whispered.

"If you don't want to be recognized, you do," Orla mumbled back.

A huge throng of people slipped by them as they stepped up to the transportation desk together. The buzzing of voices made Arian want to clap her hands over her ears. Too much noise and too many people made her shrink back into her clothing. The small black desk they stood in front of looked lost in the massive corridor filled with people traveling to other planets or friends and relatives awaiting the arrival of travelers from landing ships.

Arian wanted to stop and gape about, but knew she had to continue with their façade. As they stepped up to the desk her nose started to itch, but she couldn't scratch. With a sigh she kept her hands at her sides. She hoped this would be over soon.

"I am Norlor." Orla bowed at the waist, as was tradition when anyone introduced themselves. "My sister's future husband awaits us on Drahar."

The burly guard stared at them from his seat behind the small black desk. He checked their papers before looking back up and studying them a little longer. Then he nodded, clearing them for boarding.

They remained silent until they settled into their room. Arian sat the small crystal sphere that she had retrieved from her necklace on the floor near the door. Depressing a small button on the top, she activated the shield. Resting her fingers in two grooves in the side of the sphere activated the dampening field and the motion detector. Now they would know if someone tried to approach their room and they could have a conversation without fear of some system picking anything up.

They climbed into their appointed bunks and waited for lift off.

A soft sigh escaped Arian's lips when she felt the pull of the G forces as the ship accelerated, lifting away from the gravitational pull of the planet. "Okay, so, we've gotten this far."

"General Varal could have men aboard, following us, Mistress," came his voice from the bunk below hers.

"Orla, you can be quite depressing."

"No Mistress, just realistic," his voice floated up.

A soft smile spread across her face as she stared at the bulkhead above her. Let him be realistic, protecting her was part of his job. Even with the danger they were in, she was excited about this adventure. "So what happens next?"

"We go to Drahar and find the man we need."

Arian noticed an odd sound in his voice. He did want to help her, didn't he? She rose from her bunk and looked at him. "And just how do we go about doing this? I have no clue what Dresuer looks like, where to find him, if he'll honor the marriage contract, or if he will help me with my cause."

Orla rolled to his side, propping his head in one hand, and watched her. "Mistress, your father knew what he was doing. We will find him."

"Do you know where his camp is now?" She turned to look at him.

"I am Miran, I know where Dresuer is at all times." He sat up. "I will escort you to him."

She nodded. Her faith in him strong.

A loud beep filled the air.

Arian started.

"That is the dinner bell, Mistress. If we want to eat, we must head to the dining hall now."

"I'm not very hungry right now."

"There will be nothing again for twelve horas."

Her violet eyes widened. That would be a long time without food. She hadn't eaten since the dura before. She picked up her headdress. "Perhaps it would be a good idea to have dinner."

Orla bowed before escorting her into the corridor. They mingled with the rest of the passengers heading toward the galley. Arian had never been around this many people. She shrank back a little at the throng around her.

"Ignore the crowd," Orla whispered in her ear, gripping her elbow. "Take deep breaths and imagine we're walking in the palace garden."

She took three deep breaths, trying to gain control of her fear. Strength flowed up from his contact with her elbow, allowing her to see the crowd differently. They no longer frightened her, making her fear that she'd be crushed. Arian looked up at Orla in gratitude.

He nodded ever so slightly.

They stepped through the door way and were led along a white tiled wall. One person pushed a tray filled with food into their hands.

Arian almost dropped hers when a sudden strong stench reached her nose.

"It is not the food," came a whisper from behind her. She glanced quickly to Orla.

He nodded to the alien in front of her.

Her grip tightened on her tray. Once Orla took the lead, she followed him to a small table.

She eyed her food dubiously. "Are you sure it was that alien?"

"I'm sure." Orla chuckled. "The food might not be that pleasing to the eye, but it has a pleasant smell, and I promise it tastes much better than it looks."

"Then you have had this fare before?"

"Many times."

Gingerly she stuck her fork into the grey glob in front of her. Saying a small prayer to her Gods, she closed her eyes, slipped the fork inside the opening near her throat and took a bite. A gasp escaped her lips at the delightful flavor that exploded in her mouth.

Orla placed a restraining hand on her arm. "Remember, most of the commoners has eaten this many times. We must fit in."

She nodded as she ate quietly. Just as she put the last bite in her mouth the bell sounded again. She glanced at Orla for an explanation.

"It is time for the next group to eat." He stood.

Arian did the same. The gentle pressure of his hand on the small of her back guided her back to their quarters. She breathed a sigh of relief once they were safely in their room again.

Several horas later, Arian sat cross-legged on Orla's bunk, brushing her hair as they set plans for to find Dresuer. "What will my disguise be once we have left the city?"

"You will then be a trader. My partner and wife." Orla watched her face from where he leaned against the bulk head on the opposite side of the room.

The brush stopped in mid-stroke. "Your wife?" The heat of a slight blush crept into her cheeks.

"It will be the safest way to travel. Unless you want to disguise yourself as a man."

"A man?" Silence filled the small room as she nibbled on her index finger, contemplating the idea. "How would I do that?"

"We would have to hide your feminine form. Binding normally works for that."

"Binding?" Her brow furrowed. "What would you—oh." Her blush deepened.

"General Varal wouldn't be looking for two male travelers."

"You're right, of course." She continued to brush her hair for two more heartbeats before asking. "Will it hurt?"

Orla's brow arched in a question.

"The binding?"

His shoulders shrugged slightly. "It might be uncomfortable for you." She stared at him as she continued to brush her hair.

"And you'll have to cut your hair."

Her eyes widened in horror as she ran her fingers through the silky silver tresses. "I can't cut my hair."

"It would be safer."

"No," she said a little too forcefully. "My hair must remain intact."

A loud thunk vibrated the entire ship.

"What was that?"

A loud chime sounded, followed by a soft click of the door lock being activated.

"Citizens. Remain in your room. By the order of General Varal each citizen will show their boarding pass. There is a stowaway aboard ship."

Orla growled at the announcement. "It looks like the general has found us, Mistress."

CHAPTER TWO

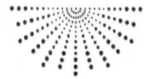

Arian sat rigidly on the edge of the bed. Fear overpowered her. "How?"

"No time for questions, Mistress. We must prepare." Orla moved to the door. "You must remove the dampening field."

Spurred into action, she knelt in front of the device and pressed the keys to deactivate it. After she palmed it, she slid it back into her necklace, hoping the guards wouldn't notice it when they came to their room.

"Now, sit back down and finish brushing your hair," said Orla. He resumed his place against the wall.

Microns ticked slowly by as they stared at each other in fearful anticipation. They waited for the door to slide open.

"When?"

Orla slashed the air in front of him, silencing her quickly. Without the damping field anyone could hear their conversation.

Arian set the brush down on the bed and clasped her hands. Her mind turned inward, as she had been taught by her mother, to create the outward appearance of calm she needed to live through the next hora. Her breathing slowed, as did her heart rate as she commanded her mind to develop the harmony between body and mind so that she could control her fear.

Stray thoughts invaded as she tried to use the exercises she had been taught. If only she could change her appearance so that she couldn't be recognized. Her silver hair color shone like a beacon, telling anyone who understood that she was a daughter of a Barou. The race of imagers. Her heritage had not manifested itself yet, so this wondrous heritage couldn't protect her. If it would, she would have nothing to fear. Only another Barou would be able to see through her creation.

She focused her attention, blocking out everything but her goal of peace. When she opened her eyes again it was to the chime of the door. In a quick movement, she hid her hair with the veil of her wedding outfit.

The door slid open to reveal two guards. "Pass," one of them ordered.

Orla handed their cards over without a word.

After glancing at the information, the guard, who held their passes, glanced up. "You are to marry?"

Arian nodded.

He then looked at Orla. "And you are her brother?"

Orla just stared back. "Yes."

He studied their information again.

Arian glanced at Orla nervously. Why were they still in the room? Didn't everything check out?

"Remove your veil."

"Wh-what?" asked Arian.

The guard raised his blaster. "I never repeat myself."

Arian swallowed hard. It wasn't unusual for a bride-to-be to wear her headdress until the day of the wedding. These men had to know that. She also knew fighting them wouldn't help their cause. Her hands shook as she reached up and pulled the veil off her hair. General Varal had won before she could even begin her quest.

Orla held his breath as the veil lifted. His body prepared to pounce. He blinked twice, hoping what he saw wasn't a mirage. Brown hair fell loosely about Arian's shoulders.

"Have you seen a woman with silver hair aboard this ship?" the guard asked as he handed back their passes.

"No." Orla moved to stand next to Arian. "Is she dangerous?"

"Very. If you do see her, report it immediately. General Varal will reward you handsomely if you do. It would be large enough to present a sizable dowry to her husband," he said as he put his blaster back in its holster.

Orla nodded.

The door slid closed just as Arian sagged against him. "How?"

Orla gently lifted her necklace, causing the pendant to swing to and fro.

Arian pulled out the orb and reactivated it. She spun on him and questioned again. "How?"

"You." Orla slipped one arm behind her shoulders and another under her knees. Lifting her, he brought her toward the closest reflective surface, the bulkhead above their beds. "Look at the color of your hair."

He watched as her eyes widened when she stared at her reflection.

She turned her head toward Orla and held up a clump of her hair. "It's brown."

"Yes."

Her laughter filled the air as she hugged him. She slid down out of his arms as she continued to laugh. "Finally, my heritage has manifested itself."

Without thought or care she pressed her lips to his in a quick kiss. The warmth of the innocent kiss spread through her body like lightening fire. She pulled back abruptly. "I'm sorry, Orla. That was very forward of me."

He didn't answer. A strange light emanated from his eyes. One she had never seen before. He lifted a finger and pressed it against her full lips. The tender touch of his finger against her mouth sent a shiver down her spine. The gleam in his eyes made her stomach tighten.

"Your hair has changed back," Orla said softly. He picked up a few strands and lifted them in front of her eyes.

Arian stepped back and smoothed her hair down. She didn't understand why her heart beat so erratically.

Orla still stood rooted to the spot. Was he angry with her for overstepping her boundaries? Her father had warned her that she must respect the wants and desires of other people, and by the way Orla was reacting she had upset him.

"I didn't mean to kiss you," she said, looking at the floor. "Please forgive me."

She didn't realize Orla had stepped close until she felt the heat of his body near hers. His hand gently lifted her chin until she had to look in his eyes.

The look he gave her was feral. She felt the heat start at her toes and flow up her body. Arian swallowed with difficulty. Why was he watching her like that?

His thumb rested gently against her throat. His eyes shifted from her eyes to her lips and back again.

Her lips parted in silent invitation.

When Orla's lips claimed hers, she felt her heart-rate triple. She grabbed his arms as an anchor against her weakening knees. A small gasp escaped her as he increased the pressure against her lips.

Orla wrapped his arms around her, drawing her closer to his body as he deepened the kiss. At first, she froze in his arms when his tongue touched hers, but the slight brushes of his tongue made her insides melt. Soon, she responded to the new sensations by brushing hers against his, joining in the dance he had set for them. Her body started to react oddly to what Orla's tongue did to hers. She could feel her nipples start to tighten, causing an ache she didn't know how to get rid of.

Orla slipped his hand behind her head and angled it to give him better access. His lips, soft against hers, slanted, drawing her with him. Her heart pounded in her chest. A soft mew escaped her lips.

When Orla broke the kiss she felt bereft. She wanted more.

The feral look in his eyes was even stronger. "I meant to kiss you."

—————

Three duras later, they stepped off the loading dock on the planet Cuckra. Arian wore her wedding attire once again, Orla gently gripped her arm as they waited for their personal items to be unloaded.

"The next ship to Drahar will be in four duras," said the gentleman who cleared them through the dock. "There are several inns locally that you can find rooms in, if you haven't already had accommodations set for you."

"Thanks be to you. We hope to see a little of this wondrous planet while we wait for our flight. How far is Faltama?"

"About a duras travel. If you go, see that gentleman right there. He will help with transportation."

"My thanks." Orla bowed at the waist. Cupping Arian's elbow, he guided her toward the center of the bustling village.

"Why did you tell him we wanted to visit Faltama? Isn't that where all the pleasure seekers go?"

"As a precaution." Orla spoke softly and kept a smile on his face as they passed merchants trying to catch their eye to show their wares. "If the general suspected you were on that transport, then this place is probably crawling with his troops. He suspects you left your world, and this is the closest planet."

Arian couldn't stop the shudder those words evoked.

"If he decides to track everyone from our flight, he will look for us in Faltama," Orla whispered as he maneuvered them through the throng of merchants.

"And where are we going?"

Orla gave her a smile that made her insides feel all fluttery. "I thought going to that tavern would be our first stop."

Arian's eyes widened at the sight of the small run-down building at the end of the short lane they had just entered. Loud music and boisterous voices spilled out of the opened doorway.

Orla stopped and swung her around to look into her eyes, even though the veil hid her face from others it had a small space where the material was see-through so she could see where she was going. "No one will harm you, Mistress. This I promise."

She searched his face for a few securs before nodding her assent. He tucked her hand into the crook of his elbow and led her toward the tavern.

As much as she wanted to, Arian didn't cover her ears against the noise when they entered the building. Her fear, a palpable thing, kept her body rigid. She felt like she would snap like a twig if someone brushed against her.

Orla led her toward the back of the establishment where he had spied an empty table. Hailing the young woman who brought food and drinks to the patrons, he ordered them both an ale and whatever the special of the dura was.

Once the steaming plates had been placed in front of them Orla urged her to eat. "We might not have another decent meal for a while."

Arian pushed her food around on her plate, trying to figure out what it was. Why didn't any of the fare she was forced to eat look like the food she had at home? The swaying mass seemed to be alive. After separating a small morsel from the large glob, she picked it up with her utensil and lifted it toward her mouth.

"It will not bite you," murmured Orla.

She looked at her food warily. "Are you sure?"

He chuckled as he ate his meal.

She held her breath as she finally put the food in her mouth. Again, she was surprised at the explosion of flavors that burst in her mouth. Her eyes closed at the ecstasy she felt from the taste of whatever she had just eaten. After eating about half of her meal she realized that her throat started to feel dry and reached for the liquid Orla had ordered.

Arian watched several others as they drank the same beverage. They literally gulped their drinks down. Slipping it beneath her veil, she lifted it to her lips, and swallowed as much as she could before slamming the tankard down, sloshing her drink all over her hand. Somewhere deep inside her, she knew she had made a mistake. The liquid burned all the way down her throat, then threatened to come right back up. She couldn't breathe. Beads of sweat popped out on her forehead. Her hands started to flutter, as if their movement would allow air back into her lungs.

Orla must have realized her dilemma because he pounded on her back three times, hard. It startled her enough to finally suck air into her lungs. The sound that came out of her as she expelled air mortified her. It was loud and deep, sounding more like the bray of a truggar than any noise a small woman should make. She tried to stop it by clasping her hands over her mouth, but the sound continued until it had finally spent itself out.

Laughter filled the air as other patrons heard her.

She frowned at Orla's lopsided smile. Just looking at him struggling to keep a straight face fueled her shame, and her anger.

"I don't see what is so funny." Orla tried to look innocent as she spoke.

"You might not want to take such a big gulp of your ale in the future." He sat his cup down. "It can have an adverse effect for the beginner."

"You mean like, like that noise?" She had never burped like that before.

Orla nodded, still fighting the smile that threatened to take over. "It is an alcoholic beverage, Mistress, something you are not use to. I would have ordered you something else, but I didn't want to bring unwanted attention to us. I should have cautioned you before you started to drink."

"I was only doing what everyone else did."

"I know." He placed his hand on top of hers. "From now on sip your drinks, and any drinks we have off world. Your body isn't used to the types of beverages we will be consuming during our travels."

"And how is your body accustomed? You have been on my planet as long as I have," she said softly.

"Except for my hunting forays. I was gone for several cycles at a time. That was when I would travel, sometimes home to see my family, or to learn about the surrounding planets."

"You didn't trust the general from the beginning, did you?" she asked.

"No, Mistress. I didn't."

"Then you have passed through this area many times."

"A few." Orla picked up his drink again.

"Did you ever visit Faltama?" Arian didn't know why she asked the question because a part of her really didn't want to know the answer.

Orla just smiled at her.

Arian remained silent as she continued to eat the rest of her meal. Any drink she took was very small. She refused to take any chances. Orla truly confused her now. He wasn't the quiet pet with whom she had grown up. Who obeyed her every whim. Instead she found a man sitting across from her. A very attractive virile man who knew so much more of the galaxy than she did.

Everything he'd done and said since they started on this quest proved he could be a great leader. If so, why had he stayed with her all this time? The question was on the tip of her tongue when a shaggy little man leaped up on the table and sat down.

"So, you return," he said.

"Yes," said Orla as he pushed his plate away. He signaled the server once again. Quickly, new drinks plunked down on the table.

Arian crinkled her nose at the offending odor that attacked her. She had never smelled anything so foul.

"It is not safe now. Goons are everywhere." The little man picked up his drink.

Her eyes widened when she realized the odor came from the little man who sat next to her plate. Appetite gone, she slid her plate away from her as well. Picking up her drink, she buried her nose in the leather cup. The grainy fragrance of the drink was better than what assailed her nose at this point.

"They don't frighten me." Orla leaned back in his chair, watching the little man.

The little man hurumped as he drained his glass dry. "You wish to travel to Drahar again? It will cost triple."

"You try my patience, little man." Orla folded his arms across his massive chest.

"No." He shook in fear as Orla stared him down. "Pilots will not travel. They fear being boarded by General Varal's soldiers. We must entice them."

"And how much do you gain from this transaction?" Orla picked up the huge knife that accompanied his meal and proceeded to clean his nails with it.

"Hardly anything. I swear, Master."

Arian noted the frown that passed over Orla's face when the smelly little man called him master. She wondered why.

"I need a pilot I can trust, little man, and you are going to find one because you will be traveling with us as well."

"Me?" he squawked. "Oh, no, Tymin doesn't leave this place, ever."

"You will now." Orla started to shift the knife through his fingers.

She watched as the light danced against the metal as he quickly sifted it from finger to finger. He knew how to handle the small blade.

Tymin's eyes widened in fear and he sputtered. "Yes, of course. I will start looking for a pilot tomorrow."

"Now."

"Yes, of course," he repeated as he scampered off the table and headed toward the door. "I will not let you down, Master."

Once the smelly little man had left, Orla turned toward her. "Are you ready to go?"

She nodded vigorously. She had been ready to leave the moment she entered the place. "Where to now?"

"We follow Tymin."

"Don't you trust him?"

"Would you?" He gestured for her to go through the door first.

"Trust is a commodity we don't have right now," she said as she inhaled fresh air for the first time in what seemed like forever. It tasted so sweet she had to inhale deeply several times to rid the tavern air from her lungs.

"Exactly." Orla crouched down toward the dirt in front of the door and studied it for a few securs before standing back up. "Our quarry headed in that direction," he said as he pointed to the south.

"But to the south is only desert," exclaimed Arian.

"And our flight to Drahar."

CHAPTER THREE

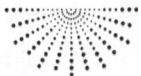

Orla led her to a small tent a few streets up from the tavern. Arian found the bright red tent a bit obtrusive against the drab brown buildings nearby, but it did catch the eye.

"We wish to rent a ride," Orla said loudly.

A very rotund man stepped out into the bright sunlight. "I don't rent, my friend, I sell."

The first thought that popped into Arian's head is that the man's green robe could have been a tent too. She squashed a laugh before it started.

"Not even for a few horas? My sister has never ridden a truggar." Orla gestured toward her, his beige sleeve fluttered with his movement.

Arian wondered why Orla didn't just buy the animals. She clasped her hands in front of her, waiting to see what he was up to.

"Then buy her one and she will be able to ride it whenever she wants." He scratched his big belly.

Orla turned toward Arian for just a few securs, acting as if he spoke to her quietly. The look he gave her made her realize that he wanted her to say something.

"It's okay, Norlor," she sighed, going along with him. "It was a wonderful idea, but I know we don't have the money to buy one."

"It would make a nice gift to your betrothed," commented Orla.

A soft frown flickered across her brow as she tried to figure out what he was trying to do. Keeping in character, she touched his arm and spoke. "We couldn't possibly add an animal to our traveling chip. It would cost too much."

"You're right." Orla looked at the man glumly. He turned around and motioned for her to follow him.

"Wait," said the owner. "I could sell you an animal for a reduced rate, then when you prepare to leave here you could sell it back to me."

"For the same amount of money?" asked Arian.

"For a little less. I have to make a profit you know."

Arian glanced at Orla.

"How much?" he asked the owner.

"Three cycle credits."

Arian's eyes widened. Three cycles of wages? No wonder Orla was trying to rent the animals. That was too much. Just as she was about to answer, Orla placed his hand on her arm.

"We'll need two animals."

"Then is it six cycle credits."

"Two," countered Orla.

The rotund man started to laugh. "Two? Are you trying to rob me?"

"It is all we can afford."

"Five and no less."

Orla shrugged. "Oh well, perhaps we can try that man over there. He seems to have a lot of truggars, I'm sure his fees will be lower."

"Four. Four and I'll throw in a cycles worth of feed."

"Three, plus the cycles worth of feed," countered Orla.

"But Norlor, we don't need a cycles worth of feed," Arian said. "Let's just go speak to the other truggar salesman you just mentioned. He seems like a nice enough fellow."

"Two and a half, and the feed, plus riding gear."

"Done," said Orla. As he stepped up to pay the man, he spoke to Arian over his shoulder. "Go pick out two sturdy ones, sister. And make sure they have all their teeth."

She shot him a glare as she did as he asked. His comment confused her since he knew she had studied animal husbandry. As she wove her way through the herd, she dismissed one after another, noticing small flaws, new wounds, and age marks in their fur. Toward the back of the corral the owner had set up, she found two magnificent truggars. Tall shaggy beasts, with wide backs that stored water for dry weather and barren areas. They were the perfect age for long rides without tiring, and by the looks of their body size they could travel at great speeds without tiring too. She stopped a few feet away from the animals and called them to her with a warble that sounded close to the call the animals made.

The male started to move first. He stood proud, his head reaching her shoulder. His long, furred head butted her hand.

A smile slipped across her soft lips as she started to rub its shaggy head. The second animal, a female, snuck up to her and butted her other hand. Her smile widened as she rubbed both of them, their unique scents filling her, allowing her to recognize them anywhere.

"Come, let's see how upset your old master will be when he finds out that I have picked the best of his herd."

The docile animals followed behind her, a small short warble emanating from them both as they approached the owner.

"You can't have those two."

"But they were the only ones who would let me near them," she complained. "The rest were just so rude."

She knew as well as he did that once the animals picked their new owner, they would follow their master anywhere, no matter what this fat little salesman tried to do to keep them in his herd. The bond had already happened and there was nothing he could do about it.

"Then I will have to ask for more."

"The transaction has been completed," said Orla as he placed the harness seat on his truggar, then secured it. Once he finished with his he turned to Arian's and did the same thing. "Besides, we will be selling them back to you."

The man frowned but nodded in agreement. "How long are you planning to keep the animals?"

"Haven't really decided yet," said Orla. He attached several sacks of grain for the truggars to the back of the seats, and their small packs behind the grain. "My sister is to be married on Drahar by the harvest moon."

He helped Arian into her seat, then mounted his truggar.

"But that is four lunas from now! They will be worthless to me by then."

Orla urged his mount forward before the man had a chance to think about it and try to stop them. His laughter rang as they sprang away.

The soft cream tunic and leggings hugged her body as she rode behind Orla's truggar. Arian was grateful to be out of her wedding attire. At least she could ride in comfort now. Orla still wore the soft ecru colored outfit he had worn since they left her planet.

Her truggar kept pace with Orla's as he followed the tracks of Tymin. How he found anything to follow was beyond her, she hadn't noticed anything that showed the little man's passage through here.

Her mind drifted back to the strange feelings that had started to affect her when Orla kissed her earlier. Although Orla had never mentioned the kiss, and acted as if it had never happened, it evoked emotions she didn't quite understand. Even now, after riding for several horas in the baking heat, she felt a shiver race down her spine as she remembered it.

She had never felt anything like that. Was that what it would be like to kiss Dresuer? Would he make her insides melt like soft foomage too? A sweet that could be poured over the local fruits to enhance the fruit's flavor.

Arian shook her head. These were thoughts she shouldn't be having now. She had to find Dresuer and she had to fulfill the promise their fathers had made to each other. Her planet was at stake. Yet, she couldn't keep her mind off the sensations she felt when Orla kissed her.

She didn't realize she had fallen so far behind until Orla reined in his truggar and started back toward her.

"Are you feeling tired, Mistress?"

"No." She looked into his deep turquoise eyes and felt her heart do a little flip. The heat of the dura was nothing compared to the heat she felt from his look.

"Perhaps we should stop for a while."

"We don't have to do that. I was just so deep in thought that I didn't realize I had slowed down."

"Are you sure?" His eyes searched her face.

"Yes." Using gentle pressure against the flanks of her truggar with her heels, she urged him to go faster. "I can keep up."

Orla nodded as he rode beside her.

"So Tymin has traveled this far on foot?" she asked, hoping to prove she felt fine.

"He has a small beast he owns. That's the tracks we follow now."

"Oh." What could he possibly be riding that could out run truggars, which are the fastest animals on this planet? "When do you think we will catch up with him?"

"Not until we reach Rolnem." Orla pulled a small cloth from a hidden pocket and wiped it across his face.

Her brow furrowed as she stared around at the empty horizon. "Where is that?"

"It's about a dura from here."

"Surely–"

"We aren't trying to overtake him, Mistress. We're following him to see if he can contact the people he promised to."

She nodded although she didn't really understand. Why follow the little man? Wouldn't traveling with him be better? It would be for her. Having another person around would keep her thoughts from veering back to Orla and that kiss.

A sigh escaped her as she kept up the pace Orla set for them. They traveled another two horas before Orla recommended that they stop and rest for a while.

"Won't Tymin continue to get farther ahead of us if we stop now?"

"Tymin is just over the next rise, resting as well. I don't want to spook him." Orla slipped off his mount, opened one of the sacks of grain and offered a handful to his truggar.

"How do you know this?" she asked as she dismounted and offered food to her mount as well. Its soft mouth tickled her palm as it ate from her hand. She could hear the crunching and popping of the grain as it chewed.

Orla touched his nose and smiled.

Arian remembered the foul odor that emanated from the little man. Orla's sensitive nose could smell him from a very long distance. "I'm glad I don't have the senses you do. His smell made me nauseous when he was in the tavern with us, if I could smell him this far away I think I'd be deathly ill."

"You'd get used to the hyper senses if you lived with them all your life. And not all things are as offending as he is."

"True. Father's garden is wonderful in the mornings when the wind blows just right. I bet you could smell it even when I couldn't."

"There are a lot of scents that I can pick up that might amaze you."

The electrifying glow in his eyes made her wonder what he was hinting at. That look penetrated deep inside her, causing her heart rate to pick up and dragged her thoughts back to the kiss. She felt flustered and uncertain. Breaking eye contact, she fussed with her truggar, combing her fingers through its thick hair.

"You are growing quite attached to that animal, aren't you?" asked Orla.

She smiled ruefully, rubbing her posterior. "In more ways than one."

Orla placed one hand on her shoulder. Within securs her pain faded.

"Thank you, Orla." She smiled at him. "You have spoiled me with that particular talent."

"I would take all your pain away if I could, Mistress."

"There are certain pains I must live with right now. The survival of my planet depends on it. If you could take that pain away, I wouldn't feel the urgency to stop General Varal before he destroys everything my family has built."

"When did you get so wise?"

"The dura my father died."

Orla was grateful she didn't ask what other things he could pick up or he would have to tell her he could smell her arousal. Her confusion was a strong scent too. She had learned about sex, he was with her all the time so learned what she did, but she had also been trained to keep her virginity. As a princess she was worth more with her virginity. The kiss they shared had started a fire in her. He knew because he started it on purpose.

Arian was going to fight her attraction to him because of her promise to her father. Why she hadn't put two and two together yet was maddening but he was going to push her until all she could think of was him and her desire for him.

CHAPTER FOUR

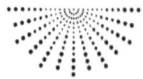

They caught up with Tymin in the small village of Breham. He stood, rooted to the ground, as a tall thin man shouted at him in a language Arian didn't recognize.

"What is going on?" asked Arian.

"It seems that Tymin has been found by one of his creditors."

"You understand the language?"

Orla smiled as he nodded. "You would too if he didn't use so many explicatives."

Tymin noticed them then and raced to Orla's side. "Master, he refuses to take you, unless I pay what I owe him."

"And he said that he would if you did?"

The thin man walked up to Orla and Arian. "We have no love for General Varal. He has cheated my captain too many times."

"How?" asked Arian. The general couldn't have gained power this far from her planet, could he? Was he planning on taking over the whole quadrant?

"That, little lady, is none of your business. Let's just say that any of the general's enemies are our friends."

"How much does Tymin owe you?" asked Orla.

"One hundred cycle credits."

Arian heard her own sharp intake of breath at that amount of money, but she couldn't help herself. That kind of money could feed a small family for over a yepa.

Tymin tried to slink off, but Orla grabbed him by the scruff of the neck. "How did he come to owe you so much?"

"He hired my captain to transport six women to Faltama, unfortunately, he forgot to inform us that they were stolen from the Pasat. When the leader demanded restitution, we had to pay."

"And Tymin refused to reimburse you," finished Orla.

Arian wondered how they could possibly repay such a high debt when Orla spoke again.

"I will pay his debt, but your captain must get us to Drahar safely first. If we are boarded by General Varal's men, I will kill you both before they get a chance to kill me."

"Thank you, Master."

"Don't thank me, Tymin, you will repay me for that money. One way or another."

The first thought that popped into Arian's head was if Tymin would just take a bath she'd call the debt paid in full.

"But Master."

"Consider yourself my servant until I think you have repaid me. All your profits will be mine, and you will now travel with us to Drahar." Orla let go of Tymin's neck. "The first thing you must do, little man, is take a bath."

"I took a bath six months ago."

"It smells like it too. A bath. Now." As Orla turned his attention toward the thin man, he added one more thing. "And use soap and water."

"Sand has always worked best before." Tymin walked toward a bathing area, his head hung in dejected misery.

"If you will pay me now, we can negotiate the fee to Drahar."

Orla remained quiet for a few moments. "The money is on Drahar, where my family lives. If you will transport us there, I will pay you two hundred cycle credits."

"Sorry, but my captain has made it a rule to get payment first." The thin man turned to leave.

"Even if I told you that I could make it worth your while?"

He stopped and looked at Orla. "How?"

"By convincing the council that your captain should be our exclusive barterer. You would get the first chance to bring in items from other parts of the galaxy and transport ours off our world."

"And just how would you go about doing that? Who are you?"

Orla didn't answer the man but showed him something Arian couldn't see. Whatever it was convinced the man immediately. Arian watched him hurry off to make preparations for departure.

"We have three horas before we leave," Orla said as he rejoined her.

"I don't think that is enough time," she commented. She wanted to ask what had convinced their new pilot to agree to transport them, but she knew if Orla wanted her to know he would volunteer the information.

"Why?"

"Because it's going to take a cycle to get Tymin clean enough for me to tolerate his smell in a closed environment like a ship."

Orla laughed. "Let's go see how Tymin is doing."

"And make sure that he doesn't disappear on you?"

"Exactly."

Arian and Orla went through the decontamination chamber, clearing it in about thirty securs. Tymin had to remain in the chamber for five microns before the computer cleared him to enter the ship proper.

"Crude machine," he spat as he finally entered the room where Arian and Orla waited for him.

"If you had cleaned yourself properly, as I requested, you wouldn't have been in there as long," said Orla. He stood up from the chair he sat in and motioned for Arian and Tymin to follow. "The captain has requested we meet him in the galley."

"How far is Drahar, Orla?"

"Three duras travel, if all goes well."

She knew what that meant. Hopefully, General Varal lost them when they landed on Cuckra, but her instincts told her that he would continue to search until he found her, and there was nowhere to run if he captured this ship.

They entered the galley to find the captain and his first mate already sitting at the large table in the center of the room.

The captain spoke first. "I guess I should introduce myself. My name is Grinnell. This is my first mate Leabo."

"I am Orla."

The captain blinked once, but didn't react in any other way, yet Arian felt some strange undercurrent. Did he know Orla?

She realized they waited patiently for her to introduce herself. "Arian."

"The Queen Arian?"

She glanced at Orla, not knowing what to say. His ever so slight nod prompted her to answer. "Yes."

Grinnell and Leabo both knelt in front of her.

Their respect humbled her. She placed a hand on each man's shoulder.

They in turn placed one of their hands on hers.

"We came from your world, my Queen. When we heard of the King's passing it was a dark time for us all."

Arian bit back a sob. He father's death had devastated her. Without his guidance in her life she didn't think she could fulfill the quest she was being forced to follow.

"My father would have been very proud to know both of you. How is it you're here, instead of on Emorai?"

"General Varal. He had conscripted pilots for mining expeditions on the third moon of our planet."

"But father had denied his request to mine that moon." She remembered when the General had approached her father, and the anger that threatened to boil over when her father said no. "The ore on that moon was what kept our planet safe from meteor showers. It worked as a natural magnet, repelling any debris that threatened to enter our atmosphere."

"I'm sorry, my Queen, but he has been mining it for the last two years."

"What can that ore be used for that makes him need it so badly?"

"Ship hulls," answered Orla.

Arian didn't like this at all. What was the General trying to do? She stepped back from the two men still kneeling at her feet. "Please gentleman, stand up. I need access to your computer."

"Of course," said Grinnell. "You may use the terminal on the bridge."

Arian nodded as she followed him. She slid into the seat he directed her to, and after a few microns she found all of the news releases on her home planet, and General Varal. He had been plundering some of the smaller planets pretty regularly, attacking any ship that slipped into their territory, slowly expanding that section of space until he had control of more than thirty percent of the galaxy.

The information coming from her planet was sketchy, but one thing glared out at her. The royal family had been painted in a very bad light. According to the records, her father had basically turned his back on his people, indulging in the mythological.

Anger gripped her. Her father wasn't into any myths. Several articles about the living conditions on her planet appalled her. She swiveled toward Grinnell. "Is this true?"

Grinnell approached the screen to read the data she had pulled up. He nodded sadly.

"How can that be? Father and I went to visit the towns regularly, we never saw any of the poverty. The reports we received showed that the people were living in prosperity." Her mind reeled at the implications. If the reports on the people were altered, then what about the treasury? She could change the conditions of the people easily by using the planet treasury, but if there was no money then she would end up just as destitute as her people. The hardest question reared its ugly head. How was she going to fix this?

She wondered if her father knew about this somehow. He had hinted as much when he urged her to go and find Dresuer. *'Go to Drahar. Find Dresuer. Stop this madness.'*

Tears welled up in her eyes. The lies propagated by General Varal had to stop. As much as she wanted to be discreet about finding Dresuer, she knew that she must also give her people hope. They deserved to know that she was trying to save them.

A gentle hand touched her shoulder. "My Queen."

She turned her tear-filled eyes toward Grinnell. "I don't deserve that title, not after learning the truth. My name is Arian."

"But–"

"Until I can resume my throne in honor, I'm in exile, my title stripped from me."

"Yes, Ma'am."

"I wish to rest now."

"Of course, my–, ma'am. Please follow me." He led her through a small maze of corridors. "We only have two cabins that are available right now. Leabo and I are bunking together so that you three can have a place to sleep."

"Where is Orla and Tymin?" As much as the thought of sharing a room with Tymin distressed her, she nodded her head in solemn thanks. She needed a little time to collect her thoughts.

"I believe Leabo is giving them a few light duties to help us run the ship."

"Once I have rested, I wish to help also."

He looked like he would refuse her, before he smiled reluctantly. "Come to the bridge when you are ready." Grinnell programed her hand print into the door keying mechanism.

"Try it now," he recommended.

She pressed her palm against the smooth surface, and the door slid open. The small room would be crowded with three people, she thought as she closed the panel and sank onto the closest bed.

The tears she had held back for so long slid down her cheek. How could this have happened? When did they lose touch with reality? All this time she thought her people were happy and healthy, not starving and homeless. What must her people think of her?

The tears continued as she wallowed in self-pity for a few more microns. Shaking her head, she stood up.

"This will never do," she said as she wiped the tears away. "I am their queen and I have to start acting like one."

She stood up and headed to the lavatory. Using the sanitizer, she cleaned her face in front of the mirror that hung there. Her reflection stared back at her. Hot angry sparks glittered in her eyes. Anger toward the general and herself. She should have known. There was always something about the general that make her leery. If she had trusted her instincts...what? Would she have been able to stop him?

Then? No, but now she knew what she had to do.

"Grinnell, what kind of armament do you have on this ship?" Arian had taken a few horas to calm down after what she had learned.

"Top of the line. I stole this prototype from the General about three lunas ago."

"Then he is searching for you as much as he is searching for me."

"Yes, but he'll never find us, Arian. I can promise you that."

Orla looked up from the weapons station, his eyes narrowed as they questioned her silently.

"But I want him to find us. How about its engine capacity?" Arian couldn't let him stop her now. This was something she knew she had to do.

"We could probably outrun and out maneuver his ships within two or three microns."

"We must be able to do that. Can you guarantee it?"

Grinnell and Leabo exchanged glances. "Yes, ma'am. We can."

"Good." She pulled on the hem of her tunic as she put her thoughts into words. "The General tried to hide the truth from me, but it didn't work. I still found out. Now the people must find out the truth as well."

Orla hadn't interrupted yet, but he might when he heard what she wanted to do.

"I want the people to know that I do care, and that I am trying to do what I can to free them. They need to know they can trust me. Rely on me. Believe in me. And the first person I must start with is General Varal."

"What are you planning?" Orla asked. His voice soft.

"To tell the truth," she responded, looking directly at him. "And when the general finds us, to face him as I should. I can't run and hide anymore."

"You can't just walk up to him and ask him to change his ways."

"I know that, Orla, but I can do the unexpected. I am going to marry the man my father betrothed me too. I am honoring his last wishes and hope to fulfill his dreams of the future, and I want the whole galaxy to know about it. I want to see it on every com channel, hear it in passing as I walk through a small town."

"And make you such a celebrity that the General can't touch you," Orla said. His smile expressing his pride at how she devised such an elegant yet simple plan.

"Exactly."

"So, what is the next step?" asked Grinnell.

"Why, go find the general, of course."

CHAPTER FIVE

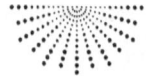

"Do you think that's wise?" asked Leabo.

"No." Orla stood up from the weapons station. "The general will come after us soon enough. We don't need to go and look for him."

"Orla, he wouldn't expect me to seek him out." Now she had to convince everyone why her decision was sound.

"That is true, Mistress, but your goal is to find Dresuer before the general can find you. This would be foolhardy. If you make yourself too much of a target, Dresuer might refuse to wed you."

She hadn't thought about that.

"We could start rumors," offered Tymin. He didn't continue when four pairs of eyes stared at him in shock.

"What type of rumors?" Orla demanded.

Tymin pulled at his hair. "People seeing the Queen here and there. Tidbits of information about her search for her betrothed. How she escaped the planet."

"That would work," Grinnell said. "And it would probably have the general searching so hard for us we wouldn't have to go look for him."

Arian had to agree. She knew time was of the essence to save her planet, and she needed to handle this wisely, but her anger toward the general for what he had done to her people wanted justification now, regardless of the consequences.

"I know the right people to contact," said Tymin. "They spread the information around like wild fire."

"Proceed," said Arian.

She sat and listened while Tymin contacted several traders on Cuckra. To some he spoke of the Queen of Emoran and her immediate arrival, to others he spoke as if she had already come and gone. Each person got just a piece of the information that they wanted to get out.

"Now we wait and see how long it takes to get into the news coms," said Orla.

"And how much of the original story remains intact," said Grinnell as he programed the ship to intercept any communiques on Queen Arian.

"Why would you be so pigheaded to want to chase down your enemy?" Orla ran his fingers through his hair in exasperation. They stood in the small quarters that he and Arian shared with Tymin.

"After what I learned? Knowing what he has been doing to the planet, and my people? You must ask that? Since when have I ever shied away from my duties?" Arian watched as his fingers sifted through the dark black tresses at the top, then down to the white tips, remembering the gentle caress of his hands when he kissed her. A quick blush bloomed on her cheeks at the thought.

"Of course not, but you have never been faced with anything remotely close to this dangerous situation."

"Can I ask you something, Orla? What would you do in my situation?"

His mesmerizing gaze captured hers. "The same thing, but there is a difference between us."

"I hope you aren't going to say that a man is better equipped to handle danger than a woman." She crossed her arms over her ample bosom.

"No, Mistress." A slow scintillating smile slid across his face. "I was going to say that I have been in enough dangerous situations that I would never go looking for them. They would find me."

That smile distracted her, keeping her from concentrating. It took a few microns for the words to sink in. "And it would be on your terms."

His smile widened. "Now you understand."

"My father taught me how to be a strategist. You even complimented me on it when we played Goltris."

"Goltris is just a game, Mistress. You are a great strategist, but you have never been in the heat of a real battle. You have never seen the best laid plans go wrong. I would wish to save you from that."

Arian stepped up to him and placed her hand on his cheek, and watched his eyes deepen into a honeyed color before returning to their normal turquoise tone. She wondered what caused the reaction but didn't have the nerve to ask him. "He is destroying the world I grew up on, the people I am supposed to protect. My heart and my mind want to stop him, now. I know you are right. I must wait and watch, then pick the battle that can do the most damage to the general when he loses it."

"How do you know he will lose?" Orla asked quietly.

"Because I will fight him until my last breath. And if he kills me then I'll haunt him from my grave."

Orla smiled at her passionate retort. Such a beautiful response. Naive, but heart felt. If only she knew how easily it could come down to that. General Varal wanted her planet. He had grand plans that included the whole galaxy and one little girl wouldn't stop him. The general would probably look at Arian as a pesky fly, swatting at her until she went away, or he crushed her.

His smile faded as determination set in. The general would die before he laid a finger on Arian. Orla would kill him first.

About a cycle later General Varal heard the first of the rumors about Arian. His demands had been curt and to the point. He wanted her found and brought back home.

But his men couldn't find that little slip of a girl. How could she evade him so easily? Who was helping her?

He growled as another communique about Queen Arian filled his screen.

Queen Arian has been greeted with open arms on the planet Cuckra. Throngs of people were there to meet her, giving gifts and well wishes.

The Queen informed this reporter that she is searching for her betrothed. Although she does know he is on Drahar, her father passed away before she could learn the exact location of her fiancé.

In other news, General Varal...

Varal pulled his blaster out of the holster and fired at the screen. Sparks shot out from the damaged video device, showering the floor. One loud pop, followed by a series of smaller ones filled the area as the screen continued to disintegrate.

"Captain," he shouted, turning away from the fried mess of metal and wires.

The man he spoke to entered the room and saluted. "Yes, General."

"Prepare one of our best ships. We're going to Drahar. I have someone I must pay a visit to."

"At once, sir."

Varal smiled. Arian might have won this small battle, but soon he'd have control of her again. All he needed to do was speak to the man betrothed to Arian. The man owed him a favor, and now it was time to call that favor in.

Arian sat in her chair on the bridge, staring at the blank screen in shock. She couldn't believe her ears. While everyone was celebrating their good fortune of the info hitting the major communique system so fast, she felt resentment.

"That reporter lied," Arian mumbled.

Orla turned toward her, waiting for her to say more.

"She never met me. How could she lie like that?" A frown creased her forehead. "How many other lies do these people tell?"

"Everyone knows that the news is always a partial truth. They embellish to make it more appealing. The information there was intact. We got what we wanted out of it," said Leabo. "Isn't that what you wanted?"

"I think Arian is upset because of the way the information was related. She has never tolerated lying," said Orla. His mind sensed a coiled tension in her, not because of the lie, but the fact that she had always believed what she had heard in the news before, and now she was learning first hand that a lot of what she heard could have been false. Her faith in people was very shaky right now, and this didn't help.

He moved toward her but stopped when she backed away.

"Mistress." He spoke softly, so only Arian could hear him. "This is not something to fear."

"I am not afraid." She brushed past him.

Grinnell, Leabo and Tymin stopped speaking when they heard her remark. Each knew that the rest of this conversation should be held privately, so after mumbling an excuse, they left the bridge. Their respect for what Arian was trying to do heightened their loyalty, and their understanding of her sheltered life before this point caused them to give her the much-needed privacy to work out these new bits of information without fear of embarrassment. There was much for her to learn, and they were thankful that the chore to instruct her fell onto Orla's shoulders. None of them would relish the job.

"Then why did you ask about how many other lies they have told?" Orla asked quietly.

She spun around to face him. "I remember the information I heard about the people on my planet. That they lived a wonderful carefree life. All lies. That the general was a good kindhearted leader of our troops. Hah! He had my father killed."

"How can you be sure?"

"Because the doctors refused to do an autopsy. They continued to pump those drugs into my father, even after I issued a decree to stop them. But they wouldn't." Her voice cracked. "He died because I trusted them. I believed they could make him well. It wasn't until it was too late that I figured out the truth. That they were killing him."

Orla stepped toward her again, but this time she didn't move. He pulled her into his embrace, allowing her to release the grief she had kept bottled up so long.

"If you must blame someone, blame the general. He is the one who is behind all of this. If your father was poisoned, the general probably issued the order. But know this Mistress, it is not your fault."

Arian turned violet tear-filled eyes up toward him.

"Your father didn't realize what was happening to him either, until it was too late." Orla gently wiped a tear that slid down her cheek. "And he was one of the wisest men I knew."

The look of sadness tore at his heart.

"Your father would be very proud of you right now." Orla paused long enough for his words to sink in.

Arian gave him a tentative smile. "He would, wouldn't he?"

Orla smiled back at her and nodded. His fingers took on a life of their own, softly grazing her bottom lip. Arian's sharp intake of breath let him know she was as affected as he from the simple gesture.

After their first powerful kiss, Orla had wanted to taste her lips again, but on the tiny ship there was no privacy. Now he had the chance. Slowly, he dipped his head toward her, giving her ample time to stop him if she wanted to. Arian didn't. Her grip on him tightened in anticipation.

He brushed his lips against hers, knowing it would be just as powerful as the first time. Her mouth opened under his, giving him access to joys he found in their last kiss. His embrace changed, from a protective one to a passionate one. Her body fit against his like second skin. By the planets she felt good in his arms.

His lips slanted against hers, his tongue delved into the recesses of her mouth, starting the dance between their tongues once again. The taste of her branded itself in his brain. He would never forget her taste, her scent, the feel of her body in his arms.

Her hand rested against his heart. He wondered if she could tell how hard it pounded in his chest, how much this simple kiss affected him. Desire raced through his veins, threatening to consume him and her in a white-hot flame.

Arian's soft mew filled the air between them, breaking through his consciousness and drowning out the roar of his blood in his ears. He felt the tremor that raced through her body.

He could take her right now and she wouldn't stop him, but he needed her to want it as much as he did. It had to be mutual. He needed to continue to seduce her.

Orla sensed someone outside the door just before it opened. The soft whoosh of air escaping mingled with their rapid breathing. Orla switched his hold on Arian's back to a protective embrace as he quickly broke the kiss. He didn't want anyone misunderstanding the tentative bond developing between them. If there was a spy amongst them this could be very damaging.

He smelled Tymin just before he entered the bridge. No matter how many baths the little man took the stench didn't go away.

"I'm sorry, Master. I mean no disrespect. I forgot something." He cast a furtive glance to the chair he had sat in.

Orla noticed the silver spoon resting on one corner. Tymin picked up that spoon when they had first eaten on the ship and had kept it like some talisman. He skirted around the room, keeping as much distance as he could between him and Orla as he hurried toward his spoon. Once he held it in his hand he smiled, then raced back out of the bridge.

Arian stepped out of his embrace the moment Tymin fled the room. She stared at him, unconsciously touching her fingers to her now swollen lips, before bolting out of the same door Tymin had crossed through securs before.

Arian felt like a fool for running from Orla, but she needed to think. She should have stopped the kiss before it started, but the desire to feel the things she did with the first kiss overruled any propriety she might have exercised. She had to see if her body's reaction the first time had been a fluke, based on the tension they had felt from escaping the general or maybe part of her over active imagination, but this time she knew it was for real. The fantasies that plagued her lately were based in reality, not some daydream she was having.

What was she going to do about it? Her blossoming attraction to Orla wasn't in her planet's best interest. She had to find Dresuer. With his backing she could defeat General Varal. But was that a good reason to marry? Her parents' marriage had been arranged like hers, but it turned into a love match for them. That was what she wanted. Her fear though, was that she was falling in love with Orla. How could she marry a man to help her save her planet when she was in love with another?

What did she know about love anyway. Perhaps this was just an infatuation. That had to be it. Her whole life had been turned upside down. It would make perfect sense that she'd latch onto the one thing in her life that was still there. She would act like nothing happened between them. That would be the safest thing she could do. Besides, Orla was probably just humoring her. He knew what her destiny was as well as she, and knew she had to find Dresuer. She couldn't believe that he would do anything to jeopardize that, unless he was the spy and was trying to distract her from her original goal.

She flounced unto her small bunk. Too many questions and no answers. If she dwelt on it too hard, she would go mad. Arian needed to center herself. Crossing her legs and placing her opened palms up on her knees she closed her eyes and cleared her mind. Now would be a good time to focus her energy on trying to control her Barou heritage.

She created a mental picture of her truggar. Flexing her muscles she deepened her thoughts to their smell, and the feel of their fur as she rode them. The rhythmic way they walked. A tingling started in her back as her body felt like it expanded and contracted to the shape of the animal. Unbidden, the memory of Orla's kiss entered her mind, shattering the exercise she tried to do.

She growled in frustration. Then stopped. Growled? She jumped up off the bed and looked at herself in the mirror. Turning her face this way and that, she didn't see anything on her body that had changed. The growl must have been her imagination.

Knowing she needed to keep busy, she decided that she should get back to her duties on the bridge. If Orla was still there she would act as if nothing had happened between them. Just like he had after their first kiss.

She stepped out into the hallway and headed toward the bridge. Something soft twitched behind her, but when she turned to see what it was she found nothing.

"It must be my overactive imagination," she said to herself.

Entering the bridge, she headed for her seat.

All conversation stopped.

Arian felt the flush of heat spread up her neck and into her face. Did everyone know about the kiss already? As she turned to confront them, she felt the same twitching sensation she felt before.

All of her nerves stood up on end. Something was wrong.

She felt the slight sensation again just as Orla whispered from behind her. "Don't look now, Mistress, but you have a tail."

CHAPTER SIX

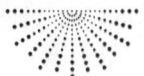

"A tail?" she squeaked.

"It is a very pretty tail," commented Leabo.

The heat in her face heightened. Since she couldn't see the stupid thing she had to ask. "What kind?"

"Um, I'm not sure." Leabo blushed at his own words.

Arian closed her eyes. Here she was, a leader of a planet, a Barou on top of that, who couldn't control her disguising abilities.

Orla still hovered nearby. She knew this because her body was on full alert. His essence called to her like a siren.

"I recognize the tail, Mistress," he breathed softly in her ear. "It is a Miran."

She wanted to hide under the table in mortification. Her last thoughts were of Orla and their kiss. Just by seeing the tail he had to know what she was thinking. So much for remaining aloof. Now she wished it would just disappear.

Trying to act dignified, she sat in her chair, carefully avoiding sitting on her newly acquired tail. Even though she had her back to them she could feel their gaze. And why wouldn't they stare? How often do they see a humanoid sprout a tail?

"I'm very flattered, Mistress," Orla said as he propped his hip against her console.

"It was an accident," she snapped. Her embarrassment running so high she didn't care how she sounded. She was mortified. Orla had to know why that tail manifested.

"Considering you have no control over your powers right now, I think that shows remarkable talent. Just like your hair on the ship."

She sniffed as she considered his words. He was right. Normally the first time the Barou talent showed itself the manifestation was something small, like changing the color of a flower. Being able to change your physical appearance didn't happen until yepas of training, yet she had done it from the very beginning.

"Well, why did it have to show itself in this way?" she whispered.

"Perhaps because of what you were thinking." His devilish smile lit up his face.

Arian ducked her head. He did know.

Orla slipped his hand under her chin and lifted it so he could look into her eyes. "Don't be embarrassed, Mistress. It's already faded."

"For now, but I wonder what else will happen until I learn to control this." She also wondered how she could learn to control her abilities while they were hiding from Varal.

"I'm sure it will be entertaining," Orla commented mischievously as he went back to his station.

"Indeed, and at my expense," she murmured.

"There is a ship heading our way," said Leabo. He depressed several keys on the console in front of him so everyone could see what he found.

"How far away is it?" asked Grinnell.

"About twenty-five clicks. At the rate they're moving they could intercept us in just a few horas."

Orla frowned as he studied the screen. "That doesn't give us much time. What if it's one of the general's ships?"

"If it is, we're in trouble. This ship is considered stolen," said Grinnell.

"Can't you disguise the ship?" asked Arian.

"Yeah, except we can't alter the beacon. The encryption is so complex we haven't been able to break it."

"Perhaps I should take a look at it," said Orla. "I've got a little talent with puzzles."

"This isn't a simple puzzle," Leabo explained. "The cap'n has a degree in logistics, and codes, and he couldn't decipher the encryption."

Orla just gave them a cat-like smile. "Would it hurt to let me try?"

"No," said Grinnell. "Perhaps you will have success where I failed. Leabo, give him the information."

Leabo nodded as he downloaded the information to Orla's console.

Arian smiled. If anyone could break that code, Orla could. She remembered when he shut down the palace's defenses. It started off as a game, to see if he really could do it. The computer system was the top of the line. No one should have been able to break into it, but Orla did. When he did, he also set it so it couldn't be reactivated again without using his code words. And those codes were still in the defense computer. No one had been able to wipe it out, even after shutting down the system, wiping the memory and reloading it.

How? No one knew. They couldn't figure out if it came from outside the system, or inside. The signature to tell them which terminal had been used was missing, yet they couldn't find any evidence that someone had hacked into the computer system from another location.

Although angry, her father was so impressed he let it stand. No one had ever tried to rid the computer of Orla's code after that. Her father also demanded that security continue to investigate until they figured out how it had been done. Four lunas went by before her father called her into his chambers. A small scrap of evidence, a security video, had been found to say she was the culprit. All the tape really revealed was that she had been at a terminal at the time the code had been activated.

Arian couldn't tell her father that Orla had done it, since no one knew he could shape-shift, and she had been standing in front of the camera to hide Orla as he hacked into the computer, so she took the blame.

Her father was angry, but not angry enough to miss the point that the saboteur had to be very talented, so he put his daughter through extensive classes in computer science. Since Orla accompanied her everywhere, he watched and learned as she studied. In fact, it was with his help she had passed her courses with high marks.

She hoped it was giving General Varal as much trouble as it gave her father. He deserved it.

As the ship drew closer, the tension heightened on the ship.

"It is one of General Varal's ships," said Leabo. "The beacon says it's from the royal family."

"That's my father's personal ship," she gasped as she recognized the beacon. "How dare he!"

Orla stepped up behind her and rested his hands on her upper arms.

Normally, his touch could sooth her, but not this time. This time her anger was a living thing inside her.

"Mistress."

"Allow me this, Orla." She shook off his hold. Meeting his comforting gaze with her angry one. "This anger allows me to keep my goal in focus."

"And that goal is?"

"You know my goal. Why do you ask this?"

He placed his hands on her shoulders. "Because I worry that you're confusing your goal with revenge. What is your goal, Mistress?"

A sigh escaped her as she closed her eyes. Once again, he was right. "My goal is to save my planet."

"And your revenge?"

"To stop the general." She opened her eyes and met his gaze.

"Never confuse the two, Mistress." Orla smiled. He wanted to be sure she knew the difference and her answer told him she did. "The danger comes when you forget they are separate."

She nodded.

A loud beep startled her, making her jump.

Orla returned to his seat. Punching a series of buttons to access the information Leabo downloaded to him. He stared at the encryption. Making small changes here and there as he found and altered the data. Finally, he sat back.

"Now what?" asked Leabo.

"We wait. Maintain speed and continue your course. Let's not give them any reason to chase us," said Orla.

They waited another hora before the interstellar com link buzzed.

Leabo stared at his consol. "We are being hailed."

"Answer it," said Orla as he took his seat once again. He pressed several buttons to make sure he did his job properly.

"Vessel 8247694 identify yourself," said a voice through the link.

Orla released the identification beacon.

"Garbage scow, Moth. What is your destination?"

Grinnell turned to him in surprise. "Garbage scow?"

Orla ignored him as he pressed a few more buttons. A small moon orbiting Drahar popped up on the screen.

"And your cargo?"

Bio-hazard waste showed up on the screen.

Orla smiled when the ship turned away from them. He had picked the one thing he knew would keep them from boarding.

Grinnell let out a loud whoop and then laughed. "Orla, you are one amazing man. How did you do that so quickly? If they had been in viewing range, they would have known this wasn't a garbage scow."

Arian smiled. Orla's ability didn't surprise her at all. In fact, his brilliance made her heart skip a beat. She didn't understand these odd feelings she was developing toward Orla, but she knew she couldn't stop them, especially when he did things like this.

While everyone else celebrated their good fortune, she remained in her seat, thinking about her blossoming feelings for Orla.

Orla noticed Arian sitting by herself. He hoped the teasing hadn't upset her. It wasn't something she was used to so she could have taken it personally. She was staring off as if she could see something no one else could.

"Mistress?" he spoke softly as he knelt beside her.

She turned to look at him. Shifting in her seat Arian turned towards him. Her face told him everything. Arian wasn't thinking about the men teasing her, she was worried about why it was a miran tail. She could have manifested anything, but she didn't. She had been thinking about him.

"Perhaps you'd like to walk and talk?"

She looked at the other men and nodded.

Orla noticed she kept her gaze averted, afraid to look him in the eyes. He took her hand in his. "Are you upset about your manifestation?"

"No, not really." She looked up at him for a moment. "The fact that it was a large apparition shows the strength of my ability. My mom said her first creation was changing the color of a glass of wine. My studies had told me it is normally something small."

"So your tail, which looked perfect by the way, was something most could only create with training."

"Yes. But I haven't been trained. I have no control. My talent seems to be powered by emotion."

Like their kiss. The clues where there. Her cheeks were flushed and the scent she gave off was the same one when he kissed her.

They had walked to the small galley. Arian wrinkled her nose when she caught a whiff of Tymin. "How do you stand it?"

"I try to surround me with scents I want to inhale." He looked over at her. "Like the sweet scent that emanates from your skin."

The color heightened in her cheeks. "I have a scent?"

"Yes, it is beautiful. Your essence calls out to me. When I'm near you it wraps around me and blocks anything else." He lifted her hand to his mouth and kissed it. "It's addictive for me."

"Really?" She was surprised.

He found them in front of their room. Pressing his palm against the panel he opened the door and gestured for her to step in. "We have been together all our lives. I've been with you when you felt joy and when your heart was breaking. Each emotion has a particular scent. They are home to me. I know it's you when I smell them."

"But I bathe as often as I can."

He laughed as he guided her to the lower bunk and sat beside her. "This is different. It is your scent, your essence. It doesn't go away when you bathe. Tymin might smell bad but I'd know him if he was the cleanest man in the galaxy because of his essence."

"What does it smell like?" Her question was so innocent.

"I'm not sure I can describe it to you properly, but I might be able to show you?"

"Really?"

"Yes, but it might make you uncomfortable."

"Why?"

"Because I'm going to touch you to try to show you how I detect your essence. How it makes me feel."

She looked at him with such trust. "We touch all the time, how is this different?"

How indeed. "Because this will go deeper than the casual touch we share. You know how you feel when my tail wraps around your waist."

She nodded. A light blush filling her cheeks when she realized he knew as well.

"This will feel so much better, but I need to be able to touch your skin." He started drawing soft circles against her hands, sliding them up her arms and beneath the sleeves of her tunic.

"So you want me to undress." She said it like a statement even though he knew she was asking a question.

"Yes, Mistress." He took her hand in his. "And it could change our relationship."

"I know what you are asking, but I promised to save myself for Drusuer."

"I'm not asking you to give yourself to me, Mistress. That is something you must offer freely. Just know that I will always be there for you. No matter what." He brushed his fingers against her cheek. "I'm your protector."

"And my best friend."

"Yes." He smiled at her. She was his world and hoped he was hers, she just didn't know it yet.

"What am I to do?"

"Enjoy."

She hesitated for only a moment before removing her clothes and laying on the bed they had been sitting on. He dimmed the lights while she disrobed to help her feel more comfortable.

She was beautiful. The lower light gave her body soft shadows as well as highlights. He knew if he stared too long, she would lose her nerve so he started immediately. He spoke softly to her.

"When we were children I always knew where you were. I'd hear that beautiful laughter of yours. There was a scent that reminded me of sunshine and laughter, your laughter, and I knew where to find you by following that." He brushed his fingers along the inside of her arms, soft feather like touches to relax her. "Your mother had a unique scent too."

"What did she smell like to you?"

"Her scent reminded me of comfort. When we were small and had taken our baths the towels she used to dry us off were soft and fluffy."

"She had such a pretty smile."

"You have that same smile." He brushed his fingers across her stomach.

"Her hugs were the best." Arian lifted one arm above her head as she became languid. "What did Varal smell like to you?"

"I don't want to talk about that right now, Mistress. That would ruin the moment and I don't want that for you." He kept his voice soft, his hands still gliding across her skin. "Let's focus on you instead."

"Me?"

"Yes." He shifted his touch to her collar bone. "Did you know that different emotions have different scents? Like when you're relaxed, like now."

"Really?" her voice came out soft.

"Yes. It reminds me of warm days next to the pond near the palace. The heat of the sun on our skin and the smell of the water and plant life surrounding the pond."

"I loved going there."

He did too. That was when he heard her laughter the most. A beautiful melodic sound that shook him to the core. He continued to touch her, soft brushes against her body. He slid his hands from her collar to her rib cage.

"Then there is excitement, like when your parents took you to the winter palace. It was just the four of us. You had your family to yourself and you loved it."

"That is one of my fondest memories. Mom baked, and we ate."

"That's what my senses remember. The scent of your parents and the food. And of course your laughter. There was such joy in the air." He brushed the underside of her breasts and along her hips. "I can still smell the food and the love."

A tear escaped her left eye and he pressed his lips to her skin to take the tear into his body.

"That was the last time I spent time with my mom."

"I know. Your sadness is a fragrance I don't like." He moved his hands, drawing a sigh from her as he changed her mood from sadness to a relaxed state again. Quick little circles across her flesh relaxed her, making her languid once more. "What I like to see is you happy. The scent makes me smile."

One particular brush made her laugh.

"There is a new scent I've noticed recently."

"Me not bathing enough," she joked.

"Arousal." He slid the soft tips of his fingers on the inside of her thighs. Arian sucked in her breath. "It's something new and something that I'm drawn to."

She shifted her legs, showing he was making her nervous.

"I became aware of it when I kissed you the first time." His fingers brushed across her lips. "So soft, like velvet to me, and so sweet. A rare nectar I find myself craving."

Her wide violet eyes stared up at him. The kiss had the same effect on her. He could tell by her scent and the way she looked at him. His finger slid down her throat to her collar bone, then he boldly brushed a finger pad across one of her taut nipples. She closed her eyes as the sensations he caused filled her.

He smiled as he moved his hands lower. They danced across her hips, up her thighs, his finger brushed against the soft hair on her mound. She reacted with a small tremor. He started drawing small circles against her, drawing closer and closer to her core. Her legs shifted, but she didn't stop him as he slipped his fingers into her folds.

Arian felt the delightful little shivers racking her body as Orla caressed her. She had pleasured herself before, but this was different. He knew where to touch her to make her body hum. She wanted more but wasn't sure how to ask. Then he slipped a finger inside her to gather moisture then started caressing her once again. When he did that her body clenched. She instinctively grabbed his hand and urged his fingers back inside her.

He smiled his sexy heart melting smile when he complied.

Her body shook at the pleasure. She lifted her hips as the pressure inside her mounted. The beginnings of her orgasm started to snake around her. It started in her core, then the heat spread out into her stomach, and continued to fill different parts of her body until it enveloped her. Arian's world melted as her climax took her over.

The next dura Arian stared into the mirror in the room she shared with Orla and Tymen. She and Orla had sat and talked after she had dressed. He hadn't asked her to reciprocate. He said that he only wanted her to know what her essence smelled like and she had to admit she did. Just as she orgasmed, he whispered in her ear.

"Can you detect it, Mistress? That faint musk scent? That is you. That is what I detect every time I'm near you."

And he was right. Their relationship changed at that moment. Their close friendship went deeper now. They talked about the chance that her marriage could be loveless and that she saw it as the only way to save her people. He was proud she wanted to stand by her decision anyway. He promised her then he would stand beside her no matter what happened. He would protect her until his dying breath. He wanted her happy and he wanted her to find love.

Three duras later, the planet Drahar loomed on the screen. Arian stared at it in awe. The large green planet looked so different to her small violet one. Huge mountains jutted up into the atmosphere. Large oceans filled three-fourths of the planet. Some of the land was obscured by light green clouds. Those same clouds hovered around the base of all the mountains.

Her heart ached to see her homeworld again.

Grinnell contacted a small landing port on the north side of the planet. Once he received clearance, he started their decent.

Within an hora they felt the soft thud of the landing gear contacting the soil. The captain shut the ship down, then disembarked.

Grinnell and Leabo stood at the hatch opening, helping Arian then Tymin out of the ship.

"Are you sure you don't want us to go with you?" asked Grinnell.

Leabo led their truggars through the cargo hatch.

Orla shook his head. "We need you here. The general can't be trusted, and we don't know how deeply he has infiltrated the galaxy. We'll need a quick getaway if he has a strong influence here." He glanced at the little man standing beside him. "Keep an eye on Tymin. He has a tendency to wander off when he's not supposed to."

Grinnell nodded.

Tymin looked hurt. He scurried around the truggar Orla saddled for Arian. "Master, I want to go with you."

"You can't, Tymin. I have a special mission for you. I need you to find out what you can about the general's visit. We need to know who he has in his pocket on this planet. Visit the surrounding towns and see what you can find out," Orla said as he saddled his own next.

"Yes, Master. Tymin can find out that for you. No problem."

"Good." After checking to make sure both saddles were secure, he turned to Arian. "Are you ready, Mistress?"

Arian had donned her royal robe at Orla's urging. She smoothed the front of the gown in a nervous gesture before meeting his eyes. "Yes."

"Then let's be off." He offered her his hand.

She placed her hand in his and let him help her up onto her truggar. The simple touch had her wanting him to touch her the way he did the other night. But now she wasn't embarrassed by her thoughts. She knew by his smile he knew what she wanted and wished the same thing. Arian smiled back and focused on the task at hand.

Orla shook out his reins, which started the truggar walking.

"Why did you want me to wear this robe, Orla? I don't understand. I thought we wanted to keep my arrival a secret." She urged her mount to follow his.

"Your robe won't stand out that much here. The lavender color is a common one, and the gold embroidery isn't much different than some of the clothing you'll see." Orla continued down the path, away from the ship. "You're still wearing your traveling clothes underneath?"

"Yes. Although, I don't know why. This heat is making me very uncomfortable."

"You only have to wear it for a short while. We will be passing through a small village in an hora. You can remove it after we leave the village. If they don't react to your robe, then I'll know it's safe."

"Why?"

"It would mean that they haven't heard about you yet. I know they have no communique there, so the only way they would know about you is by other people telling them. That robe is the same hue and cut of ruling family's. They should just assume that you are a member of that family and ignore us."

"And if they do react to my presence?"

"Then we'll know that the general has been here, and we can trust no one."

CHAPTER SEVEN

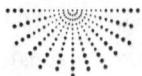

Arian sat, perched up top her truggar like a stiff piece of wood, fearing that someone would recognize her and run to the general with the news. She didn't realize how silly she must look until Orla leaned over and whispered. "You look like you could break into a thousand pieces any micron."

She relaxed in her saddle and gave him a sheepish smile. "Sorry."

He patted her hand.

The small village bustled with people. Shops were set up along the main road, selling trinkets, fresh vegetables, breads, leather goods and other items the people needed.

When no one stopped and stared at them as they passed through, Arian relaxed a little more. She would have liked to stop and look around, but Orla kept a steady pace to the edge of town.

Just before they reached the edge of the little village an elderly man stepped out in front of them.

"Where are you going?"

Orla stared down at him in surprise as he fought to calm his truggar. The man appeared out of nowhere, startling their animals.

"We are traveling to the Priesat compound."

"You must turn around."

"Why?" asked Arian.

"It isn't safe out there now. You are welcome to stay here as long as you like, but we can't help you once you pass this point."

"Help us?" Orla wondered what the old man was trying to warn them about. "I am of the Priesat. I have come to visit my family."

The man's skin turned ashen. "My apologies, excellency."

Orla glanced at Arian before he responded. "I have no title. My family is insignificant."

"Then your family could be in grave danger."

He heard Arian's sharp intake of breath at the man's words. The heat of her hand burned through him when she laid it on his arm. Once he covered her hand with his, he spoke to the man. "I think we need to talk."

"Of course. Come with me." He led them to a small thatched roof house near the road. "My wife has just finished fixing biscuits for the bazaar tomorrow. She makes the best in the land."

Holding Arian's hand, Orla stepped into the small home, with her close behind.

The elderly man gestured toward two handmade wooden straight-back chairs.

They murmured their thanks as they seated themselves.

"Grenta? Grenta! We have guests," shouted the old man as he eased his tired body unto a small stool near a hearth. A loud pop filled the air as a bone didn't quite move the way it should have, then snapped back into its proper socket.

"What are you hollering about, Metan? I could hear you clear out in the—oh. Company." She stopped in the doorway, the sunlight framing her.

Orla blinked when he thought he saw a halo surround the woman's head. Wishful thinking? He stood up and bowed when she entered the building.

"Ah, a gentleman. And the lady?"

Arian stood and gave her a shorter bow, which was customary for women. "I am Arian."

"Very pretty name," she commented as she busied herself in a cloth draped cupboard. She pulled out freshly baked bread, two leather cups, along with two ceramic cups, a wooden plate, a sharp knife, and several crocks filled with jelly and honey.

Metan retrieved a bottle from under the floor near the hearth, uncorked it and poured a small amount into each cup. He lifted his glass. "To your health."

Orla lifted his glass. "And to yours. I am Orla."

"I am Grenta and that is my husband Metan." She started to slice the bread. The heavenly aroma of the butter and yeast wafted through the room. She laughed when she heard Arian's stomach rumble. "I see I'm breaking this bread at just the right time."

Arian blushed. "Sorry."

"Don't be sorry, child. At least I'll know it will be eaten. So what brings you here?"

She looked over at Orla. "We are traveling to the Priesat compound."

The woman clicked her tongue.

"I have tried to explain that they should not go, wife. But these stubborn young ones don't want to believe."

"That place is very dangerous. People from this village have gone to the compound to sell their wares, just like they have always done, but never came back."

"Never?" Orla sat up straighter in his chair.

Arian stifled a soft moan when the taste of the bread Grenta had spread with honey exploded in her mouth. The warmth of the honey mingled with the melting texture of the soft bread.

"Perni, the tinker, went to the compound two lunas ago. We haven't seen him since then, and he left a wife heavy with child. One luna later, his wife's brother went to see what happened. He also hasn't returned," said Grenta.

"We don't know what happened to them, but we have our theories," interjected Metan. "Ships have been landing out there on a regular basis. Every time one lands the ground around here shakes."

"What type of ships?" asked Orla.

"Don't know. Their markings were strange to us."

"When was the last time you felt the vibrations?" Arian wiped a stray bit of honey off her chin.

"Two or three duras ago. We should feel them again sometime today. The ships normally don't stay longer than three duras," said Metan.

Arian laid her hand on Orla's arm, asking an unspoken question. Could it be the general's ships?

"How many people have disappeared?" asked Orla.

"About seven so far." Metan placed his cup on the table. "Before this started three people would travel there once a cycle, carrying the wares of the rest of the village. We did this because the distance is so great, and to honor the pact our ancestors made with the Priesat. That we would leave them alone and send no more than five people to visit them at once, only when we had items they needed."

"What do you think is happening to these people?"

"Those ships. I think they are being taken in those ships." Just as Metan spoke the floor vibrated before a loud roar filled the air.

Orla and Arian dashed to the door in time to see a ship lift off and blast up through the atmosphere. Arian grabbed his arm for support. Her knees went weak when she saw the general's marking clearly on the ship.

"Oh Planets. He's been here," Arian whispered. "What are we going to do?"

Grenta looked at her with concern. "We should get her back inside. Her face has lost all its color."

Orla nodded as he led her back into the small home.

Grenta knelt down in front of Arian once she had taken her seat. "Child, you don't look good. Are you feeling all right?"

Arian gave her a shaky smile. "Yes, thank you. I guess the bright sunlight and the heat has taken its toll."

"Perhaps you should go and lay down for a while. We have a spare room that has a nice cool breeze this time of dura. It will make you feel better." Grenta pressed the back of her hand against Arian's forehead.

"A small rest might be a good idea." Arian stood up, then gripped the table when her world swirled around her.

"Oh dear. Orla, could you help? I don't think this old body can guide her into the room alone." Grenta took one of Arian's arm as Orla took the other. They maneuvered her into the small room in the back of the house.

"If it is all right with you, Grenta, I would like to stay with her."

"Of course."

"I'll get something cool to lay on her forehead. That should help." She ducked out of the room, returning quickly with a soft cloth and a bowl of cool water.

Orla smiled at her. Once she made sure Orla could have anything he might need to make Arian more comfortable, she slipped out of the room and left them alone.

"Mistress?"

"I am fine, Orla. Just a little flushed." She touched her hand to his face. "This is not unknown with someone just gaining their Barou talents."

"I know that some people have hot flashes, and others have had headaches, but I have never known a Barou to swoon."

"I didn't swoon. Consider it a massive hot flash. Mother warned me that this could happen."

"She did?" Orla glared at her. "And you didn't tell me?"

"How was I to know that the Barou talent would be so strong in me?" She couldn't tell him her suspicions started when the tail appeared earlier. That she knew the things she had created only happened to those who had extensive training, or a lot of talent. If she was having these so soon, what else would happen? She had to learn control, and quickly, but who would be able to help her?

"Is there more I should know, now that you are sure about the strength of your talent?"

"Well." She paused for just a moment. "I don't know if my talent is that powerful or not. It needs to be tested. This could all just be a fluke. Some have had giant peaks like I have and have had minimal talents."

"But others have become some of the most powerful Barou of your race."

"Mother was average, with a few special talents that rated a little higher than normal, and she was full blood. I am not."

Orla watched her for a few moments. "But you could still develop into a very strong talent."

"I don't know."

"How is a Barou tested?"

Arian felt heat spread up her neck. "Mother never really told me. All I know is that it would take a master."

"And how do you find this master?"

"I don't know that answer either."

Orla ran his fingers through his hair in frustration. "Mistress, we can't have this happening now. How am I supposed to protect you when your talent can cause more trouble than we need? We must find you a master and get him to teach you to control this."

She shot up into a sitting position. "Not now! We are to meet Dresuer! My planet!"

"You will do your planet no good if you can't control this. We've already been told that the Priesat compound could already be compromised. Do you want to take the chance of the general catching you before you learn to control this?"

"No." Her shoulders slumped.

CHAPTER EIGHT

Arian's goal was within her grasp, yet she knew Orla was right. She didn't want to agree with him. Her people suffered more every dura she was gone, but what good would she be to them if the general did capture her. Her talent needed to be controlled before she took another step.

A loud sigh escaped her. "You're right, Orla. I don't agree with it, but you're right. Except, how are we going to find a Barou out here? Most don't advertise their talent."

"We'll have to go back to the ship and talk to Tymin." Orla smiled. "If anyone can find a Barou, he can."

One of the truggars roared, drawing their attention outside.

Arian glanced toward the window. "I wonder what has upset them." She slid her feet off the bed and onto the small carpet that covered the dirt floor.

Orla stood up and grasped her elbow. "You shouldn't be up."

"I'm fine, Orla." She smoothed down the front of her dress. "Let's see what cause the truggar to roar."

Arian exited the small house first, with Orla right at her elbow. A smile slid across her face when she spied Grenta arguing with their smelly little friend.

"It looks like we didn't need to go find him after all," murmured Orla. He addressed the little man in a clear voice. "Tymin, why are you here?"

Tymin whirled toward Orla's voice. "Master! I have searched for you everywhere. Grinnell had to take the ship into orbit."

His eyes narrowed just a hair. "Why?"

Tymin looked at the older couple, not sure if he could speak plainly. "It's not safe right now."

"You know this little man?" Grenta asked. Her face pinched from standing downwind of him.

"Yes, Grenta. He is a friend."

"He can't come in my home unless he takes a bath."

"Another bath? Tymin has never been so clean!"

Arian laughed. "He always smells that way, Grenta, much to my disappointment. I have learned to never get too close."

"How long will they be gone?" interrupted Orla.

"Three cycles."

"Three cycles?" Arian felt her heart pounding in her chest. Three cycles was too long for them to wait. They had to find a Barou, then convince Dresuer to help her save her planet. Three cycles would put them too far behind. Too many of her people could be hurt during the time.

"But Mistress." Tymin worried the ragged hem of his worn brown cloak. "They said it couldn't be helped. Something about a window."

A warm hand settled on her arm. "It's all right."

She turned to look at Orla. "How?"

"It will give us time to look for your Barou master."

"Here?" Arian wanted to laugh. A master on this planet would be a feat indeed.

"You are looking for a Barou Master?" asked Grenta. She looked at her husband and saw him give her a slight nod before she continued. "Will I do?"

"You?" Arian stared at Grenta. "You are a master?"

"Of course dear, that's why I knew you needed to lie down. I have seen the signs many times." Grenta gestured toward the house. "Why don't we go back inside? You need to explain to me why you haven't been trained before this. I don't get to exercise my talent as much as I would like, but I can train you properly, once you've been tested."

Tymin remained where he stood.

"You may enter too, just make sure you sit near one of the windows."

Arian wiped her brow as she concentrated on the task at hand. The cool air of the morning didn't keep her from sweating from the mental exhaustion she put herself through. Grenta wanted her to create a three-dimensional sphere. The last several duras had been spent with the mechanics of using the imagery. How to make it look real, using her memory to make the size and shape of a particular item.

"You are trying too hard, Arian. Relax, let you mind free itself. Use the meditation your mother taught you to open your mind." Grenta sat under the shade of a fruit tree in their backyard, the place where she had been training Arian for the last few duras.

She nodded, then sat on the ground opposite of Grenta. Starting the breathing exercise, Arian noticed a small Garron, a scaly creature with wings and a tail, watching her. She wondered how he got here. A lot of people captured them and kept them in cages as pets. She felt sorry for the poor thing. She cooed and held out her hand, hoping it would come close enough for her to pet.

The Garron took a few steps toward her then stopped. Then a few more before stopping again. It did this until it stood close enough for her to reach out and touch it.

A gasp escaped her when her hand passed right through it. Then she watched the animal grow in size until it was twenty meters high, towering over the small village. A soft laugh escaped her. "That is wonderful."

"And very easy to do." The image shattered into thousands of pieces, light flickered and danced through the air as it dissolved.

"Why didn't I know that it was fake? Mother told me that a Barou should be able to spot someone else's illusion."

"True, once you are trained to recognize what to look for and will be able to spot them easily. But you knew it was a fake the moment you touched it. Only a Barou can do that. To everyone else it's real." Grenta stood up and dusted herself off. Walking over to Arian, she sat down beside her. "We have worked on this one exercise all morning. Let's move on to something else."

Arian breathed a sigh of relief. She felt her sphere was very poor and trying to focus wasn't working for her.

Grenta patted her hand. "You are just starting your training, give it time."

"Time is the one thing I don't have."

"Let's start with something simple." A small sphere appeared in front of them. "Now what do you see?"

"Something I couldn't do a few microns ago." Her sphere wasn't opaque like Grenta's. You could see straight through hers.

"No." She shook her head. "What do you notice that is different than the real thing?"

She stared at it. Her shoulders slumped. She didn't see anything different.

"Don't look at it directly."

She let her gaze go unfocused, using her peripheral vision instead. A slight golden edge appeared for just a secur. She furrowed her brow, not sure if she had really seen the edge or had conjured it up herself.

"I think I saw a slight golden edge to it."

"Very good. That is what you saw."

The image blurred for just a secur before the edge stood out very prominently.

"This edging is around all images. The color might be a little different, some have a more copper edge."

The sphere shifted again, and the edge turned copper.

"Or a silver."

A silver edge appeared around the sphere.

"A true master can actually manipulate that edge to where it is so slight you miss it, unless you are a master and know what to look for."

The edge of the sphere darkened until it was undetectable.

"Now, Orla told me that you have done two manifestations so far. You were able to change your hair color and you grew a tail."

She felt the heat of a blush raise up her neck as she nodded.

"What were you thinking each time?"

"I don't know." She picked up a stick and started to dig in the dirt. "The first time I remember wishing that my talent had shown itself so I could..." Too late she realized what she said.

"Have no fear, Arian. Anything you reveal is safe here." Grenta shifted a little, getting a little more comfortable. "So you needed to disguise yourself. Can I assume you were petrified the first time?"

"Yes."

"And the second?"

She ducked her head and continued to doodle in the dirt. "I was remembering something."

"Another strong emotion?"

"You could say that." She couldn't dare tell her that she was remembering Orla's kiss.

"Then strong emotions bring it to the forefront." Grenta stood up. "We're going to try the sphere again."

"All right." Arian stood up beside her. Closing her eyes, she spread her hands in front of her. In her mind she pictured the sphere perfectly, but the barely visible apparition paled in comparison.

"Come on, Arian, you can do better than this."

"I'm trying."

"Not hard enough."

She opened her eyes and glared at Grenta. Although she was right, she didn't have to be so rude. Anger flared in Arian. She was doing the best she could.

Grenta didn't look at her though. She was looking just to the left of Arian's shoulder. There, suspended about one meter above the ground was a sphere, perfect in shape and size. The glimmering edge almost invisible.

"It seems your emotions need to be in play for you to get your talents to work properly." She crossed her arms over her chest. "Let's go in and replenish ourselves. And we'll continue later this afternoon, once the heat of the dura has passed."

The sun seemed to rest against a far-away mountain as Grenta resumed Arian's training.

"Now let's try something new. Let's create that sphere again. This time I want you to think of one instant that was emotional for you while you do it."

The death of her father leaped into her mind. To her that was one of the most emotional things she could remember. The sphere appeared once more, as perfect as the last time.

"Give the sphere wings."

The sphere started to wobble a little and lose its shape.

"Keep that emotion in your mind."

The sphere regained its shape, but the wings never appeared. Arian stared at it, knowing that if she continued to dwell on the death of her father, she'd break into tears, and be no good to anyone. "I can't. That moment is too much to bare."

"Child, I didn't mean for you to pick a sad emotion, just one to help you create the images. Pick a happy one, something that causes some sort of strong reaction in you."

Her thoughts conjured up the time they spent together in the ship, and the sphere sprouted wings.

"Very good." Grenta studied the sphere intently. "Now make it vibrate."

It started to oscillate slightly.

"Now make it bounce."

The sphere bounced up and down.

"All right. Let's try something different. Create a Whala desert flower."

The sphere slowly dissipated and, in its place, stood a delicate flower. Long pointed petals of yellow with small orange dots running through the center and all across the tips of each petal.

Grenta even noticed small dots of dew on the petals. "Can you make it larger?"

Arian concentrated, trying to expand the image. The flower disintegrated when she tried too hard. "I don't know how."

Metan came forward with refreshments. "I thought you might be a little thirsty."

"Thank you," said Arian. Taking a glass, she wondered what Orla and Tymin were doing right now. She hadn't seen either since lunch earlier.

"Why don't we quit for the dura? This is a lot of mental stress." Grenta must have noticed that she was unfocused.

"Yes, thank you." She set her drink down on the small tray Metan still held. "Do you know where Orla is?"

"Yes, dear. He's with those animals of yours."

Arian smiled. "Truggars." She bowed slightly before racing to find Orla. His voice carried across the air, making it easy to find him.

Both truggars lay on the ground, with Orla rubbing their stomachs. Arian covered her mouth, not wanting to laugh aloud and have him see her. He'd stop if he knew someone watched him.

She stood there for a few microns before the moment was broken by Tymin.

"Master," he said. "Grenta has invited us inside for a quick repast."

Orla stood up and stretched, his muscles flexing with his movements. Arian felt her mouth go dry. Watching him move this way made her want something she knew she shouldn't. His kisses made her knees weak, his touch made her crave it more, and watching him move made her mouth go dry. He did things and said things that made her not want to meet with Dresuer and fulfill her vow. Why was she having these feelings?

Orla felt her eyes on him when he rubbed the truggar's stomachs. Having her watch him made his blood thicken. He knew she wouldn't be watching him if she wasn't attracted to him.

The truggars soft fur caressed his hands as he contemplated what he should do next. Should he look up so she would know he was aware of her watching him? Would it embarrass her? There were times when he wished they had already mated, then he wouldn't have these questions of what she was thinking. He would know.

Tymin disappeared in to the small house before Orla stood up and looked at Arian. Her shy smile warmed his heart. At least she didn't run and hide in embarrassment. Silently, he offered his hand to her. Her young body moved gracefully as she hurried to his side. He felt the warmth of her hand when she clasped his. After wrapping his fingers around her hand, he led them into the house.

Tymin sat in a chair near the largest window. The wind pulled his scent out of the window instead of making it linger inside. Grenta and Metan's house had several of these large windows. Tymin's chair moved when the wind shifted so he could enter the home, yet not offend anyone with his unique scent.

Orla offered Arian a chair, then sat on the floor next to her.

Grenta entered the room, bearing a small tray loaded with bread, meat, fruit, plates and napkins. She set the tray on the table before turning to Orla. "You shouldn't be sitting on the floor. Please take my chair."

Orla smiled up at her. "I prefer the floor, Grenta."

"But you are a guest in my house, and our tradition is to make sure our guests are comfortable."

Orla stood up and took Grenta's weathered hand. "My father also taught me to respect my hosts. I show that respect by allowing you and Metan to use your own chairs instead of forcing you to stand while I sit in a chair when I know I can be just as comfortable on the floor."

"Perhaps a pillow for Orla will satisfy you both," Arian ventured.

Grenta smiled at the thought. She exited the room and returned with a large pillow.

Orla took the pillow from her, placed it on the floor next to Arian's chair, and sat down. Arian's suggestion was the perfect solution. He looked up at her, marveling at the wisdom she held.

"Why are you staring at me that way?" she asked him.

"Once again your training has shown itself. What made you come up with the idea of a pillow for me?"

"I know how stubborn you are and thought the pillow would be the perfect compromise." A slight blush filled her cheeks as her gaze dropped from his.

He loved the way the color spread slowly up to her hairline. "Thank you for your insight." The color deepened, making him smile.

"You're welcome," she murmured. Shyly, she accepted the leather cup Grenta offered her. Lifting it, she busied herself with taking a drink, trying not to squirm under his gaze.

He grinned as he took the other cup Grenta offered. He kept

watching Arian, knowing sooner or later her curiosity would get the best of her and force her to look at him again.

Metan had entered the small abode and their meal had been served before Arian did look at him. Her eyes widened slightly when she looked into his eyes. He wondered what she saw there that surprised her so much.

His gaze slipped to the table when he noticed that a second cup had appeared on the table next to Arian's. Was this because of her training sessions with Grenta? Were they pushing her too hard?

Arian picked up one of the two and took a drink. The other cup disappeared. Each time she went to drink, the second cup appeared. Sometimes to the right of her real one, other times to the left, and always a few securs before she started to reach for her real cup. It kept moving so much that Orla couldn't tell the real from the fake, but somehow Arian could. She unerringly picked up the real one each time.

"I can assume I have passed your little test?" asked Arian.

Orla looked at Grenta and noticed a smile on her face.

"Yes, my dear, you have."

"Then is my training complete?"

"No. Arian, you know this takes yepas. How can you think that you would learn it in a dura or two?"

"Because I am on a mission that doesn't give me much time." Arian set her cup down. "I only wanted to learn to control it enough so I don't jeopardize my friends. Any further training can wait until after."

"You can't stop the training once you start it. If you lose control again, the Barou power could destroy you."

"I'll have to take that chance."

"No you don't." Grenta smiled. "I have the perfect solution."

Orla turned his attention to Grenta as the woman continued to talk.

"I will travel with you."

CHAPTER NINE

Metan gasped as he gripped Grenta's shoulder. "You promised!"

Arian wondered what she had promised. Perhaps her promise would keep her out of the danger she could be in if she tried to travel with them now. She was already responsible for several lives, and she didn't want to add to the list.

Grenta placed her hand on his. "I promised because it suited them. As a Barou I can't shirk my duties. You know that."

Metan frowned at her words.

"What did you promise, Grenta?" Had she been banned by the Barou? She knew that although a very rare thing to happen, some members had been expelled because of their evil tendencies. Although she feared what Grenta had to say, she hadn't sensed any evil in this woman, or her creations.

A sigh escaped Grenta. Folding her hands in front of her she watched Arian. "You deserve the truth. Several yepas ago I—"

"Twenty yepas," interrupted Metan.

"Hush," she admonished. "It's my story so let me tell it."

Metan rolled his eyes but kept his hands on his wife's shoulders and remained silent.

"I am a Barou master. A trainer from the academy. My pupils were some of the best. For yepas I trained young people like yourself. In fact, I trained the queen of Emorai, and the present leader of the Barou."

Arian's eyes widened at the mention of her home planet. "You trained my mother?"

"Yes, child, I did."

"Continue with your story, Grenta," Orla said.

Arian wanted to interrupt but knew that the story about her mother would have to wait until another time.

"One dura I gained a new student. I could sense that he had a small streak of maliciousness in him, but it was something I thought I could control. I knew with the right training he could learn to fight that side and use his Barou powers for good. So I worked with him, teaching him how to control the evil side of his nature. He followed my training, learning to control it, but one dura something happened. We were working on a particularly difficult lesson that he had trouble with. His anger started to control him, allowing his evil nature to overpower all of his training. He started to fight me." Grenta rubbed her hand over her face. "In the end, the boy was killed. The Barou council understood I did what I had to do, but I could no longer train. They kicked me out to save face. I agreed, under one condition. As long as I didn't try to approach the council again to regain my position, they would allow me to leave the planet and live where I want and as I wanted. If a student came to me, I could train them, but what I taught them wouldn't count when they approached the Barou council. They would still have to go through the Barou testing."

"What you are teaching me doesn't count?" Arian asked.

"It counts, but you'd have to take a test to prove your training. Just like anyone else who approached the academy without training."

Arian's brow crinkled. "I don't understand."

"I can't certify your training. In order to do that I must be a member of the Barou academy. If you wanted to be certified, then you'd have to approach the council and take the test like an untrained person would. You just wouldn't have to go through the classes. Your training would be very evident when you pass the test."

"Then there is no problem," said Orla.

"There is if another Barou were to find out I'm traveling with you to train Arian. They would assume that I pursued her instead of her coming to me."

"Even if we told them differently?"

"I'm not sure if they would believe you. Never-the-less, I'm going with you. Your training must continue until you gain complete control. The few lessons you have had won't do that."

Arian played with the soft material of her gown. She knew they couldn't jeopardize Grenta's life to continue her training. It would be too dangerous. "I can't allow that."

Grenta grabbed Arian's hand. "If you don't take me with you then I'll follow you. I can't let you walk out of here with such little training. You'd be a danger to yourself and your friends."

Orla placed his hand on Arian's. "What if we come back and get Grenta after we visit the encampment? Tymin can't come with us anyway."

Arian remained silent. She knew as well as Orla that they were probably walking into a trap, but she still had to go on the off chance that Dresuer was there and would be willing to help. "Then she must know all of it."

Orla nodded in agreement.

"I know who you are, Arian. You look too much like your mother for me not too. We have also heard the rumors of you traveling to your betrothed. It's one of the reasons Metan stopped you. Something is wrong in the Priesat camp, but no one knows what it is."

"Then that is what we must find out," Arian stated as she stood. "I need a little time to prepare before I leave."

Grenta stood up with her. "There is something I must teach you before you travel."

Arian gave her a slight nod before exiting the house.

Just as Orla rose to follow her, Metan placed a hand on his arm. "She doesn't know, does she?"

Orla looked at the man, wondering just how much he really knew. "No, and I want to keep it that way."

The truggars growled nervously when they were saddled the next morning. They could sense the tension.

Metan stood near the small lean-to that functioned as a barn for the animals. He handed a bag of food to Arian. "Remember what my wife taught you, child. Come back safe."

She nodded silently. Her nerves, taught as a bow string, had her head pounding and her knees shaking. Speaking was out of the question. If this were a trap, she would have to fight for her life to escape. If their fears were for naught, then she'd be marrying a total stranger. Something she wasn't sure she was prepared to do.

Her truggar followed Orla's into the sandy wilderness. Horas passed as they passed dessert-like flora and fauna, but Arian didn't pay attention to them. She was busy trying to convince herself that she must fulfill her father's request.

The thought of being married to a strange man made the lumlights in her stomach take flight. Not knowing anything about her future husband made them soar all around her insides. Fear gripped her hard.

What if he refused to help her? Where would that leave her? She needed a champion to bring back home. Her people had to be free. The lumlights quieted down when that thought took root. She was doing this for her people after all. Her desire to keep them safe drove her to go on this quest. That and the promise to her father. Arian straightened her back. She could do this. She had to do this, and any fear she had would just have to get in line with the rest of her jumbled emotions ricocheting throughout her body right now.

She glanced up toward Orla sitting proudly on his truggar, leading the way to the encampment. He understood destiny so well. All along he had kept them on the path to Dresuer. Arian wished she could figure out what her destiny was as easily. One microns she was a child, then a queen, then an escaping felon. She knew she had to find her betrothed, but instead found feelings for her closest friend, and opened her heart to a strange assortment of new friends.

Her thoughts scattered within her mind, like leaves dancing about in a strong gust when she saw the first hints of the encampment just as the sun started to set. Up ahead she saw Orla dismounting. Curious, she reigned her truggar in to see why he stopped.

"We should walk from here."

She slid down off the back of her animal.

"And I must change back into my Miran form."

"Why?" Her curiosity got the best of her.

"Because you left with only your pet. You'd raise too many questions if you arrived with a man."

"Couldn't you be my guide?"

Orla smiled at her. "You are a queen. Would the queen travel with one man alone?"

She felt her cheeks heat up. "Of course not."

A slight shimmer surrounded Orla's body as he shifted into his Miran form. The large sleek cat wrapped his tail around her.

She sighed in contentment. "God, I have missed that." A low purring sound emanated from Orla. She guessed he missed it too. Straightening her shoulders once again, she headed toward the encampment, with Orla guiding her in case she veered off track.

Arian crested a small dune and gasped at the view before her. A huge black tent dominated the area. The smaller tents, even though they were all the colors of the rainbow, paled in comparison to the luxurious design of this one massive tent.

A soft whir from Orla sent her moving down toward the main tent.

She didn't know what to expect but was prepared for just about anything. Her hand closed around the heavy damask material, preparing to lift it when a sharp pain pierced her hand. She pulled back her hand before much damage could be done.

"How dare you!" she said haughtily, just the way a queen should react. She stared at the cut on her hand for a secur before looking up at the guards. "I am here to see Dresuer."

"Our master sees no one."

"Oh, he'll see me. I am Arian, queen of Emorai and his betrothed." She never saw men scurry so fast. The drapes that covered the threshold parted for her entrance. A regal nod addressed her thankfulness for the men holding the curtains open.

It took her a few securs for her vision to adjust to the darker interior. The tent walls arched high above her head. A chandelier hung from the center pole. "How very odd."

Orla bumped up against her.

"All this opulence in a temporary dwelling," she whispered to him. She walked across the richly carpeted floor to a huge throne sitting atop a large dais. A frown burrowed its way across her forehead. This is not what she expected. What if Dresuer didn't want to leave this luxury to help her? Although she hadn't really thought about how Dresuer would live, she did expect something more befitting a hero.

A soft laugh escaped her. Her imagination had created a superhuman hero. Something she was already judging Dresuer against without giving the man a chance. Taking a deep breath, she guided Orla as she approached the throne.

The young man she came to see slouched in the chair, acting bored. Until his eyes landed on her. Suddenly, he sat up straight, threw back his shoulders, and smiled at her invitingly.

"My Queen."

She gave him a slight nod.

"I must say that I'm surprised that you are here, without escort, and looking very well. Your trip must've been very harrowing."

"I will admit it had its moments," she responded. Her hands clasped in front of her, she paused for a moment. "You know why I'm here."

"To fulfill the vow my father made to your father."

"Yes. And to ask for your help."

"Help?" Dresuer rested his arm against the arm of his chair then rested his chin in his hand.

Arian didn't know how to continue. Verbalizing this request was a lot harder than she realized. Why would a total stranger help her?

She dipped her head in thought. They would be his people too. Arian would have to make him realize the power he would gain when their houses joined. If he fought and won, he would not only be a hero to her, but to her people as well, and nothing surpassed their loyalty.

Orla, who had sat passively at her feet, started to growl low in his throat.

She absently started to pet his head, hoping to calm him. Not knowing what bothered him worried her. If only she could talk to him and allay his fears.

"What is that animal you have with you?"

"The gift your father gave me when we were betrothed." Didn't he remember?

"Of course." He leaned back in his chair. One of his guards stepped up and whispered in his ear.

Orla started to scratch her leg, growling all the while. Arian tried to disentangle herself from him, but his tail had wrapped around her so tight it was a futile attempt.

"Um, I wish to be excused for a few moments. Or—my pet needs to be tended to."

"Of course, my dear, and perhaps you'd like to freshen up a bit too." He snapped his fingers. Two servants raced to his side.

"Take the Queen to the guest quarters."

"Thank you." She followed the servants out of the tent, fighting to control Orla.

"You must stop this," she whispered when Orla pushed past her escorts and dragged her away from them.

One quick tug pulled the leash she held out of her grasp before he dashed away from her, forcing her to chase after him.

The servants forgotten, she raced after him. He wove through several tents before he finally stopped and allowed her to catch up. She was breathing heavy when she did. He had already shifted by the time she had caught up with him. "What was that all about?"

"Something is wrong."

That got her attention. "What?"

"This encampment normally bustles with activity this time of the evening, yet I have seen very few people milling about. Dresuer's father is nowhere to be seen, but I know he hasn't turned control over to Dresuer yet. There is an underlying tension that I feel but can't explain."

"Do you think Dresuer is in danger?" She noticed an odd flicker in Orla's eyes before he answered.

"I don't think so. To be sure I need to look around. For now will you take yourself to safety? Dresuer did dismiss you so you could clean up."

"All right, but where?"

Orla glanced around. A large tent loomed in front of them. Snagging her hand, he pulled her with him as he investigated the tent. The floor was covered with pillows.

"My goodness! Who would ever try to walk on these things," Arian commented when she saw the floor.

"I wouldn't worry about this right now, but it would be the perfect place for you to hide for now."

"Here? Under the pillows? Orla what aren't you telling me?"

A lot, he thought. Instead, he touched her elbow, hoping his touch would still calm her. "Just trust me. Once I feel it is safe, I'll come for you."

"But in the meantime, you want me to bury myself under all those pillows."

Orla gave her his best smile.

A sigh escaped her as she opened the flap into the tent.

As he shifted back into his Miran form his sensitive ears picked up her last comment before she buried herself under the pillows. "You owe me."

Orla smiled again. He loped toward the main tent, then hesitated. If he went through the main entrance, he knew he would be spotted. Following the edge of the tent, he found a small gap where he could enter without being detected.

Using his snout, he lifted the edge of the tent and slipped back in. He wove his way around the poles and columns toward the throne. Orla inched close to it, then found a hiding spot nearby, hoping he'd over hear something useful.

Dresuer stood up and stretched. After he stepped down the steps from the dais, he addressed the guard standing there. "So, when is the general arriving?"

"Within microns. He has explicit instructions on how he wants to find the Queen."

A low growl emanated from Orla when he heard those words. Arian was in danger.

He wished he could have told her that Dresuer was the name of the heir apparent and the man she thought was Dresuer was his younger twin brother. Then she might believe what he wanted to tell her. Instead he crept closer, hoping he had misunderstood.

"Find her and bring her here. We can't keep the general waiting."

"But I thought you wanted to ask for more."

"Oh I do," said Dresuer. "But in order to do that she must be here. Can't ask for a higher payment without the bait, now can I."

Anger filled Orla. Only one thing would help this situation. The death of his brother.

CHAPTER TEN

Another low growl emanated from Orla as he contemplated his options. If he killed his brother now, he could take his rightful place and marry Arian. But he wouldn't know what promises his brother had made with the general. Without that knowledge he couldn't help Arian and could jeopardize them all.

"I just wonder where my brother is."

Orla's ears pricked up at that. So his brother knew about him. Interesting. As far as Orla knew his father kept their twin birth a secret, even from his brother.

"If Queen Arian came here to meet her betrothed then she doesn't know that you had a twin. Why do you worry about such a small detail?"

"Because my father told me that my brother has the true birthmark of the leader. All he has to do is show that birthmark and the people will follow him."

"But you have been their ruler. Why would they follow a total stranger?"

"Because he would be my father's first son. This people are steeped in tradition. They would fight to maintain that stupid tradition."

"But we have taken care of that. They have no weapons, and we have crushed their will."

"Ha! That wouldn't stop them if they knew the truth," said Dresuer.

"Since the general will be here soon, you really don't have too much to worry about."

"True. All I have to do is give him Queen Arian and I will have total control forever, brother or no brother." Dresuer stood up from the throne. "Make sure she has freshened up and bring her here."

One of his protective guards bowed then headed outside.

A loud searing noise filled the air above them. Startled, Orla glanced up to see the ceiling on fire. Bits of flaming cloth dropped to the carpeted floor.

Orla twitched his tail in annoyance. He moved quietly around several of the main poles, avoiding the burning canvas as it dropped to the floor.

Did the general change his mind and decide to kill them all off instead of trying to capture Arian? Or was he trying to eliminate the middle man by killing off Dresuer?

A scream pierced his thoughts, jerking his attention back to the dais. Dresuer sat on the throne, curled into a fetus position, wailing in fear. The air filled with a loud whistling sound just before the top of the tent exploded off completely, snapping the supporting poles as a missile burned its way through. The ground vibrated with its impact. Smoke rose from the hole it created.

Orla snuck closer to the hole, wondering what type of missile had impacted the earth. Keeping an eye on his sniveling brother, he crept close enough to recognize the bomb. His brows shot up at the sight of one of General Varal's pulse missiles. It was designed to knock out all electromagnetic activity. Anyone who got caught in its wake would be rendered unconscious for microns. That would give the general plenty of time to take everyone to his stronghold, lock them up and take control.

He turned and raced out the tent, tearing through the darkened evening and into the tent where Arian hid. He hoped it would be far enough from the bomb. Quickly, he dove into the pillowed floor and crawled through them, searching for Arian.

A muffled sound to his left allowed him to locate her quickly. Wrapping his tail around her, he pulled her into his protective embrace and pushed her beneath him.

The air roared with exploding bombs and the anguished cries of wounded members of the encampment. He gritted his teeth in anger, if Varal didn't kill his brother, Orla vowed to do the deed himself.

The pulse bomb exploded in a white heat, effecting almost half the camp.

A slow lethargy seeped into Arian and Orla's systems, but they didn't take the full brunt of the explosion.

They should be safe if the general didn't search the tents thoroughly for Arian. There was no way they would be able to outrun the troops if they tried to flee.

Orla heard the tent flap snap open then he heard voices inside the tent. He ran a hand over Arian, hoping to keep her calm and quiet.

"The general wants us to search each tent."

"I know, but there is no one here."

"Do you want to face his wrath if we don't do what he asked?"

"No. You check those curtains and I'll check the floor."

Orla felt Arian stiffen at their words.

The pillows muffled their footsteps so Orla and Arian didn't know where they were until one of the two guards stepped right on top of them.

"Any sign of her?"

"No."

"Did you move any of the pillows around to see if they are hiding underneath?"

"I had a better idea."

Orla wondered what that idea was. Securs later, he knew when the sharp point of a blade sliced through the pillow, missing his face by only millimeters. The lethargy in his bones kept him from jumping up, which probably saved his and Arian's life.

"Well, I don't think they're here. We'd see some evidence if they were."

There was silence for a few microns. "All right, if they were here you probably would've stabbed them by now. But let's continue to work our way across the floor just to be sure."

Orla waited tensely until he heard the door flap open and close.

"Are they gone?" whispered Arian.

"Yes, but let's stay put until we are sure the area is cleared."

Once the screams and cries moved away from them, Orla took a chance and lifted his head above the pillows.

"I think we can try to get away from here. Can you move?"

"I think so." She sat up, leaning against the pillows. "I'm so tired all of the sudden."

"The general used a pulse bomb on the main tent, although it didn't knock us out, it drained our energy. We can stay here and rest if you need to."

"No. I don't want to take the chance of the general's men coming back and capturing us." She stood up and arched her back. "Where should we go?"

"Good question. Stay here and I'll go look around and see if I can find a safe route for us."

She sighed her agreement and slipped back into the pillows.

Orla slipped out of the tent and snaked his way around several others. He hesitated when he grew close to a large open space. Peeking around the side of a tent he spotted a group of people surrounded by the general's men.

"We are looking for Queen Arian. We know she is here. Everything will go better for you all if you tell us where she is."

No one spoke.

Orla watched in horror as one of the guards drew his laser and fired upon one of the older women in the small crowd. She disappeared in a flash of light, leaving behind the odor of burnt flesh, and charred ground.

"Now. Where is Queen Arian?"

Silence greeted the guards once again.

The guard sighed as he raised his weapon again.

"None of these people know where the queen is. Most of them didn't even know she was here."

"Who said that?"

"I did." A young woman stepped from between two tents. The simple robe with silver trim denoted she worked in Dresuer's private quarters. "The queen was sent to the women's quarters to freshen up."

She pointed toward a badly burned tent. "No one knows what happened to her once the tent caught on fire. As far as we know everyone got out, but there are still five women missing. Your queen is one of them."

"Go search the tent."

Two of the four men trotted off toward the tent. When they returned a few microns later, they returned empty handed.

"There was no evidence of anyone inside that tent. It looks like everyone escaped."

"Then where is she?"

"Perhaps one of the other squads found her," the young woman said. "Or she could be part of the people you have ready to be transported."

Orla's heart pounded. He hoped Arian was where he left her.

The lead guard glared at her suspiciously but ended up contacting his commander to relay the information. "You are to—where did she go?"

None of the other guards realized she had left.

"Search for that girl. The general will want to talk to her."

Two of the guards bowed before starting their search. The leader herded the rest toward the center of camp where other encampment members were already waiting.

Orla shifted his position so he could follow them. Although he told Arian to stay put, he feared she didn't listen and had ended up being captured.

He hovered as close as he could without being spotted, watching the guards and searching the faces for Arian. The heat in the area increased when a ship approached and hovered over the people. A bright green ray filled the area, transporting all the people that were touched by the ray. The ship fired up its engines and sped toward space.

Orla stood in the darkness, fearing he would find himself all alone. He didn't see Arian in the crowd, but she could have been transported without his knowledge. Steeling himself for the worst, he looked around the area to see if he could find Arian. The tent he told Arian to stay in was the first place he searched and came up empty handed.

"I told you to stay put," he grumbled. Rescuing her would be very dangerous. But Orla knew he couldn't leave her in General Varal's clutches. A warm hand touched his arm.

He jerked around to find the young woman who spoke to the guards earlier.

"Looking for me?"

"Have you seen Queen Arian?"

"You are looking at her." The young woman smiled. "Do you like my disguise?"

"Arian? Are you crazy? Those guards wanted to take you with them."

"Grenta taught me a special trick to keep me safe. Once I spoke to them to stop them from searching for me, I blended into the background. No matter how hard they looked they wouldn't have been able to find me."

"Why?"

Arian spread her hands out in front of herself, then slowly faded out of sight.

"Arian? Arian!"

She slowly materialized in front of him. "Unless a Barou master was one of the guards, no one would know where to look. My parents never broadcast my heritage to anyone, since they didn't know if I would even show any type of ability. General Varal doesn't know about my Barou blood so he wouldn't have hired anyone to look for another Barou."

"You still took quite a risk. One I didn't want you to take."

"Orla, I couldn't stand by, knowing that people were dying because of me."

"And what if they had grabbed you the moment you spoke to them?"

"But it didn't happen."

"It could have. As queen you must think of these things. What would have happened if General Varal had gotten his hands on you?"

"Orla, I understand your worry, but I was in no danger."

He grabbed her arms, forcing her to look into his eyes. "You just don't understand, do you? You can't risk your life like this. Too many people would be hurt if something happened to you."

"Who? The people on my planet? Orla, I don't have delusions of grandeur. I know that most don't even know who I am, except that I'm now their leader, and not a very good one at that. I might be queen but that doesn't mean I'm not expendable."

He wanted to shake her and make her realize how much she would be missed. Especially by him, but he knew he couldn't. To reveal his heart to her now would make matters worse.

Arian studied Oral's rigid pose, not understanding why he was so angry. He knew she held no power while she was in exile. Hopefully her people already knew what the general had planned and were trying to fight him on their own. As much as she wanted to show up with reinforcements she knew if something were to happen to her, the people of her planet would go on. They would still fight for their planet, with or without her.

One question did niggle at her. No one seemed to be left in the compound. Did General Varal take everyone and press them into his army?

The real question was what happened to Dresuer. Had he been killed? Without him, she didn't think she would be able to defeat the general.

"Orla, is everyone gone?"

"Yes. I saw Dresuer in that last group that left. He had four guards surrounding him and his hands were bound. As much as I wanted to get to him, I couldn't."

Arian noticed an odd glint in Orla's eyes. Did she see hatred or was it the night sky that reflected such an odd light into his eyes?

CHAPTER ELEVEN

"Genral Varal has taken him prisoner?" Arian frowned, but not because she was upset that Dresuer had been captured. A part of her felt relief that she had been given this reprieve. Why wasn't she upset over what had happened to Dresuer? She should be very angry that the general had him.

And why was she happy that she could spend a little more time alone with Orla before she had to fulfill her vow to her father. These feelings she was having for Orla were obviously affecting her better judgement. Dresuer was her betrothed. The man her father had picked for her yet knowing she didn't have to fill her vow for now almost made her giddy, and it was all because of Orla.

She rubbed her hand across her face, the futile gesture acted as a way to rid her mind of these wayward thoughts. But she knew better, the only way she would get rid of them was to focus on the fact that she had to free Dresuer and do what was expected of her. Even if she didn't agree with it anymore.

"So what now?" she asked.

"We go back to Metan's home and prepare to follow the general. We know where Dresuer is right now, and I don't think the General Varal will hurt him until he has you."

"I hope you're right."

Metan, Grenta, and Tymin stood at the door as they approached.

"What happened there? We saw the ships and heard the bombs exploding." Metan put a protective arm around Grenta as he spoke to them.

"Yes, master," piped in Tymin. "We feared the worst."

"Things didn't go as planned," said Arian. "The camp was attacked, and the people were taken away."

"And your betrothed?"

"Gone as well. General Varal has captured him."

Grenta stepped away from her husband. "Come inside and have some food. While you eat you can discuss what to do next."

Arian and Orla followed Grenta willingly. They knew what would come next would be very hard.

Sitting down in a chair Arian started to do her meditation, trying to relax the tense muscles in her body. What would they do next? They couldn't go back to her planet yet. She didn't have the reinforcements she needed to fight the general.

She gripped the leather cup she had been using, thinking about what their next move would be. She knew the first thing that had to be done.

"Grenta, you told me that the Barou council said you couldn't go looking for students but could train one if they went looking for you."

She nodded as she popped the last bite of a biscuit in her mouth.

"Then I have come to you willingly, and now ask you to accompany me to continue my training. I can't stay here to finish it, yet I know I can't leave in the middle of my training. Would that appease the council?"

"I don't know." Grenta stood, picked up her plate and carried it to the side board near her cupboard. After setting her things down she turned and looked at Arian. "But I accept."

"Before you accept you need to know the whole story. General Varal is hunting me. He has taken my fiancé captive, and I must rescue him. It could be very dangerous, and I can't promise you will live to see your home again."

"I can't let you go alone without finishing your training. My life has been long and full. I will go with you."

Arian watched Metan out of the corner of her eye. The man paled when his wife promised to travel with them, knowing the dangers.

"Metan, will you accompany us as well? Asking you stay here while your wife risks her life to travel with us is cruel, but you have to understand that your life may be forfeit. If we don't accomplish our goals all of our lives may be."

Metan touched his wife's face tenderly. "Thank you for the offer, but Grenta knows I will stay here. My old bones wouldn't be able to keep up with you and I fear that I would be more of a hindrance than a help."

"Are you sure? We will do everything in our power to keep you safe."

Metan turned to Arian. "I know that, child. But Grenta must do this alone. All I ask is that you try to bring her back safely."

Arian bowed, a time-honored act of respect. "We will do everything in our power to keep her safe and send her back to you unharmed."

Metan smiled at Arian's hopeful words. "But not unchanged."

He stood up and gestured toward his wife. "Come, we have much to do before you leave here."

Orla stood as well, gesturing toward Arian and Tymin, knowing that Metan and his wife deserved some time alone before they headed back to rendezvous with the ship. "We must prepare the animals for travel."

Orla and Arian stepped under the lean-to where the truggars were tethered.

"That was very kind of you." Arian felt the heat of her truggar's breath on her hand when she stepped up to brush it down. She knew how difficult this separation would be on Grenta and Metan. They doted on each other. Knowing Orla had the insight to give them these last few moments together melted her heart. It proved to her that Orla understood what love was. Something she knew her parents had and hoped to achieve one dura.

Orla remained silent.

Arian continued to comb her beast, wondering if she could love Dresuer. She might have promised her father, but it didn't mean that hers would be a love match. What if she had no love for the man. She looked at Orla. He had promised to be there for her. Was that what he meant? If her marriage was a loveless one would she be able to turn to Orla?

Her first impression of Dresuer didn't sit well. He didn't strike her as leadership material. In fact, he acted like a sniveling fool. The fact that the general could overrun the camp so easily didn't speak well for him either. Why didn't he stand up and fight for his people? If he wouldn't do it for his own people, what could she say to convince him to do it for hers? The big question was would convincing him be worth it? Or had she misread everything?

She shook her head. It was all so confusing.

Once she had her truggar completely combed and saddled, Grenta stepped into the small barn wearing her traveling cloak and carrying several small bags over her shoulder.

"Here, I've prepared some food for us to take," she said as she handed a small bag to Orla.

Arian looked at Grenta's saddened face. "You don't have to do this."

"Yes I do. Metan understands as well as I do." Grenta stepped out of the barn first, to be followed by Orla, then Arian. Tymin sat in the dirt near the front door.

He kept his distance from the truggar, which they seemed to appreciate because any time he drew near they growled. Did his smell bother the animals as much as it did the rest of them?

Metan stepped out the door, carrying a large cloth bag, and four smaller skin bags. He handed them to Orla. "There should be enough bread for the four of you to last three duras. I also packed some fruit and some jerky to help keep your strength up."

"That was supposed to be your provisions for the next few weeks," said Grenta.

"I don't need that much food, wife. It will perish before I can eat it all."

"Metan." Her voice carried the concern she felt for her husband.

"I will be fine."

Orla handed out the smaller drinking skins to everyone.

Grenta slipped hers over one shoulder just as her husband took her hands in his own.

"You are being very brave here, Grenta. You do me proud."

"Must you stay here?" she whispered, fighting back the tears that threatened to spill.

Metan nodded. "Just come back to me," he said, his voice sounding a little coarser than usual.

"If the planets permit it, nothing will keep me away."

Arian nudged her truggar forward. They didn't need to watch this farewell. Orla followed her, with Tymin bringing up the rear. Once they cleared the house they stopped and waited.

It didn't take long before Grenta caught up with them. She said nothing, just stepped in beside Tymin as they started out toward the port where the ship should be landing.

Arian wondered if their ship had been able to land without any more incidences. "How long before we can try to contact the ship?"

"Several horas. With Grenta and Tymin walking our return trip will take a lot longer." Orla scanned the horizon. "But that is going to work in our favor. It will be dark by the time we reach the port so we shouldn't be noticed."

"Do you think General Varal realizes I'm not in with the people he captured?" Arian fiddled with the reigns. She knew how angry the general would be when he learned the news that she was still free. That port could be swarming with guards, blocking their escape route.

"Probably. But the general still doesn't see you as a threat. If he did, he would have been in that tent instead of Dresuer. It's possible that he sees this as a game."

"A game? Millions of lives are at stake."

"You know he doesn't care about them. He only cares about what he can gain from this." Orla turned to look at her. "With you as the prize."

"What makes you so sure about that?" She didn't like the way this conversation was going.

"If he controls you, he can control the planet. The people will follow you and he knows that."

"My people know that I would never do his bidding. I proved that by coming to find Dresuer."

"And somehow General Varal convinced Dresuer into turning you over to him. How can you think that the general couldn't persuade you?

What if he threatened to kill off groups of your people if you fought him. Then what would you do?"

She saw anger in his eyes as he watched her. Was he mad at her, or what happened at the encampment? Times like these made her wish she knew what he was thinking.

Arian knew one thing though, once again Orla was right. She would do anything to protect her people. What ruler wouldn't. With that thought, hope blossomed in her heart.

Perhaps that was why Dresuer made a deal with the general. Maybe he had to, the general had threatened something he held precious and in order to protect it he had to go along with the general's plan. That one thought lifted her spirits. It made perfect sense, reinstating her faith in Dresuer.

The night sky, littered with a million stars, was the only light they saw as they approached the transport station.

"It is too silent," whispered Arian.

Orla agreed. He motioned for Tymin to scout ahead.

The smelly little man returned a few microns later.

"Master, there are guards everywhere."

"Any sign of the ship?"

"No. The port is completely vacant."

"Then where are the general's ships?" asked Arian.

The whirring of an engine directly above their heads caught everyone's attention. Looking up, Orla felt the frown crease his forehead.

"Never mind."

Grenta literally pulled Arian from her mount. "We must cloak ourselves. Combining our power should keep us from their sensors and their eyes."

"Tell me what I must do."

Arian and Grenta linked hands as they spoke softly to each other. Orla hoped what they planned would work. As quickly as he could, he led the animals into a small shelter nearby. Hopefully, they hadn't been detected yet.

A shout, followed by the pounding of heavy boots let him know that the guards knew they were in the area. He looked around for anything he could use for a weapon, all he could find was a few rocks and clumps of dirt. It looked like General Varal's troops had picked the area clean before they got there.

Orla and Tymin crowded Arian and Grenta into the shadows of the shelter, blocking them from a casual glance. But not interrupting their work.

Voices grew closer.

A hoarse voice penetrated Orla's thoughts.

"Join us."

He felt Grenta grope for his hand just as Arian gripped Tymin's.

"Now you complete the circle," said Grenta.

Tymin grabbed Orla's just as the guards came around the building.

CHAPTER TWELVE

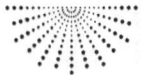

One guard stepped into view, weapon drawn. He glanced around the interior of the small shelter, looking straight through them.

He turned to his left. "No one is here, sir."

A voice floated back. "But we saw movement there just a few microns ago. Check again."

The guard retrieved a large light from a pocket in his uniform, turned it on and shone it into the darkened interior.

"There's nothing here, sir."

"Damn it, man, use your sensor. They could have hidden themselves."

The guard shrugged but did as ordered. "Sir? The sensor doesn't detect anything either."

Grenta jerked Orla's hand. "Help—concentrate."

Orla closed his eyes and tried to will his strength to Grenta and Arian to give them all the help he could. He offered comfort to Arian where their hands touched. He felt her tension flow out, and his strength flow in. Her breath slowed, becoming more rhythmic, alerting him to a deeper concentration.

Outside the shelter, another voice joined the first one. "We tracked them to this spot, they have to be here."

Orla kept his eyes closed as a second beam scanned the area. "But they're not here, sir. Could they have slipped out another way? Or created a false image for our sensors?"

"The only way they could have done that is by being on a very sophisticated ship."

Orla recognized a small beep that sounded as the second man pressed a comlink.

"Check for any ships nearby."

"We already have—"

"Check again," he thundered into the mouthpiece. Another beep closed the link. "They couldn't have just disappeared."

They could have if they had two Barou cloaking them. Orla listened as their footfalls became softer, letting him know they moved off in another direction.

"It is time to move," said Grenta.

"Where?" asked Orla.

"I noticed a small copse of trees nearby. That would be our best bet."

Orla nodded, leading the way. He pulled Arian with him. Her movements sluggish, he feared letting go of her hand. Once they had found the haven of the oasis, he took point, watching for the general's troops to search their hiding place.

Arian slumped against an outcropping of rocks.

Grenta rested a hand against her forehead for a moment, nodded to herself, then joined Orla.

"She will need to rest."

Orla shot her an angry look. "After draining herself like that she should."

"Your anger is unjustified. Every untrained Barou drains themselves at least once. Be glad it was for such a good cause, and that I am here."

"She shouldn't have been put into such a situation."

"You must understand Orla, Arian did this to save you." She paused. "Each time she drains herself like this she becomes more powerful."

"I don't care about her powers."

"I know." Grenta rested a hand on Orla's arm. "But she is a very powerful, untrained Barou, and she would have tried this on her own if I hadn't been here."

"She would have died if she'd tried this on her own."

"I'm not sure about that. Arian would have been able to keep you hidden, but not for long. And she'd be at General Varal's stronghold before she'd have the time to rejuvenate enough to protect herself."

"How long will it take before she is back to her normal self?"

"Out here, it could take duras. Under proper care, a few horas."

"We need to get her on the ship."

"Tymin said the ship wouldn't be back until the moon's zenith. She'll be fine, it just might take her a little longer to recuperate for now."

Orla nodded, keeping his vision on the guards that paused near where they were hidden. He didn't like it, but knew he had to trust Grenta on this. "As long as they don't find us."

"They won't," said Grenta as she moved back to Arian's side.

Even though Orla was upset Arian had pushed herself too hard, he was grateful that Grenta had decided to travel with them. She proved she was a true master by being able to still shield them after the tremendous use of energy. Orla did wonder how long she could keep it up before she started to feel the drain on her powers.

He wished he could contact Grinnell to set up another pickup someplace safer. They could be waiting for duras before they get off the planet.

The roar of a ship descending into the atmosphere drowned out the sounds of the night insects in the area. The nearby guards ran toward the port.

Orla glanced behind him to see if anyone watched him. Quietly, he slipped further into the brush, then shifted. Keeping to the shadows, he snuck closer to the transport.

The ship landed just as the guards surrounded it, weapons drawn. The door opened with a soft click. Two men stepped out, baring weapons.

"Is this the way you greet messengers from General Varal?" said one.

Orla studied the two men. They wore their full uniforms, which included the space helmets, that kept the new soldiers' bodies completely covered. Their odds just got worse. He knew the rest would all end up in their full uniforms unless these two took theirs off. If they didn't, his plans of taking them out one by one wouldn't work. Nothing could penetrate those suits.

"General Varal has reassigned you. You are to report back to base now."

The leader of the guards stepped forward. "But what about the search?"

"Since you have failed so miserably, he has ordered us to dust the area."

"But I thought he wanted her alive."

"I only follow orders, mister. Just like you are supposed to do."

The troop leader turned on his heel and called his men in from the field. Within fifteen microns they lined up and awaited their ship's arrival.

Orla loped back to the small copse of trees where everyone else was hidden.

"We must get out of here," he said as soon as his friends came into view. "They're going to dust the area."

Grenta looked a lot paler than she did just a few microns ago.

"We can't move. I can no longer shield us."

"If we don't move, we'll be captured." Orla bent to scoop up Arian just as he heard the soft foot falls. He spun with Arian in his arms.

The two men stood before them, guns in their hands. Then one handed his weapon over before releasing the claps to his helmet. Gripping it with two hands, he pulled it off.

"Grinnell!"

Grinnell grinned at Orla. "How'd you like a ride?"

Orla laughed. "Once you tell me how you found us."

"I can smell Tymin a kilometer away."

Once aboard ship, they hovered above the port. Grinnell pushed a button to release the dust.

Arian sat in her chair, still a little tired, but doing much better. "Why are you dropping the dust?"

"Because we did intercept a message from the general with those orders. If we follow through, then General Varal will think his men followed his orders. It helps buy a little time for us to get away."

Arian nodded. By the time the general figured out what really happened, they would be long gone.

"So where to?" asked Grinnell.

Arian looked at Orla.

"For now, let's head for Calsindar. It's the first planet out of General Varal's jurisdiction. And will give us time to regroup."

"We need to get back to Emorai." Arian didn't want to head to the frontier planet. It was in the wrong direction.

"General Varal will be looking for us. If we try to go back home now, he'll catch us before we can get there." Orla placed a hand on her shoulder. "I know this isn't want you want right now, but if we are to save your people we must retreat. How much good could we do if we are locked up in one of General Varal's cells?"

She felt the hot sting of tears but refused to let them fall. "Every dura we are away gives the general more time to kill off my people. I can't just walk away from that."

"We are not asking you to do that," said Orla. He stared at her stricken face. They needed to speak privately. "Come."

Arian took the hand he offered and followed him into their small quarters.

"Mistress, you must separate your emotions from the situation. We don't have the ability to take on the general right now."

"And how do you plan on fixing that problem? By heading in the opposite direction?" Hands on hips she glared at him, not understanding why he refused to go back to her home planet.

"Yes. We won't be able to find anyone to help us within the general's influence. They will be too frightened of him." Orla watched her, making her nervous.

"Are you talking about hiring soldiers of fortunes?" She started to pace in the small room.

"I'm not dismissing any avenue right now. First, we need to get somewhere we feel safe, where you can train, and we can come up with the right strategy. We can't do that on the run, which is what we would be doing if we stayed here." Orla stepped up to her and cupped her chin. "When we face the general it has to be on our terms. You know that."

She remained silent. Anger rolled off her in waves, but she knew he was right once again.

"Do you have a better idea?"

"No, but that doesn't make your decision right." Arian pulled her chin free. She started pacing again.

"I know the thought of taking your planet back by force upsets you, but we must look at every contingency. You did say at all costs."

She nodded. "But must we leave this quadrant? This is one of the general's best ships."

"And reported stolen."

Arian wanted to huff at him. "It can outrun most of the other ships in the general's fleet."

"True, but do you want to constantly run from Varal's ships? How long do you think the general will take to set a trap for us and we are caught?"

"Orla."

"Mistress, look at this logically. We have five people in our troop. The general has thousands. How can we fight against those odds?"

Arian stared at the plain white floor, fighting the tears that threatened to spill once again. "I feel like I am abandoning them, Orla."

"Because we are leaving this quadrant?" He stepped up to Arian, placed his hand on her chin again and lifted her face. The heartbreak etched on her face shook him to the core. "This is a smartest move we could make right now."

She gave him a half-hearted smile. "I know it is. In my head, I think it is brilliant. If the general learns we have fled the quadrant he might believe that I gave up. If that happens we could sneak up on him when we do go back. But my heart says I must stay and protect my people at all costs, even if that means my own life."

Orla's heart constricted at the thought of her losing her life to save her planet. Brushing one of his thumbs across a cheek to catch a tear that slipped down the soft flesh, he vowed that he'd die to protect her life.

The soft light reflected in her eyes drew him in. He continued to brush his thumb across her velvet skin. Orla didn't realize his own intent until he pressed his lips against hers. She tasted like the delicate fruit, tajha, from his home planet. The honeyed nectar, like an addiction, made it difficult to stop once you started. He knew he couldn't stop now he'd started.

A soft gasp escaped her when he nibbled on her bottom lip, but he couldn't help himself. The delicate tidbit beckoned him, tempting him beyond the control he had kept himself locked under.

His arms slipped around her soft body, drawing her against his, then he twined his fingers in her hair, so he could hold her head at just the right angle to give him the greatest access.

Arian hesitated for a secur, but then she softened against him and started to return the kiss. As her response became more eager, he deepened the kiss. Hesitantly, she opened her mouth for him, then she twirled her tongue around his, growing more confident with each stroke.

Passion rose inside him, threatening to overpower both of them. Orla knew Arian hadn't initiated this and he promised himself it had to be her decision. He knew if he didn't stop now, he couldn't be sure he would be able to stop later.

Breaking the kiss, he looked at her face. Her eyes, overly bright, showed the unmasked passion he had awakened in her with that kiss. Her swollen lips beckoned for more.

"Mistress, I need to get back to the cockpit."

She just looked at him.

He wished she would say something instead of gazing at him with those passion filled eyes. If she kept it up, he wouldn't be able to leave.

Unable to resist, he gave her one more kiss then walked out of the door before he could do something he would regret.

CHAPTER THIRTEEN

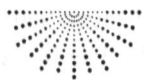

A rian continued to stare at the door Orla had just exited, every nerve in her body sparking from the emotions he lit with that kiss. She touched her thoroughly kissed lips. What was she going to do? The more time she spent with Orla the deeper her feelings for him ran. So deep she feared she was falling in love with him.

Why was this happening now? She had to fulfil the vow she made to her father, yet now the thought of marrying a man she didn't know scared her. Especially since she knew that Orla would still be her pet. The bond they had developed as children would last their lifetime. How could she perform her wifely duties knowing that Orla was there in the same house, possibly in the same room?

Arian crossed to the small alcove that held the sink, shower, and refuse receptacle. Two hands braced on either side of the sink, she wished water poured from it instead of the sonic lights that would clean her face. Right now, she wanted to feel the cool liquid against her hands as she splashed it on her face and neck.

A soft chime filled the air, making her turn toward the door.

"Enter." She wondered if Orla had returned. Nerves taught, she held her breath as the door slid open.

"I had hoped we could start our lessons," said Grenta, standing in the doorway.

"Of course." Arian brushed her hands down the front of her tunic, realizing she still wore the outfit from the planet. What a fright she must look. "Let me change first."

"Meet me in the mess hall."

She nodded. The door slid closed, allowing her privacy to switch her soiled traveling clothes for something clean. She picked out one of the soft dresses she had, knowing if nothing else, it would lift her spirits.

After a quick sonic shower, she slipped the silky material over her head and felt it slide down her body. Training would be the perfect thing to take her mind off Orla. It would also help keep her away from him for a few horas. Hopefully long enough to sort through her thoughts.

Orla found concentrating to be the hardest task he had ever undertaken. All he could think of was Arian's soft body against his as she opened herself to him. If this didn't stop soon he'd be walking around with a permanent erection. Grinnell and Leabo noticed his state when he first walked onto the bridge. A wry grin spread across his lips. It was hard to miss. He not only had the same physical arousal signals that most humanoids did, but he had to add the Miran's signals to the mix. Eyes black as a Daruvan cave bat, and sparks of electricity snapping in his hair. Over all very hard to ignore.

Luckily, neither of the men made a comment.

Tymin, who had just entered, was not as smart.

"Master, what is wrong?"

Orla knew all he could see was the sparks in his hair. He wondered how he would react when Tymin saw his eyes. "Leave it be."

"But, Master."

Orla spun in his chair and stared at Tymin, who cringed under his stare.

Tymin swallowed hard. Giving Orla a wide berth, he edged toward his chair, all the while keeping an eye on his master.

Grinnell spoke, breaking up the heavy tension that hung in the room.

"We are about three duras away from the planet. Most of it is rural, with the exception of the cities with landing ports."

"We still need to keep a low profile. Can this ship be landed without using the landing ports?" Orla welcomed the change in topic. He needed to keep his mind off Arian.

"We can't enter the atmosphere without being detected."

"That is not what I asked, Grinnell." His sharp ears heard Grinnell swallow hard.

"Theoretically, yes. This ship is equipped with landing gear, but it has never been used. I'm not sure the gear even works."

"Then it must be tested." Orla waited for Grinnell to argue with him. Instead the man looked at Leabo before agreeing.

"The schematics are in the archive."

Orla pushed a few buttons. This was just what he needed to occupy his mind. Grinnell and Leabo were wise enough to realize this as well, since they turned it over to him instead of asking who should do it.

When the schematics popped up on the screen, he started to study them.

By the time the dinner bell chimed, Orla's eyes had returned to their normal color, and the electricity in his hair had died down. The only thing still evident was a certain part of his anatomy that remained at attention. This worried Orla. How was he going to continue to share a room with Arian if he couldn't control his desire for her? Of course, he'd still have to make it through dinner without the other signs showing back up first. Arian might not know what a miran looked like when aroused, but her curiosity would push her to ask questions. Questions he didn't want to answer. Once she learned the truth, she might not want to be around him at all.

Her desire to fulfill the vow she made to her father was strong. As long as she believed that his twin was the real Dresuer, she would try to rescue him. If he told her the truth now, would she accept him? Or even believe him? Or would she think he told her this for his own dark reasons?

Orla rubbed a hand over his face. He couldn't reveal the truth yet. It was much too soon. Arian's sheltered life still had a strong hold on her, making her believe in the best in everyone. Until she learned who she should and shouldn't trust he had to keep his secret to himself.

Frustrated with the dilemma, he approached the door to the mess hall. He hoped she wore a huge bag over her head. The doors slid open to reveal Arian laughing with Grenta. An image hovered between them of a small Miran prancing about with its tail switching back and forth.

Orla took one look at Arian in the soft blue dress that molded to every curve on her body and groaned. Dinner was going to be hell.

Arian looked up when she heard the groan and blushed. The audience she had suddenly acquired wasn't supposed to see what she had created. The Miran dissipated as she tried to draw her wits about her.

Grenta noticed very early that Arian couldn't concentrate on the lessons. Her suggestion was for her to confront what was bothering her. Instead of revealing the intimacy that was starting to develop between her and Orla, Arian created the Miran to help her confront the feelings that she had for Orla that wouldn't go away. Feelings she wasn't sure how to act on, or even if she should act on them.

This was the one time she wished there was someone she could confide in, and maybe explain why every time she was near Orla, she wanted to find out what it would be like to be with him. Trying to talk to Orla was out of the question, and she didn't feel close enough to anyone else to reveal this problem to yet. Her thoughts kept her from noticing the arrival of the rest of the crew.

Grenta stood and addressed everyone. "My goodness, we didn't realize it was so late. I hope I haven't kept Arian from any of her chores."

"No," said Grinnell after he glanced at Orla. "Besides, we would have paged her if we needed her."

"Dinner won't take but a moment. Why don't you have a seat while I program the replicator?" Leabo had already started to push the proper buttons before he finished speaking.

Arian stole a quick glance at Orla, feeling highly embarrassed. Knowing how much Orla enjoyed teasing her, she waited for some barb about the image they had all walked in on. His silence worried her. Had she done something wrong and angered him to a point where he refused to talk to her?

Almost on cue he lifted his head and looked at her. The intensity of his gaze trapped her. Suddenly they were alone in the room. She felt herself responding to his deepening gaze. The lumlights were doing loops and swirls in her stomach and blood roared in her ears. Not expecting such a strong response, she gripped the edge of the bench she had sat on a few moments earlier.

She let out a soft cry when a small sliver of metal sliced through her skin. Lifting her hand she stared at the linear gash in the center of her palm. Blood pooled in her hand, edging closer to the side of her hand before it started to drip a steady beat on the table top.

Orla grabbed her hand, staring at the wound. Without thinking he placed his mouth against her palm, lathing it with his tongue, trying to stop the flow.

Grinnell jumped up and raced to the first aid kit kept in sealed wall in the mess. When he returned, he placed the kit on the table next to Arian's other hand.

Orla held her palm in his as he opened the kit and pulled out what he needed to seal the wound.

Arian held her breath as Orla licked her wound clean. There was something about the way he did it that was almost sexual. The warmth of his mouth against her palm had her heart jumping. Heat pooled in places she didn't expect. Orla was her pet. Nothing more, but her body wanted more.

As he continued to lathe the wound he looked up into her eyes. The heat that emanated there sent a tingle through her that went straight to her toes. Something passed between them. Arian didn't know what it was, nor did she understand it, but she knew that Orla felt it as much as she did.

Once he used the first aid kit to wrap the wound properly, they both sat down and at their meals in silence.

Grinnell spoke about the planet they were going to, with Leabo adding a few comments here and there. Grenta smiled and nodded, watching Orla and Arian the entire time.

Once Arian finished her meal she stood, excused herself and headed back to her quarters. Her stomach lurched when Orla stood as well. The quarters they shared would become very tiny the moment Orla would enter the room.

Before Orla could follow her though, Grenta asked to speak to him.

Arian felt a small reprieve, knowing that Orla would be detained for a few securs. She didn't know what would happen between them, but she knew it was something she couldn't ignore.

Grenta waited until everyone left the mess hall before speaking to Orla.

"You are her true mate."

"Yes." Orla couldn't see lying to the woman. Sooner or later she would learn the truth.

"And if Arian were to confront you, she would learn the truth too."

"Yes."

"Then why don't you tell her the truth?"

"Because she isn't ready for it." Orla placed his hands on the table between them. "If I were to tell her now, she wouldn't believe me. You know that, you have worked with her."

"But the emotions that are passing between you two are powerful. It is too strong to ignore, and soon it will start affecting all the members of this crew."

"Don't you think I know that? I know the power of the Miran passion, but there is nothing I can do about it now. She needs time."

"Yet you still share a room with her."

"I have to," he nearly shouted. "I can't trust anyone. To be sure she is protected I must be with her."

"And who is going to protect her from you?"

Her question stunned him. "She doesn't need protection from me."

Grenta just raise an eyebrow at him. "Then why won't you trust her with the truth."

"I do trust her." Orla started to pace back and forth, like a caged animal.

"But she doesn't know who you truly are."

Orla stopped and glared at the woman, the hairs on the back of his neck stood up. How much did she know? "What are you talking about?"

"Who you are." Grenta held up her hands before Orla could speak. "My boy, I have lived near your compound for a long time. Metan and I knew who you were the first time we saw you. That is one of the reasons he stopped you that dura."

A low growl emanated from Orla.

"Your father spoke to Metan just before he disappeared. He knew something could happen and feared you would come home looking for him."

"Then you know what happened at the compound."

"No." Grenta sat down in a chair as she gathered her thoughts. "I only know that your father suspected something. He came to Metan with a warning for the villagers not to go to the compound for a while. Those that didn't listen never came back. When those people started to disappear, I feared the worst about your father. Rumors have it that he is still alive. General Varal has him detained some place."

"And how did you learn this?"

"Some of your people have been escaping the compound. One or two every so often. They were the ones who gave us this information. I don't know how accurate it is, but I never doubted their sincerity."

"When was the last time you saw my father?"

"Six lunas ago."

Orla looked at her in shock. His father disappeared before Arian and her father had any inkling that general Varal was trying to take over the planet.

"But this has nothing to do with the feelings between you and Arian. She is my main concern right now."

At just the mention of her name Orla felt his mating drive increase. How was he going to be around her without taking her?

"There is a complication." Grenta paused just long enough to gain Orla's full attention. "She is a Barou."

"I know that." Orla fought hard not to roll his eyes. By now everyone on the ship knew of her talents.

"An untrained one."

The air on the back of his neck prickled at the words. What now?

"There is that one instant where each of us reach that moment of bliss, where we lose control. For an untrained Barou that could be deadly."

"So you are saying..."

"Yes." Grenta clasped her hands in front of her on the table. "I didn't think I'd have to evoke the Barou law of abstinence between you two, but I will if you can't control your mating desire."

"How would you stop me?" Orla couldn't help himself. Curiosity got the best of him.

Grenta only smiled. "Do you really want to know?"

CHAPTER FOURTEEN

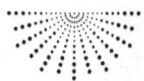

"I'd make you see something that is not there."

Orla narrowed his eyes at Grenta. "Who said there would be lights on?"

Grenta laughed. She knew Orla was just rebelling against the fact that someone might actually be able to stop him. "No one."

It was Orla's turn to laugh, before he sobered his thoughts. "I would never do anything to jeopardize Arian. But you must know that if she asks, I can't deny her. My mating drive wouldn't let me."

"And if she loses control?"

"Each time her talent appeared it never harmed a soul. I have the faith that she would never hurt anyone, no matter what."

"And what if she does?"

"No offence, Grenta, but I have known her all my life. She would rather chop off her own hand than harm anyone. Her subconscious would stop her. This thing between the two of us is natural and would have happened even if we hadn't met you. I will never push her into something she isn't ready for, but I must protect her. I can't protect her as well if I'm not with her."

"But I can," countered Grenta.

"And if another Barou would accompany one of the general's raids?

You wouldn't be able to use your powers to shield her. I can protect her no matter what." Orla smiled apologetically. "I am here for Arian. If she tells me to stay away then I will, but if she wants me at her side that is where I'll be."

Grenta nodded, knowing she wouldn't change Orla's mind. She had to keep them apart until Arian had a better handle on her powers. Grenta also knew that Arian needed to understand the feelings she had for Orla before she became his mate. They were just asking for trouble if it happened too quickly.

Orla walked back to their room, pondering Grenta's words. He knew the woman was right, if Arian lost control there could be danger. Yet he knew he was right too. Arian would never do anything to harm anyone.

Pressing his palm to the door he stepped inside the room once it opened. His eyes adjusted to the darkened room while he shifted into his Miran shape.

It wasn't hard to spot Arian in her bunk, her features softened in slumber. He itched to touch the soft silver hair that spilled across the pillows. His mind imagined burying his face in those long silky tresses as he made her his.

His tail twitched angrily. How was he going to make it through the night without touching her?

Arian woke the next morning with a purring noise in her ear. Orla, in his Miran shape, had draped himself over her sometime in the night. She shoved at him several times before she finally moved him off enough to escape the bed.

"Orla, Can you purr any louder? I don't think Grinnell and Leabo heard you on the bridge."

Placing his weight on his hind legs, Orla stretched out on the bed, claws extended, as he gave her a feline yawn.

Watching his graceful moves had her blood pounding. He was

beautiful. He leaped off the bed and walked up to her, wrapping his tail around her, triggering sensations Arian had never felt before. Her body reacted to the sensations, raising her body temperature, making her eyes dilate and shortening her breath.

She moved away from him by heading to the sonic shower. "Grenta has asked me to join her for some early training, since I'm not needed on the bridge that much I agreed."

Her skin prickled when the shower turned on, she noticed soft shimmer surround Orla as he reverted to human form through the frosted glass door. She hoped he was fully clothed. Arian wasn't sure if she could handle seeing him naked again. Her feelings for him had her all mixed up inside.

She stepped from the shower with her night shift on. After a quick dart to her closet, she donned another simple outfit that matched the type of cloths everyone wore on the ship. A soft aqua shift that covered her from head to foot.

She thought she had covered everything until she looked into Orla's eyes. He watched her as if he could see straight through her cloths. She noticed his eyes start to darken and wondered what caused it.

"Um—I'll go ahead and meet Grenta." Arian came real close to stuttering. She also didn't want to leave right now. Something drew her to Orla, making her want to touch him, and have him kiss her again. Before she could follow through on the feelings zipping through her body she slipped out the door and headed to the mess hall.

She found Grenta waiting for her. If she noticed anything different about her, she didn't comment on it.

"So are you ready to start working?"

"Yes." She sat on the floor opposite from where Grenta had just sat. This should help keep her mind off of Orla.

They worked together for several horas before Arian finally fell back onto the floor and said. "Enough."

Grenta laughed. "Why don't you rest for a while and we'll start again after dinner?"

"Oh. I'm supposed to help on the bridge after dinner for a few horas."

"Then how about after you finish?"

"I guess I could for a few horas." Arian wanted to question why

Grenta wanted to meet so late but knowing they had dragged her from her husband and home stopped her. Perhaps Grenta needed to keep busy so she wouldn't miss her husband.

"Good. We'll meet here once you're finished." Grenta stood up and headed out the door.

Arian stared after her. How very odd. Not knowing why Grenta wanted to work with her again so soon caught her off guard. She suddenly seemed to want to push Arian to train harder, yet she always seemed happy when their training sessions were over.

Arian retired to her room for a few horas before she wandered down to the bridge. Boredom kept her from resting for too long.

"Arian! You're not needed here until this evening," said Leabo.

"I know, but I thought I'd come up here and see if you had anything you needed done right now."

"A bit free now, huh?"

She nodded.

"You could help scan for info on General Varal," said Grinnell.

"I thought you had the computer set to scan for him automatically."

"We do, but we haven't had the time to read through anything the computer found lately."

Arian smiled as she took her seat. At least that would keep busy for a while. She read through several posts before she felt someone watching her. Turning she found Orla observing her.

A light blush spread across her cheeks. She turned back to the screen, hoping no one else would notice how just looking at him affected her. What was he thinking about when he looked at her that way?

Her mind started to daydream was she read through more posts. She imagined her and Orla alone in their room, both acting a little nervous because of the intimacy. Then Orla would step close and take her in his arms like he had done before. This imaginary kiss was just as potent as the real ones had been, making her blood boil and her heart race.

She shook herself mentally. Thinking about his kiss wouldn't help her concentrate at all. Arian cleared her throat and proceeded to read more posts, trying to keep her mind off her fantasies about Orla.

Something caught her attention in the fifth post she read. It was an obscure remark, but it seemed to jump out at her. She reread it several times before she was sure she had read it right.

"Where is Nortura?"

"About a duras travel. Why?" asked Grinnell.

"This post says something about the general making a side trip there to visit an old friend from Drahar." Arian turned her chair so she could look at the three men.

"Put it up on the main screen."

"There is also a newsclip with it." Arian pushed a few buttons so the post could show up where everyone could see it.

"Show us the news clip," said Orla.

In a few securs an image of a young female news reporter popped up on the main screen.

"...General Varal is taking a quick side trip to his stronghold on Nortura. A long time friend has fallen ill."

A picture of Dresuer leaped unto the screen.

"The General hopes to give support to his friend in his time of need. But he says for everyone not to worry, he'll still maintain everything from there for as long as he needs. In other news..."

Arian sucked in her breath at the sight of Dresuer. It must be a...

"Setup," Orla said out loud. "He wants us to jump at the bait."

"Why? Wouldn't he know that we'd ignore it?" asked Grinnell.

"I'm not sure. Perhaps the general is so sure we'd want to rescue Dresuer that he didn't deem it necessary to try to make it look real."

"But what if it is real?" Arian couldn't stop the question from spilling from her mouth.

"The general would never tell anyone where he was going without a good reason. The fact that he leaked it to the press smacks of paruka."

Arian wanted to agree but she couldn't help but think that they should jump at the chance while they knew where Dresuer was.

"And if it is false, then Dresuer might not even be there."

Arian turned to look at Orla, who had been the one who spoke. She hadn't thought of that. In fact, she didn't know if Dresuer was even still alive.

Later that evening she sat on the floor across from Grenta, the thoughts of Orla never too far from her mind. She hoped that Grenta didn't plan anything too difficult tonight.

She put her through a series of simple exercises in the beginning.

"Now that you have warmed up a bit let's start working on something a little more difficult. I want you to create a new image for yourself."

"What sort of image?"

"Whatever you want."

Arian thought about it. The only thing she could come up with was a different hair color.

"No, my child. You have to be able to fully disguise yourself."

She concentrated a little harder and changed her eye color along with the hair.

"Your face is still the same."

Arian huffed. "What do you want? All my features changed? Like this?" In an instant she had altered her features to resemble one of the truggars.

"Not bad, but how about a humanoid?"

She rolled her eyes as the first image dissipated. After a few microns, she created a second image of one of the older cooks that always had a sweet for her when she snuck into the kitchen without permission.

"Very good." She walked around her to make sure the image went all around. "Now, how long can you hold it?"

"I don't know." Arian shrugged.

"How long have some of the other uncontrolled manifestations lasted?"

"That stupid tail lasted quite a while."

Grenta nodded. She noticed the image start to waver. "Hold it as long as you can."

"I am."

"Once you develop the strength to maintain the image for a long time then we'll work on giving the image depth. That will help stop the flickering that is happening."

"I don't see anything."

"That's because you don't have a mirror." Grenta clasped her hands in from of her as she concentrated.

Arian found herself staring at a mirror where Grenta had been only moments before. "That is amazing!"

"You will find something like this very easy in no time. The inanimate objects are much easier to manipulate. I can hide in any room in full view."

The doors behind them slid open, halting the conversation.

Arian felt the room shrink when Orla stepped into the room. The image she had created dissolved instantly.

"I'm sorry. I came down to get something to drink." He looked around and found her by herself. "Am I intruding?"

"No." She glanced at the mirror, wondering why Grenta hadn't dropped her illusion. "I was practicing a little."

"I saw. You seem to be progressing very well. Wasn't that one of the cooks?"

A slight blush filled her cheeks. "Yes. She was always so nice to me, so I found her image easy to create. Do you really think that it looked like her?"

"From what I saw, yes." He moved with feline grace to the replicator.

Arian watched Orla's long finger punch the buttons as he selected the beverage he wanted. She flushed when she remembered those fingers on her body bringing her to heights she had never reached before.

Drink in hand, Orla turned back toward her. "Well, I'll leave you to finish your work."

She nodded, afraid to speak. Her jumbled emotions didn't want Orla to leave her just yet, but she knew Grenta was there and she wanted privacy.

Orla stood there for a few microns, as if he didn't want to leave. Then finally started to move toward the door.

Once the door closed, Grenta dropped her mirror image. "So, you are in love with him, aren't you?"

CHAPTER FIFTEEN

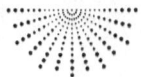

"What makes you ask such a thing?" Arian feared that Grenta could see something she didn't want known. Her goal was to marry Dresuer and save her planet, not seek some sort of formal bond with Orla. Her promise to her father on his death bed won't allow her to do anything else. The feelings she had for Orla didn't matter. Her planet came first.

"You deny that you're attracted to him?"

Arian glanced around the room. She couldn't answer her unless she was willing to admit what she feared was happening between her and Orla.

Grenta seemed to let her non-commitment slide. At least until she spoke. "I know the truth, Arian, even if you won't admit it."

"I don't know what you are taking about." She started to wander around the mess hall so she wouldn't have to look Grenta in the eye. Arian couldn't lie to her if she did.

"You have feelings for Orla."

"I have an obligation to my father. One I must fulfill." She ran her fingers over the buttons Orla had pressed earlier.

"Even if that means you'll never be happy?"

"Saving my planet will make me happy." She wasn't sure if she said that to reassure Grenta or herself.

"Arian, you are only looking at the goal you want to achieve by marrying Dresuer. How will you feel about this after you achieve that goal? Are you sure you will still want to be married to him lunas or yepas later? What if it is a loveless match? How will you cope?"

That was a question she didn't really want to answer. She had asked herself the same question a lot lately, but she didn't want to face the feelings she had for Orla. Once she saved her planet then she would face this.

Arian sat at her station, reading more posts as her mind wandered. What if Grenta was right and she found herself in a marriage she didn't want? How could she be married to one man while loving another?

"I must do what is required to save my planet," she said out loud. Arian looked around after her outburst. Thank goodness the bridge was empty at the moment.

Scanning the posts they had received for the dura she didn't see anything mentioning General Varal. Clearing her screen, she figured that Grinnell, Orla, and Leabo must be right. As much as she didn't want to admit it, the general had set a blatant trap, hoping they would be dumb enough to fall for it.

Orla, Grinnell, and Leabo had gone forward with their plan to leave the sector to regroup. They should reach that planet on a dura or two.

The doors slid open, drawing Arian's attention. The room filled up with a foul odor before Tymin had even entered the room. This was the first time she had seen him in a couple of duras. He usually kept to himself, but on this ship he practically hibernated.

"Good dura to you, Tymin."

He stopped and stared at her, acting like he didn't expect her to speak to him. "Mistress."

He had to use the one phrase that would make her blush. Only Orla called her that and only when they were alone. How did Tymin learn of the nick-name Orla had given her? The few times he might have used it around other people couldn't have been over heard. Orla could pitch his voice in such a way that only the people he wanted to hear him would.

Tymin must have noticed a frown start to pucker on her forehead because he launched into an explanation of why he had come to the bridge.

"Master asked me to get something for him. I no want to disturb you."

Master. That's what Tymin always called Orla. She smiled, realizing that was why Tymin called her mistress. In deference to Orla.

"You are not disturbing me, Tymin. I'm sorry if I acted rude."

Tymin's little body jerked at her words. "On no, mistress. You never rude. Not like other people, but Tymin use to it. He don't care."

"You and master take good care of Tymin." The smelly little man walked to Orla's station and picked up a small bag. "Make Tymin want to help."

Arian had the good grace to blush at his words. All this time she couldn't get past his smell, and here he was willing to lay his life on the line for her and her cause, and for no real reason.

Tymin shuffled out of the room, leaving Arian with her thoughts. She wished she didn't think so much, but all the inactivity left her with very little else to do. Her training with Grenta moved quickly along. She could feel the difference already, more in control. Those episodes of uncontrollable shifting had stopped, and she could shift into any of the images she had been trained to do quickly and easily now. In the beginning she could only hope she would be able to make simple things. Now she was working on much more complicated imaging.

Maybe taking this side trek would be a blessing in disguise. Arian wanted to try to shift into other things than what she could remember and being on that planet would give her all sorts of items to copy. Although Grenta hadn't said anything to her she sensed that the next step would be for her to practice her shifting on strangers to see if she could fool them.

Excitement started to zing through her blood at the thought. If she could fool strangers, then she could practice on her friends. Once she could hide in plain view of them, she would be able to walk right under the general's nose and he would never know she was even there. Then she could free Dresuer without fear of being caught. All she needed to do was formulate a plan.

She needed to talk to Orla, and she went in search for him the moment she finished her shift. Since Tymin had been on the bridge retrieving something for Orla just a little while ago, she assumed they were still together. Arian let her nose lead her to Tymin and hopefully to Orla.

Turning a corner, she heard them long before she would be able to see them.

"But master, Tymin not know this place we go. How can I find a safe place if I not know?"

"I have faith in you, Tymin."

Arian paused outside the door instead of walking into the science lab where the two men were.

"No, Master. Tymin not do this."

"Tymin, you must do this. There is no one else."

She heard him shuffling around, knowing he was trying to think of another way to get out of the task that Orla was asking of him. Arian decided to step up to the door instead of hiding just outside. Eavesdropping was not something she liked doing. It felt wrong to her.

Orla looked toward the door, spotting her quickly. The moment they made eye contact his dilated. Arian wondered if hers did the same thing. She felt a reaction the moment she saw him but didn't know if it showed. Instinctively she looked down, breaking eye contact with him.

Tymin tried to sneak out the door then she walked in. Just as he made it to the door Orla spoke. "Tymin, you know your job when we land, right?"

His shoulders slumped. "Yes."

Orla smiled as Tymin disappeared around the corner.

"Orla, I need to talk to you," said Arian, suddenly feeling nervous. What if he didn't agree with her idea. "I have an idea on how to free Dresuer."

He stiffened at her words.

"Once I have mastered my Barou training—"

"No." He stood up and moved away from her.

"But you haven't heard what I was going to say."

"You want to disguise yourself and sneak in where the General has said he is holding Dresuer." He turned back toward her. "I can't let you do that. What if the general has a Barou working for him? You'd be spotted."

"But we don't know that."

"Arian, I don't want anything to happen to you."

"I will be careful."

"I know that." He took her hands in his. "But you aren't a warrior. What if you have to fight for your life? Could you take another life if it came to that?"

She looked up at him, not knowing how to answer that question. She didn't believe in killing, but if it comes down to her life or someone else's she hoped she could protect herself. "Then train me to be a warrior."

Orla stared at her. "Why?"

"You said yourself that I can't protect myself. What if I find myself isolated from everyone else?"

"All right. You can be trained, but not by me. I'll speak to Grinnell."

"Why can't you train me?"

"Grinnell has had professional training and knows how to train others. He is the best choice for this."

Arian nodded. Although she felt like Orla was avoiding her by having Grinnell train her, she saw the logic of his suggestion. Besides if she really thought about it, she wouldn't be able to concentrate as well if Orla was training her. She'd be too busy trying to keep her emotions in check.

Orla released her hands, she thought, reluctantly, but she figured she was just imagining it. He walked over to the com pad and paged Grinnell to the science lab.

A few microns later, Grinnell entered the room.

"You wanted to speak to me?"

"Yes. Arian has a request," said Orla.

Her eyes widened at his words. She didn't expect she'd have to ask him. "Um yes. I want to be trained to protect myself. Orla suggested you."

Grinnell seemed to pale a little at her words. "You want me to train you?"

"Oh, yes."

"I don't know. I mean, it is very difficult."

"I can handle difficult."

"Not for you." He gave her a sheepish smile. "For me. Arian, you are still my Queen, I don't know if I can push you the way I would have to, to teach you properly."

"Forget I am your queen."

"I can't."

"Grinnell, you must help me. Think about what could happen to me if I don't have the training and get into a situation where I would need it."

"I will try, but you must do everything I say. You can't get angry, or cry. Everything I do is for your own good."

"When can we start?"

"Tomorrow, after lunch. I won't have to be on the bridge for several horas."

"Thank you, Grinnell."

"Don't thank me yet. Let's see how you do first."

Three duras later, everyone stood on the bridge as the planet loomed into view. The lush green planet grew larger and larger until it filled the view screen.

"Are you sure we should approach the planet cloaked? What if they detect us?"

"It is better to learn the cloaking devise doesn't work here then when we try to get in without the general finding out." Orla pressed a few buttons. "The shield is holding. Let's tap into their communications to see if they suspect anything."

Leabo opened the ship's com link to monitor the planet. The noise that filled the air didn't say anything about their approach.

The ship entered the atmosphere undetected.

"So far so good. Now we get to see if the landing gear works."

"It will work," said Orla. "I checked them several times to make sure."

They landed a little outside of the only large city on the planet. Within a few horas they set up camp. After testing the weather, and learning the temperature stayed at a steady comfortable temperature they decided to set up several tents so everyone could get out of the ship for a cycle or two. The length they had planned to stay.

Orla made plans to visit the city. He needed to ferret out anyone he could to help with their cause. People had been escaping the general's influence for lunas, some had to have arrived here. Some of them should be willing to fight for their queen, but he knew he had to be careful too, he wouldn't know who he could trust.

Of course he never straightened out Arian's misconception that he was looking for soldiers of fortune. If she knew he was looking for people from her planet she'd want to accompany him. He didn't need to worry about her safety as he searched for help. Finding them would be hard enough. He'd have to ask the right questions. Talk to the right people.

Luckily between Grinnell and Grenta she'd be too busy to even think about accompanying him.

He set out the next morning, before anyone was awake and started to travel to the city. This first visit was just to feel it out. Tymin had left the dura before to see if he could find a place for him to stay while he searched for recruits.

As he came up on the edge of the city he found a group of young children playing in a small garbage pile. It didn't take long before a woman, he assumed was the mother of the children, came out, shouting at the children to get out of the trash and into the house. Orla smiled at the grumbling children as they did what their mother told them to do. By the different piles of rubbish he saw in front of most of the small homes he passed Orla assumed it was trash day.

That assumption was verified later when he passed the workers clearing a small pile in front of one house. Although the men used a small cart to help them collect some of the discarded items, most of the items were disintegrated on the spot. The small silver rod they used to remove the trash didn't look familiar to Orla. It was possible the general's influence hadn't reached here as they suspected.

He worked his way down the small road toward the center of the city. The closer he drew the bigger the homes became. Then the small shops started to crop up here and there. Vendors stood outside, chatting instead of guarding their wares.

"...the Browlman swears that visitors arrived last night," said one of the older men in the small crowd.

"Pah, the Browlman is just an old busy body who wants everyone to think she is some sort of oracle," responded another.

"She did help my daughter find her promise ring when she lost it the last time."

"Heacen, your daughter would lose her head if it wasn't attached to her shoulders, and everyone knows she bakes pastries for you to sell. I could have guessed where she left that ring."

Laughter filled the air.

Orla continued by them, wondering who this Browlman was. She could definitely cause trouble for them if they weren't careful. Deep in thought, he passed by one shop without paying attention.

"He's one of them." An older woman, wearing a flamboyant gown of purples and yellows came screaming out of her small shop.

Orla gaped at the little woman who practically tackled him in the street. The purple and yellow gown flowed around her as she moved. The material didn't look familiar, but it shined and glowed in the sun in such a way it reminded him of the iridescent gowns Arian wore at home.

"You are one of them, aren't you?" She flitted around him in her excitement.

"I'm not sure what you are talking about." The woman's height barely cleared his hip. Yet she had a commanding presence.

"You are one of those travelers I saw in my vision." Her shriek earlier had drawn a crowd.

"Browlman, stop accosting that poor stranger."

Orla recognized the man. He was one of the merchants who had been talking about this woman earlier.

The Browlman glared at the crowd before taking Orla's hand and dragging him into her shop. Although he could have refused to go with her, he didn't sense any kind of threat from her, and he had to admit that he was curious.

"Those old clucking pricos don't understand my abilities. They think I'm some addled old woman who misses her husband too much." She gestured toward a chair. "Please sit, we have much to talk about."

Orla watched her as she hustled around the small room. After closing her curtains, she prepared them a drink. She offered a cool glass to Orla, then took a seat opposite him.

"I'm sorry I stampeded you the way I did earlier. I was just so excited to see you I forgot myself."

"We have never met." Orla took a sip of the beverage she offered him. It's sweet/sour taste was new to him. He decided after several sips that he did like the flavor as it slid down his throat.

"Yes we have," she replied. She tapped her head. "In here."

"Explain, please."

"For the last few cycles I have dreamed of your coming." She leaned over and patted his hand. "You are here to fulfill a great quest. Let's see, you are traveling with three other men and two women, the young one is the one who has the mission. Something about defeating someone to regain control of her planet. The rest is a little fuzzy to me."

Orla stiffened at her words. Had he stepped into some sort of trap set by Varal?

CHAPTER SIXTEEN

"I want to join you on your quest."

Orla choked on his drink. "I don't think—"

She went on like he hadn't spoken. "Everything I need is packed. Oh, this is going to be such fun."

"I don't think you understand." He set his drink down. What had he gotten into? "I can't take you with me."

"Yes, you will. I have dreamed it." She stood up and grabbed the pack she had prepared. "When do you want to leave?"

Orla stood as well. "Um, thank you for the drink, ma'am, but I think I'll be going now."

"Of course, of course, just lead the way."

"You can't come with me." He stood a step back.

His words finally penetrated. "And why not?"

"Because." Orla didn't know what to say. He couldn't reveal the truth of why he was there, even if she seemed to know all about their mission. His special senses didn't detect any evil in her. His instincts told him to believe her. "I didn't come to recruit a woman, but warriors."

"I can take you to some warriors, if that is what you really want."

"It is." He inched toward the door.

"Then let us go and find your warriors." She stepped out into the sunlight and waited for Orla to join her.

"Ma'am."

"Please, call me the Browlman, everyone else does." She fell into step beside Orla. "The men you are seeking are in the eastern section of the city. It is not the safest part of town, but most people leave you alone as long as you act like you belong there."

"So you have traveled there before?"

"Yes." She bowed her head a little. "I venture in there about once a luna. My husband disappeared in that sector yepas ago. I keep hoping that one dura I will find him. That is why I wish to go with you. I believe that helping you will show the gods that I am sincere in my quest and they will lead me to my husband."

"What if you don't want him once you find him?"

"Then I can abandon him, like he did me all those yepas ago."

Orla couldn't help but smile. The little lady had a lot of spunk. He knew he couldn't take her with them, but he knew she'd be a unique addition to their group if she were to accompany them.

They traveled along the streets of the city in companionable silence. Orla watched the people they passed. Many noted the Browlman walking beside him and gave him an apologetic smile. As if they felt sorry for him being saddled with the woman. He couldn't help but smile back. He didn't find her that taxing, as long as she didn't speak of traveling with them.

He noticed a change the moment they crossed into the eastern section of the city. The tension was stronger. A lot of the buildings were dirty and rundown. Several vagrants sat on steps that led up to the overly plentiful pubs that littered this part of the city.

"Hey Browlman, you back looking for your man? I could be him this week if you like." One of the two men on a nearby porch sneered at her.

"Ha, that shows how low you would stoop, huh? What makes you think I would want a big gangly man like you?" She acted like she had conversations like this all the time, but Orla sensed the nervousness in her. She didn't like the attention these men gave her.

"Who's your friend? A new husband? Have you come to show him off to your old one?" said the second man.

"He's a better choice than you are."

The first man laughed at her words. "She is still above us lowlifes, even though she searches for a man who must be lower than us to leave such a woman on her own."

"Have you heard anything new?"

"No, Browlman, we haven't."

"Speak for yourself," said the second man. "I heard that there is a new man in the area that at least fits an important part of the description you have given us. The height."

"Thank you." She threw them each a coin. "Go have a drink on me."

Each smiled as they stood up and entered the bar.

"You pay them for information?"

"These men always say they have information for me. They can't get decent jobs around here. I give them a coin when I can, they in turn try to keep up my hopes on finding my husband."

"So you give money to all these men you see?"

"Only certain ones. Those that were forced here and can't go home."

Orla's ears perked up at that. These were the type of men he was looking for. "Do you think those men want work?"

"Not sure. I always find them outside when I come by. You could ask. All they could say is no."

"True." Orla scratched his chin. "But are they trustworthy?"

"Only time will tell."

Orla started up the steps to the tavern.

"Where are you going?"

"To recruit those men." He walked up the steps and entered the tavern. The Browlman right on his heels. He found the two men sitting at a small table near the bar. To his surprise, they were drinking a heated cup of Chickoran instead of an ale.

They both stood when they saw Orla and the Browlman approach their table.

"So, you have changed your mind about us, Browlman? And have decided to take us up on our offer?"

"Of course not. This man wishes to speak to you about work. I have come with him to make sure nothing happens to him."

"As if you could protect him if someone did threaten him."

"I can take care of myself," Orla said quietly. He sat in a vacant chair.

"What type of work are you talking about?"

Orla chose his words carefully. He wasn't sure if these men could be trusted. "I need warriors."

"Then continue on your way. There are no warriors here," said the man who had been the first to speak outside.

Orla knew he wouldn't get any more information from them if he didn't reveal a little himself. "Good enough. Too bad, my queen would pay well for the protection she will need to go home."

The men didn't say anything while they sipped their warmed beverage.

"There are very few queens who would need such protection from strangers." The first man set his drink down. "Who are you?"

"I am Orla." He thought he saw something flicker in the man's eyes just before he looked away.

"I am Pusha, this is my brother, Kushem," said the first man.

Orla nodded, knowing he was making headway by getting their names.

"Which queen would want such useless men to protect her," asked Pusha.

"She doesn't want useless men, she wants loyal men who fled her planet when they could no longer stay. Her goal is to take back her planet from the evil that is controlling it right now."

"General Varal."

Orla looked at the two men. He wasn't sure which one spoke the name out loud.

"No," said Kushem. "I can't go back there now."

"Why? Your queen needs you."

"Ha," Kushem laughed. "She doesn't need two men who watched as their families were killed in front of them because they refused to join the general's army. Who were pressed into service and escaped as soon as they found the chance."

"When did the general do this?" Rage filled Orla.

"Several yepas ago. He was looking for elite soldiers to help him with a special project. When we refused to leave our farms, he marched our family out one by one and murdered them. When he got to the children, we begged him to spare them. We would join if just left the children alone. He agreed."

"But we found out lunas later that he killed them anyway. It was a lesson to others to accept his invitation or their families could meet the same fate." Pusha shuttered a little at the memory. He pushed his cup away. "That's when we started planning our escape."

"We can't go back there now. Tell your queen we're sorry," said Kushem.

"General Varal has killed the king, forcing Princess Arian to be queen before her time. He has slaughtered thousands, trying to control the population. He is spreading that control out to other planets with a goal to take over the whole galaxy." Orla watched at Pusha started to shake at his words.

"That frewmas has to be stopped." Kushem slammed his cup on the table. "I will help."

"Brother..."

"No. I can't turn my back anymore," he said to Pusha. "My wife and son were killed because of the general. How many people are we going to let die because we hide here? It is time to face our demons." Kushem looked up at Orla. "How can we help?"

Several horas later, Orla and the Browlman sat on the veranda of a quaint little restaurant sipping a fruit drink. Once Pusha and Kushem were convinced to help him, it was easy to enlist their help recruiting many of the people who escaped from Arian's planet. According to the two men, there should be about twenty people in the area that should be willing to fight the general. Orla hoped so, they needed all the help they could get.

"Thank you for all your help today. Your knowledge saved me a lot of time."

"I told you I would be helpful." She sipped her drink, pleased with herself.

"But you still can't come with me."

"Yes, I can."

"No. You can't. What we are trying to do is very dangerous. I won't be responsible for any harm coming to you."

"Is that what you say to your queen? Don't let this little package fool you. I can protect myself. How do you think I can venture into the eastern section of the city every luna and come out unscathed?"

"Browlman."

"Oh no you don't. You need me. Whether or not you realize it now, you need my help and I am offering it."

Orla could tell she wouldn't budge on her desire to come with him. It was time for a different tactic. "You would be a better help if you stayed here and be our eyes and ears for evidence of the general's influence."

"You have a smooth tongue. I can say that about you Orla, but you'll not convince me to stay here. I must accompany you, if you try to leave me behind, I'll follow you. Even if I have to travel with the men you have just hired as warriors." She crossed her arms under her breasts to accentuate her unwavering desire to follow him.

Orla smiled at her backbone. "Why?"

"Because if I am not there you, all of you will be killed."

His eyes narrowed. Did she know something he didn't, and used that as a threat to force him to take her with him? "How will we be killed?"

"My vision hasn't revealed the details yet."

"That is very convenient."

"It is the truth." Browlman became very agitated as she spoke. "These dreams come to me in pieces. I never get the whole thing at once. That's why the people here come to me for my guidance yet laugh at me behind my back.

"All I know is that you and Arian will be in a dark tunnel when you are attacked. You will be killed, and the Queen will be captured."

"How do you know her name? I never mentioned it." Orla didn't like the feel of the hairs on the back of his neck starting to stand up. Something wasn't right here.

"The broadcasts. We've been hearing about Queen Arian traveling to Drahar for lunas now. When you spoke of General Varal it was easy to put it all together." She studied him for a few microns. "You don't believe me, do you? Let me prove it to you."

She grabbed his hand and closed her eyes.

A strange tingling sensation shot up his arm, making him jerk his hand free.

"My god." She stared at him.

Orla knew he couldn't leave her behind now. Somehow, through her special powers, she knew the truth. He could see it in her eyes.

A sharp odor assailed his nose. Tymin had to be nearby.

"What is that smell?" someone from the next table asked. "I hope that isn't coming from the kitchen."

The couple got up and left before they could find out the source of the odor.

Orla scanned the area but didn't see Tymin anywhere in sight. Then, he saw the tangled mass that was Tymin's hair.

The little man shuffled toward them quickly. He pulled up a spare chair and climbed up on it.

"Hello master."

"Tymin. I thought I smelled you."

A little squeak escaped the Browlman, making Orla glance in her direction. She stared at Tymin like she had seen a ghost.

Tymin stared at her as his features paled. He tried to climb down before the little woman spoke, but one word stopped him.

"Husband."

CHAPTER SEVENTEEN

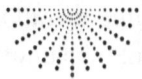

"Your wife, Tymin?" Orla couldn't help himself. He never thought of Tymin as a married man.

"I told you I didn't want to come here. I told you," he murmured as he looked for some place to hide.

"You low life frewmas," she screeched as she threw her drink at him.

Frewmas was the belly of a serpent that crawled in refuse piles. Orla ducked his head to keep his smile from showing. Tymin had a lot of explaining to do to his wife. Time to break up the party.

"Tymin, it's time to head back." Orla fought the grin when he noticed that Tymin walked on one side of him while the Browlman walked on the other. They shot angry glances at each other, but neither spoke. He knew it would only take one comment for them to start voicing what they were saying in their heads.

They walked through the eastern section, winning startled looks from passersby. Orla figured they made quite a sight.

The small party passed the Browlman's house. She dashed into her house, emerging a few microns later with a small carpet bag in her hand.

"Master?" asked Tymin.

"Your wife is traveling with us."

His face turned ashen when he heard Orla. The Browlman beamed.

Orla wondered just what kind of trouble he had created by allowing Tymin's wife to join their group.

"Master?"

"Your wife knows too much to be left behind. We can't take the chance that the general might stumble across her. She is safer with us."

"Perhaps we can take her to a safer planet?"

Orla just shook his head. Tymin would never believe that the Browlman had planned on joining them long before she knew Tymin was part of the group, and she wouldn't allow them to deposit her anywhere for safe keeping.

They came to a narrow copse of trees and Orla gestured for the Browlman to go first so they could continue to the camp.

"Such a gentleman." She gave Orla a bright smile. "Unlike this piece of trash we travel with. Must he accompany us?"

"Yes. He's proved his worth to me."

Orla listened to the barbs she threw at Tymin all the way back to camp. By the time they reached it, he hoped there would be something to pull him away from those two. He wasn't sure if he could handle much else.

He found Arian working with Grinnell, concentrating so deeply, they didn't know he had arrived. Orla couldn't help watching her mimic Grinnell's movements as he guided her through training exercises. She moved with a sensual air, so fluid, so beautiful. The entire time he had been away he never felt his libido take control of him. Five microns back in her company and the desires that had haunted him before came back in full force.

A loud crash caught everyone's attention. Arian turned toward him and gave him a shy smile when she spotted him. She looked past him, a frown starting to crease her features. The Browlman must have just come into view.

Orla turned to confirm his suspicion. The Browlman stood there, gesturing and shouting at Tymin, who listened to her tirade with a grimace.

Arian walked up next to him. "Who is that?"

"Tymin's worst nightmare."

"What do you mean by that?"

"That is Tymin's wife. It seems he left her a long time ago, without any explanation. She's a little upset with him."

"I'd say." Arian watched them a few microns. "Do you think he has tried to explain yet?"

"Don't think so. I don't think she's actually given him a chance to say anything. The Browlman has been too busy either glaring or shouting at him."

"Oh, dear. How long?"

"Time wise has only been three horas but that was the walk back here, so by my standards it has been a whole cycle, and if they keep it up much longer it will feel like four."

"It can't be all that bad."

"Why don't you go over there and see how long you can put up with that incessant anger."

"This doesn't sound like you, Orla. I've never seen anything bother you before."

"True, but this was different. You will have to see what I'm talking about for yourself."

"All right." She slipped past him and walked over to where the Browlman was berating Tymin. The moment the Browlman spotted her she turned her back on Tymin and greeted Arian.

Orla wished he could hear what they were saying. He smiled as he moved closer, this was going to be good.

Arian smiled down at the petite woman.

"My, you are pretty." The Browlman looked toward Orla who walked up to join them. "You never said she was so pretty."

"You talked about me?" Arian asked.

"No."

"Yes, he did." The Browlman tapped Orla on the arm. "He didn't say a lot, but it was what he didn't say that I heard. So you are the Queen now."

"No. Not until General Varal is stopped." Arian changed the subject. "Orla tells me you are Tymin's wife."

She glanced over her shoulder at Tymin, who still stood nearby. "Unfortunately, yes."

"He has been a great help to us."

"Did he tell you he left me? One dura I woke up and he was gone. No reason, no explanation. Nothing."

"Did you ask him why?"

The Browlman took Arian's arm and urged her to walk with her. "I will, once I feel he has suffered enough."

"I think we have all suffered enough now," Orla murmured.

The Browlman laughed.

"How did you find Tymin?" Arian assumed it was his smell, but she wanted to hear the Browlman's story.

"I, um, came close to tackling Orla when he came into the city. You see, I have a visionary gift. I dreamed of all of you long before you came here and knew that I would find my husband if I went with you."

"Then why are you here?"

"Because I have a destiny, like you. Somehow, I am tied in with your quest. Although I'm not sure how yet, I must go with you, even if that Frewmas is with us."

"That Frewmas is your husband," countered Arian.

"True, but he is still a Frewmas."

"When will you forgive him?"

"I don't know." The Browlman set a leisurely pace through the camp. "Have you seen his sadness? Does my heart good."

"Why? Haven't you missed him?"

"Dreadfully." The Browlman sighed. "But has he missed me?"

"That's a question you must ask him."

"You are very wise."

Arian shrugged. If she really was wise why didn't she see what the general was planning a long time ago, before he started plotting against them?

The Browlman sniffed and frowned. "Has he always smelled so bad?"

"Oh yes. Even after several baths that particular odor stayed with him." Arian glanced back. Tymin and Orla followed behind them. "I try to stay down wind."

"You poor thing. I brought my supplies. That smell will be gone in no time."

"Not another bath!"

Tymin's outburst let them know that he could hear what they were saying.

"It could take a full cycle of bathing every dawn for you to get rid of that smell," said the Browlman.

Tymin's moan made her smile.

"When will you forgive him?" asked Arian.

"In time. All in good time."

Arian wondered what she meant by that.

Grinnell and Leabo gestured at them as they turned and headed back toward them, letting them know that it was time to prepare dinner.

Flames from the bonfire snapped and swayed with the soft breeze that blew. Arian cupped the mug she held, watching the flames as they leaped and danced before her. Tymin's wife had added a breath of fresh air for her. She didn't realize how much she missed having a simple conversation until the little woman had joined them.

Tymin sat close to the ship, probably to avoid his wife more than protect their noses. Grenta sat next to the Browlman and engaged her in a lively conversation about what she had seen so far. The woman was a great story teller. She would have a lot to tell her husband when she finally returned home.

Orla sat down next to Arian.

She glanced up at him, seeing the flames snap and dip in the reflection in his eyes. Her heart started to flutter as she looked into his eyes.

"How is your training going?"

"Oh. Very well." Nervous lumlights took flight in her stomach.

"Grinnell is a good teacher then?"

"I guess. There isn't a lot to compare him with." She held her cup out toward the flames, wondering why she felt so edgy around him. She thought her feelings for him would have faded by now, instead they seem to have grown. That couldn't be a good thing, knowing she was destined for another man.

"And Grenta?"

"Oh I have learned so much!" She thought about showing some of the things she was now able to duplicate, but she knew the moment the image showed up, Grenta would jump into her teacher mode and force her to make it better. She wanted to just enjoy Orla's company right now, not worry about whether or not the image was perfect.

"Were you successful?" Arian felt silly asking him this question, but she wanted to keep his attention for a little while longer.

"Yes. I'll know how successful in two duras."

"How did you meet the Browlman?"

"The way she said." Orla gave her a lop-sided smile. "She came flying out of her shop shouting 'you're one of them'. It definitely caught my attention. She is a seer, and believes we need her."

"Why?"

"Don't know. She never explained other than saying she knew she'd meet her husband with us. I'd say she fulfilled the first vision."

Arian laughed. "I don't know how happy Tymin is about her first accomplishment."

Orla glanced over where Tymin sat. "Not very."

They ran out of words, yet, kept looking into each other's eyes. Arian felt her heart flutter as she looked at him. She didn't realize how much she missed him until she had him back beside her.

A frisson of heat slid up her arm when Orla took her hand in his. The warmth of his palm against hers felt right.

The Browlman stood up from her conversation with Grenta and walked passed them, grazing her hand across each of their shoulders before making her way over to Tymin. She crooked her finger at Tymin, then headed away from the fire. Tymin hesitated few a few microns before leaping to his feet and scurrying after his wife.

"I think the forgiving has begun," said Orla.

Arian wasn't sure what he meant but nodded anyway. Anything

to continue to have him look at her that way, like she was the center of his world. Times like this made her wonder why she had to fulfill her vow to her father. Orla was doing everything her father had asked of Dresuer. He was the real hero to her. Would Dresuer do the same things? Could he do them as well, or even better?

She sighed, wishing she could sort out her feelings better than this. Her heart wasn't letting her make a smart decision. When she was around Orla she didn't even think about Dresuer. No that wasn't true, she kept comparing them.

"A jewel for your thoughts."

"Oh." She blushed as she looked away. She hadn't planned on floating away on her thoughts on him like that. "It's nothing, really. Just thinking."

Orla lifted her chin until she looked into his eyes.

"What are you looking for?" She placed a hand on his chest, reveling in the strength she felt beneath her fingers.

"The truth." His fingers glided up and down her throat while he searched her eyes.

She felt the soft caress all the way to her toes. "Orla."

"Yes."

The soft rumble vibrated through her fingers.

"I believe it is time to call it a night," said Grenta, who stood beside them.

Arian started at the sound of her voice. She was so busy marveling in the sensations, she hadn't noticed Grenta move.

"Already?" She didn't want retire so soon.

Orla placed one of his hands on top of her hand resting against his chest. "Grenta is right. I'll see you in the morning."

"But—" Arian had never slept without Orla before. His company was a comfort. One she would sorely miss.

"We've only the two tents. The Browlman and Grenta will keep you company tonight." Orla pressed his hand against her face.

"I will miss you."

"And I, you."

Arian went into her tent and sat on the soft pallet she had laid out earlier. Her loneliness a palpable thing. This was going to a very long night.

Arian awoke from a fitful sleep to the beautiful song of the Cewell, a native bird to the planet. Stretching, she sat up.

"Oh, dear. You didn't sleep well, did you?" asked the Browlman.

Arian blinked and looked at the Browlman. "I slept quite well."

"Not by the dark circles under your eyes. Let me get you some of my special tea. It will make those circles fade quickly. Now, don't move until I come back."

Arian watched the tent flap drop into place after the Browlman left the tent. She brushed out her hair and slipped on a clean tunic while she waited for the little woman to return.

The Browlman returned with a steaming cup of tea.

Arian accepted the tea and inhaled deeply. The pungent odor made her eyes water.

"I know it doesn't smell that great, but it will make you feel better."

"Are you sure?"

"Of course, dear. Go ahead. Drink it."

Arian took a hesitant sip. She smiled as the smooth beverage slid across her pallet and down her throat. "It is quite good. My thanks."

"Enjoy. The medicinal qualities will work very quickly."

By the time Arian finished the drink she felt one hundred percent better. Stepping outside, she had to shield her eyes from the overly bright sunlight.

"Good dura, Arian," Grenta said to her.

She turned toward Grenta's voice and got a little light headed. Must have turned a little too fast. "Good dura."

"You look very chipper this morning."

"Thanks be. I feel wonderful." She gave her a very happy smile before she headed toward the ship.

Arian stood in front of the stairs that led up to the ship doors. It seemed to be a little higher than she remembered. She stepped up two of the five steps easily, but when she tried to maneuver the third one, she lost her balance and landed on her rump against the hard earth. A loud oof escaped her.

She stood up and dusted herself off. A slight stagger entered her step as she tried to climb the stairs once again. Arian couldn't figure out what was wrong. Each time she tried to place her foot on the steps she ended up tripping over and finding her face a little too close to her feet. She had to brace her arms against the stairs in fear of finding her face pressed against it or toppling over completely. This odd feeling was most bizarre to her.

Looking up at the door that could have been one hundred meters above her instead of the fifteen meters distance she knew it to be, she decided to wait a few microns and allow her head to clear.

She was still sitting there when Orla came out of the door.

"Arian? Weren't you supposed to be on duty by now?"

"Yes." She swung around to look up at him. Oh, that wasn't smart. Orla doubled for a moment. "But I couldn't quite make the stairs."

"Why not?" A slight frown creased his forehead.

"I don't know. 'Tis the most bizarre thing. I just couldn't climb the stairs."

He jumped down onto the earth and helped her to her feet so he could examine her. He placed a hand on her forehead and released his pent-up breath. "You don't have a fever. What have you had to eat or drink to break your fast?"

"I haven't broke my fast yet, but the Browlman made me a cup of tea earlier. It was very good. Really made me feel good." She leaned heavily into Orla, as if her spine has turned into frumas.

He took her weight easily. "What type of tea?"

"Ask her?" Arian gestured toward the woman, almost smacking Orla in the face at the same time.

"Ask me what?" The Browlman stepped up to them and looked Arian over. "What is wrong with you, child?"

"Nothing," she said a little louder than she needed to.

The Browlman tilted her head up.

The bright light in Arian's eyes made her blink in rapid succession.

"Oh dear."

"What?" asked Orla.

"She's acting like she's had spirits."

"Spirits? What's that?" Her words slurred a little.

"You're drunk, dear," said the Browlman.

"Am not."

Orla helped her to her feet. "So what should we do?"

"Let her sleep it off."

Orla nodded as he helped her up the stairs and into the ship.

Arian snuggled against him as he carried her to the room they shared on the ship. Her eyes felt heavy.

"Why don't you rest for a while? I'll wake you a little later." He deposited her on to the bed.

"But what about my shift?"

"I'm sure we can get someone else to cover you for now. You rest. I'll check up on you a later."

"'Kay," she murmured as she smuggled in the bed. Maybe a little rest wouldn't be too bad right now. She could barely keep her eyes open.

When Arian finally woke up, she felt extremely rested. She sat up, adjusted her clothing and headed toward the bridge. She found Leabo standing watch.

"So you're finally awake."

"Finally? How long have I been sleeping?"

"Long enough." Leabo smiled at her.

Arian glared at him. "Where's Orla?"

"Outside."

She grumbled to herself about Leabo's vague answers while she walked toward the main doors of the ship. She pressed a button. The doors slid back, revealing twilight on the planet. How long had she been sleeping?

Arian found everyone around the bonfire once again.

"Ah, there's our sleeping queen. I hope you had a good rest." The Browlman spoke, being the first one to spot her exiting the ship.

"Yes." She descended the stairs. "Was I asleep for long?"

"One dura," said Orla.

Her eyes widened. "One whole dura?"

"Actually," said the Browlman. "In a couple of horas it would have been two duras, but who is counting."

Arian felt the heat spread up her cheeks. How embarrassing. First she made a fool of herself by becoming inebriated from tea of all things, then to top it off she had to sleep like a Three-eyed Tree Fron, a hairy little creature that burrowed into the roots of trees and could sleep for cycles before rousing, eating, and then sleeping again. If she could crawl under a rock right now she would.

Warmth surrounded her shoulders. Looking up, she found Orla standing beside her, his arm around her protectively.

"Don't let them get to you. They're just teasing. It isn't every dura they get to see a queen get tipsy."

"Everyone saw me?" She wanted to run back into the ship and hide in their room.

"No, but after they noticed your absence they had to be told. Telling is the same thing as seeing for these people. They now have a story to tell on you and each time they tell it a new embellishment will happen. In fact, considering how much it has changed in the short time they have known about it, I doubt you'll even recognize it."

"Oh, how will I ever live this down?" Arian wanted to cry.

"Now, Mistress, don't worry. You'll laugh at this in the yepas to come."

"I don't see how, this is the most mortifying thing that has ever happened to me."

Orla smiled. "Then you have just begun to live. Everyone has embarrassing moments that they wish had never happened. This is only your first one."

"Second."

He looked at her curiously.

"My tail."

He laughed. "Okay two, but everyone was in awe of your powers, not laughing at you."

"Sure. That's what you'd like me to think."

"Mistress, you know how much I liked your tail. You flattered me."

She could feel the heat of her blush creep back into her cheeks.

A small commotion just outside the camp snared their attention.

Orla stepped forward when he recognized two of the dozen or so men who approached the camp. "Pusha, I didn't expect you until tomorrow."

He nodded. "I know, but I had gathered who I could earlier today."

"You know you are welcome. Would you like to introduce everyone?"

He nodded absently. Glancing behind him first he turned and faced Orla. "There's more."

Orla waited.

"General Varal is on his way here."

CHAPTER EIGHTEEN

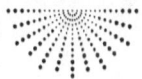

"Are you sure?" asked Orla.

"Yes. We heard it on a news communique."

Arian turned on her heal and raced back to the ship. She had to see this communique for herself. As quickly as she could, she traversed the hallways to the bridge and sat in her station. Keying in a few commands, she found the news blip.

"So what did you find?"

She nearly jumped out of her seat at Orla's question so close to her ear. She didn't know he had followed her.

"According to this, he left Nortura three duras ago. You know what this means, don't you?" She knew Orla would be totally against what she wanted to do, but Arian couldn't hide her excitement.

"No."

"That Dresuer is without his guards now. We can go and rescue him."

"It would be too dangerous." Orla crossed his arms across his chest.

"How? General Varal has pulled his troops from the planet to come here."

"Arian." His voice a warning.

"No. Orla, you keep telling me that everything is too dangerous." She spun her chair around so she could look him in the face. "How am I going to fulfill my quest if that is true. We must try."

"I don't think it is a good idea."

"Why?" she questioned him. "What is it about Dresuer that you don't want me to know about?"

"That is a very good question."

Arian wondered who spoke and looked toward the door way. She found the Browlman standing there. The little woman walked deeper into the room.

"Orla, she must do this."

"Are you out of your mind?" he growled as he turned toward the Browlman. Anger radiated off him.

"If she is to succeed she must try to find the man she has vowed to marry."

The very simple statement shook Orla to the core. He stared at her, furious at what she implied. Then the words she said sank in. The Browlman was right. Arian needed to find the man she had vowed to marry. It just might not be who she expected. "What if I disagree."

"It's not really up to you, now is it. It is Arian's quest. She must fulfill it her own way."

He turned back toward Arian, who looked like she was holding her breath, waiting for his decision. Orla didn't speak right away. His mind told him to squash the idea right now, before she could get hurt, but his heart knew she needed this experience to make her a stronger woman.

"You will do exactly what I say."

Arian leaped up out of her chair and hugged him. "Oh, yes, Orla, thank you."

"Don't thank me yet, you haven't heard what you must do."

Seven duras later, Orla wished he hadn't gone along with this crazy scheme. It was a trap, he could feel it in his bones, but every time he even thought about canceling it, he saw Arian's hopeful face while they trained for the rescue and couldn't bring himself to stop their plot to rescue

Dresuer. He sat in his seat, feeling his lunch turn into a rock in his stomach as the planet grew closer.

Arian rested her hand on his shoulder.

"I know you don't believe we should be attempting his rescue but thank you for going along. You don't know how much this means to me."

Orla didn't respond. If he said one word it would be no, and he'd stop them from stepping one foot on the planet. He also knew if he stopped them, Arian would never forgive him. Something he didn't want to face.

He could feel Arian's excitement humming through the touch of her hand on his shoulder as she watched the planet get closer.

Orla took her hand in his and stood up.

Grinnell maneuvered the ship behind one of the moons to help keep them undetected.

"Are you sure you want to do it this way?"

"Yes. You're our only way to escape. We have to use that derelict ship we found. If we don't and get captured, they will start looking for the ship that brought us. Although that ship normally wouldn't be used for intergalaxy travel, it could make the flight from the closest inhabited planet without any trouble. That's what I want General Varal to think if they capture us."

"All right." Grinnell sighed. "I'll stay in orbit around this moon for two horas. If I don't hear from you by then, I'll head to the closest planet as you instructed."

"Don't worry Grinnell, we'll be there," said Orla. Placing the palm of his hand against the small of Arian's back, he urged her to move. The sooner they started this, the faster it would be over. They entered the cargo bay and opened the doors to the small ship.

Arian went to the co-pilot's seat and waited for Orla to join her.

He hesitated for just a secur, before he climbed into the pilot's seat and closed the small hatch. He started up the engines, opened the viewing portals, and watched as the bay doors silently slid back into the ship. Gently, he eased the smaller ship out into space and headed toward the planet.

Arian remained silent, watching their progression toward the atmosphere with a childlike excitement. Although he could feel her elation strumming through her, he knew she realized the seriousness of this rescue. She did everything he had trained her to do to make their approach safe, never questioning his commands.

He landed the ship close to the compound, but well out of view of any surveillance that might be watching.

Using hand signals, he led her toward the towering building his brother was supposed to be in. They crouched behind a small outcropping of rocks and waited.

"That should be the guard's entrance," whispered Orla.

Arian nodded.

They had monitored the compound's pattern for a cycle to figure out how they would enter. They decided their best bet would be to disguise themselves as guards to gain entrance. Now they waited for the sentries to exit and check the surrounding areas. If all went well, they would be the ones returning in the sentry's place.

The doors slid open, allowing two guards to exit the towering building. They moved away from the massive walls, scanning the area for intruders. Something they did about every fifteen microns.

Orla gestured for Arian to follow him and they shadowed the guards. The guards separated at the third outcropping of rocks to cover more territory. Orla followed one, while Arian followed another.

He snuck up behind the guard he followed, and with two blows, knocked him out. After taking his uniform, Orla tied the guard up and stuffed him into a small outcropping in a cluster of rocks. That way, the guard wouldn't be able to escape and the cameras shouldn't be able to detect him.

Adjusting the uniform, which was a little too small, he silently moved where he hoped Arian would be. He found her standing over the prone body of the other guard, snapping the front of the pants closed. His blood pounded as he watched her peel off her tunic to put on the uniform top. Viewing her without her notice made him feel like a voyeur, but he couldn't stop himself. She was too beautiful. Her skin glistened in the soft sunshine, her soft curves kissed by the sunlight. His desire had a stranglehold on him, wanting to take her then and there.

Without knowing it, he must have made a sound because she suddenly looked up and spotted him.

"Oh!" She placed a hand against her collar bone.

A collarbone he wanted to trace with his lips.

"Orla, I didn't hear you approach." He felt the heat of her gaze on his body. A soft smile stole across her lips. "It seems your guard was a little smaller than you are." She pulled on the shirt. The tail of it fell to her knees.

"And yours seems a bit too big."

Arian glanced down at the oversized outfit. "Should we exchange our clothes? These might fit you better."

"No." Orla crossed his arms over his chest. He wasn't sure if he could watch her strip in front of him without acting on it. "They were about the same size, so either uniform will be too small for me."

Arian put the belt on and pulled it past the holes to make it tight enough to fit. "I hope my Barou talent is strong enough to confuse the cameras. There is no way they'll believe we are the guards if it doesn't."

"If you aren't sure." He let the comment hang in the air between them, hoping she'd change her mind.

"We are going through with this, Orla. We have to." Arian straightened her shoulders. She tilted her head back a little, then looked at Orla. "I am ready."

Following the timing they had observed all cycle, Orla and Arian headed back toward the compound as if they had finished their survey and were returning to duty. The doors slid open and they stepped into the darkened hallway.

Following the corridor, they moved warily toward the set of metal doors in front of them as the doors behind them closed. If Arian's image didn't record on their cameras, they would be caught. There was no way out of the corridor they were in.

A loud grinding noise filled the area as the doors started to lift.

"Report you our assigned areas," a loud voice boomed out of the intercom.

They nodded as they walked through the doors and entered the security section of the compound. Following the plan they laid out before they left the ship, Orla and Arian headed toward the center of the building, hoping to mingle with other guards and find the area where Dresuer was without raising anyone's suspicion.

The corridor seemed to go on forever. Each time they pasted a check point they feared they would be detained and captured, but Arian's imagery worked through them all. All of the guards barely glanced at their identification before allowing them to pass.

They found the center bustling with people moving from one position to another. Not all were security. They saw doctors, scientists, and several others they couldn't identify by their clothing.

Their steps faltered when they found a dozen doors. The blueprints they studied so diligently only showed eight separate corridors. Which one held the corridor they needed to find? Orla scanned the area quickly, looking for something he would recognize from the blueprints that would show them where they were supposed to go. Nothing stood out.

Arian tugged on his arm before heading toward the sixth door. She calmly moved into the corridor and headed to the left when they came to a fork.

"Do you know where we are going?" Orla breathed.

"I think so," she whispered back. "I remembered that the corridor we wanted to take had the tallest arch of them all. That's the door way we took. I just hope it was the right one."

They traveled deeper into the bowels of the place before they hit another guard post. This was the first time they were stopped.

"We have been assigned to guard Varal's guest." Arian presented her pass. Orla did the same.

The guard studied their I.D.s for a few microns, then nodded, allowing them to pass.

"That was too easy," Arian murmured to Orla. The security around Dresuer should be a lot heavier.

"I agree. Be on your toes." Orla felt a small fissure of unease snake around his back and settle on his nape, causing the hairs on the back of his neck to stand up. He glanced around, not liking the sensation at all.

She nodded. They went around a turn and found themselves confronted by four guards.

CHAPTER NINETEEN

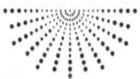

"I.D.s"

Arian pulled hers off of her shirt and handed it to the guard who seemed to be the one in charge. Orla mimicked her movements.

The guard scrutinized their's before handing them back. "You aren't authorized to be here."

"We were assigned to guard the prisoner," said Arian.

"What prisoner?"

Orla shrugged. "Prisoner, guest, whatever his title is today."

The guard didn't comment.

Arian pulled a slip of paper out of her breast pocket and handed it to the guard.

He, in turn, studied the form, glancing up at them several times before handing the paper back to her.

"General Varal didn't inform me you would be coming to move his guest."

She slipped the paper back in her pocket. "Since when did General Varal let you into his confidence?"

The guard stiffened at her words. "I have been told to question everything."

"And you are going an excellent job. I will inform the general of your good work."

The guard straightened at her words. "Come this way."

Arian barely inclined her head as she followed the guard down another corridor toward the only door in the area.

"He's in there. We have followed the general's strict orders."

"Very good." Arian waited for him to open the door to the cell. The door creaked open slowly to reveal a very posh room. She looked around but didn't notice anyone in the room.

"Where is he?" she asked.

"Over in that corner."

She stepped in, looking into the corner the guard indicated. "Are you sure he hasn't escaped?"

"You're kidding, right? This guy couldn't fight his way out of a duras sack if he tried. Why would he want to leave the comfy prison General Varal has placed him in?"

"A cell is a cell. Never underestimate anyone."

Orla stared at her, not believing she would be so militant. He stepped into the cell after them, looking for his brother. It didn't take long for him to spot him in a corner piled high with pillows.

He heard Arian instruct the guard to leave them alone with the prisoner as he headed toward the pile of pillows. Although she continued to cloak them from the cameras, the moment the guards left she dropped the images so Dresuer would recognize her.

Orla stood at the base of the pile, watching his slovenly brother try to find a soft spot in the overstuffed pillows. "Having a problem?"

Dresuer jerked his head in Orla's direction. Shock filled his face. "So brother, you have come to rescue me?"

"No." Orla wondered how he knew what he looked like. His father kept no picture of him.

A well sculpted brow arched over one eye. "Then why are you here?"

"Because of her."

Dresuer's gaze slid over to Arian. A predatory look entered his eyes as he drank in the vision in front of him.

Orla felt rage fill him when his brother's eyes darkened with passion. Before he could say one word, Arian stepped up, grasped his arm and gave Dresuer a beaming smile.

"Thank the Gods you are all right," said Arian. "I feared that General Varal had hurt you."

Dresuer stood up from the cushions. His gaze devoured her. "Why would the general want to hurt me?"

A frown creased her brow. "Because of me?"

"Because of you?" He paced around her, checking her over from head to foot.

"I am Arian." Surely he hadn't forgotten what she looked like that quickly.

"Very pretty." He then looked at his brother in triumph. "General Varal would never hurt me, my dear. We're friends, so to speak."

Orla glared at Dresuer.

"Then why are you being kept under lock and key?"

Dresuer didn't answer right away.

Orla wondered what his brother was thinking. He didn't like the scheming look that had entered Dresuer's eyes.

"Gu—"

Orla moved quickly, stuffing a pillow in his brother's mouth before he could finish the word.

"Orla!" Arian tried to pull the pillow from Dresuer's face.

"Arian, stop. This tree slime was just about to call the guards on us. You forget that the general has a very handsome reward on your head. Our friend here knows what he could do with all that money."

"No."

"Yes," said a voice behind them.

Arian cringed at the sound of the general's assistant. Spinning, she turned to face him.

"Well, my Queen, we meet again." He gestured for six guards to enter the room.

Arian, Orla and Dresuer found themselves flanked by two of them.

"What is this?" asked Dresuer. "I was the one who got her here. Is this the way you are going to treat the captor of Arian?"

Orla stood rigid. If he could move it would be straight for his brother's throat. He glanced over at Arian's pale face.

"How could you?"

"How could I not? You don't know how much you are worth to the general."

"But you are my betrothed. What happened to your loyalty?"

He laughed.

"Shut up, or I will have you silenced," snarled the general's assistant.

Dresuer's laughter died quickly. The last of the echo bounced around the huge room one last time before the air hung silently in the room.

Orla kept looking over at Arian, hoping to catch her attention without being noticed. When she did look up at him with tear filled eyes, he wished he didn't have to see the betrayal etched across her face. He wished he could send her signals to explain what he wanted to do, but he could tell just by looking in her eyes she thought the same thing he did. They must escape.

"Move these two out of here. Leave our fat little lord here until the general arrives."

Dresuer tried to break free of the two men who held him. "I demand to speak to the general right now. He won't allow you to treat me this way."

"Silence him."

Orla heard the blow. By the time he looked at his brother he was sprawled on the floor.

The two extra guards joined them.

"You," the general's assistant said to the first extra man. "Go get the doctor to take care of that sorry piece of man. You," he said to the other. "Keep an eye on the room until the doctor sedates him. I just don't trust him."

He signaled the other four to follow him, bringing Orla and Arian with them.

Orla glance furtively from side to side as they walked through the maze-like corridors, hoping to find some weapon to knock out his captors. If he had been alone, he would have shifted and attacked them, but with Arian here, he feared they would harm her before he could take them all out.

Just as they reached a tight bend in the building, Arian cried out and crumpled to the floor, pulling her two guards off balance.

Orla stumbled and gripped the arms of his guards, causing them to crash into each other and knock each other out.

"Hey, now. What is going on here?"

Arian sat on the floor, massaging her ankle. No one noticed when she took a blaster from one of her guards.

"This oaf stepped on my foot and made me twist it," she whimpered. "I think it is sprained."

The assistant knelt to inspect her ankle.

It took Orla a few securs for him to realize she had shielded the blaster from their view. He watched as she pointed it and fired at the assistant, evaporating him. She then turned the weapon on the two guards, dispatching them with an efficiency that frightened him.

She stood and reached for his hand.

Together they raced toward the way out. Arian shielding them from the eyes of the guards they flew by. They made it as far as the main hall before they were detected.

Orla felt a tremor flow through Arian when the first cry went out.

"Someone here must be Barou." Arian continued to keep up the deceptive image she had created for them.

Rock exploded just to the left of them as they entered another corridor.

"How far?" she asked as they rounded a turn.

"Another twenty meters. But don't expect those doors to be open."

"I don't. But how are we to escape if we can't get out that way?"

"I don't know, mistress."

The doors loomed in front of them. They could hear the clamor of their pursuit.

Arian released Orla's hand, closed her eyes, and pushed air out of her lungs. Interlacing her fingers together, she bowed her head in concentration.

The sounds grew louder as their pursuers neared.

"What are you doing?"

"Shhh." Arian spread her hands out in front of the massive doors.

"Arian."

A loud clanking noise filled the air as the doors started to lift.

Orla grinned as he looked at Arian. He didn't know how she did it, but he knew she was somehow responsible.

The microns there was enough room for them to squeeze under the door, Orla grabbed her hand and pulled her toward the small opening.

"No, not yet." Her brow beaded with sweat. "The secur I let go, the door will start descending again. I need to make sure we both will make it."

The door crept up as their pursuers drew closer.

"Mistress." Orla glanced behind him.

She waved at him as she concentrated harder.

The inched up a little more.

"There's no more time." Orla grabbed her shoulders and steered her toward the door. "We have to go."

"You first," Arian said through gritted teeth. "I'll keep working on the door."

Orla wanted to argue with her, but instead did as she asked. He slid under the door, then positioned himself on the floor facing their pursuers so he could protect her with the weapon he appropriated when she started for the door.

He heard them just before they crested the turn in the corridor. "Now, Arian."

Arian glanced behind her before she dove toward the small opening.

"Hurry!" Orla felt his heart stop when the door started to slip back down at an alarming rate. He kept his blaster trained on the people running toward them, as Arian rolled under the door.

Just as she cleared it the door slammed shut. He grabbed her and pulled her toward him, grateful she made it through unscathed.

"You were wonderful." The sound of pounding against the door made them turn toward the door.

"We're not out of here yet." Arian stood up and offered Orla her hand.

He pulled himself to his feet. "Can you do that again?"

"I hope so. I'd hate to get caught after all we've been through."

They ran quickly to the next door and their escape to freedom.

Arian stood in front of the door. Closing her eyes, she spread her hands out and closed her eyes.

Once again, the door started inching up.

"You have to tell me how you do that," murmured Orla.

"Later."

A whoosh of air let them know that the other door had opened. They were running out of time.

Orla squeezed through as soon as there was enough space for him to go under.

"Can you keep the door open while you exit?"

"No. It takes all my concentration."

The pounding of footsteps vibrated down the corridor.

She dove straight through the opening.

The moment Orla could, he grabbed her arms and pulled with all his might.

The door slammed down just as Arian's feet cleared the door.

Orla urged her to her feet, grabbed her hand and pulled her behind him as he ran toward the ship.

As they drew near their ship they slowed their pace. Ducking behind a rock outcrop, they scanned the area to see if anyone from the compound had already found their ship and were lying in wait for them.

Orla picked up a palm sized stone and threw it at the ship, then waited to hear voices or a blaster firing, but they heard nothing.

"Do you think it's safe?" asked Arian.

"I don't know, but we can't wait out here all dura. The entire compound is probably after us now." Orla inched around the outcropping, once he was sure there was no one within sight, he grabbed Arian's hand and ran the short distance to the ship. Quickly he entered in the access code, scanning the area while he waited for the pod doors to open.

Once they had entered the small ship, and secured the door, Orla slipped into his seat and started up the engines. Just as they started to lift off, they saw a large battalion clear the rock and start shooting at their ship.

Arian turned on their radio and contacted Grinnell. She appraised them of their situation. "We're under pursuit."

"We'll be there in microns."

"No." Orla took the mike from Arian. "Follow our backup plan and we'll contact you when it is safe."

Arian gave him a worried look.

"But Orla," said Grinnell. "You have no weapons on that ship."

"Grinnell, I need to make sure they think we did this by ourselves. I can fly circles around most of these pilots. How difficult will it be to evade them? Once I can get this ship off this planet and into the normal shipping lanes, we should be very hard to detect, and we'll contact you then. It should only take a couple of horas."

Several shots across their bow made Orla cut the communique short. "We'll contact you as soon as we can."

Using all his concentration, Orla started taking evasive action to avoid being hit.

Arian turned on their tactical systems screen to watch for damage as they tried to outrun the ships in hot pursuit.

The ship jumped when one missile seemed to have found its mark.

"The shields are down to eighty-eight percent."

"What did they hit?" His fingers flew across the display screen, constantly changing their flight pattern.

"Looks like they grazed the ship on the right side." She punched a few buttons. "It doesn't look like they did any structural damage."

Orla nodded. As long as they don't take a direct hit, they should be able to make it. Their assent into the stratosphere should have them out of the planet's gravitational field within a few microns. Once out there the ships chasing them should turn back. They weren't long range ships, so weren't designed to go too far out of the atmosphere.

One of the displays blew out when the ship rocked from another missile. Orla felt the sting of metal biting into his skin from the flying debris. Casting a quick glance at Arian, he saw several cuts and abrasions on her face and hands. "Are you all right?"

"Yes." She wiped her forehead, leaving a streak of blood in its wake. "That was a direct hit. They took out one of the two back up engines, and part of our navigational system."

Orla tried another series of evasive maneuvers, but they couldn't shake their tail. The sky above them started to turn black as they left the atmosphere.

"Get us out of here, Orla."

"We're almost there."

"And they are firing up weapons again." Arian placed her hands on the console in front of her. "One more direct hit and we will lose all navigation, and our shields."

"Can you shield us from their view screens?"

"No. I've been trying to do that since they started to follow us. I'm either too weak, they are too far away, or their ships are too advanced for me to fool them."

Orla figured it was a combination of all three.

Sweat broke out on his brow as the next barrage of missiles exploded around them. Some were a little too close for comfort.

The entire ship shuttered when another missile hit their engines. Smoke filled the ship as the engines sputtered and died. Orla fought to control the screaming ship as it plummeted into the atmosphere.

One more missile struck the ship. An ominous groan filled the air just before the main console started to pop and snap.

Orla pushed the console away. "Abandon ship."

Leading the way, he headed toward the two escape pods on the ship. Something he made sure were in working order, just in case.

Orla never made it to the pods. Part of the bulkhead collapsed on top of him halfway down the corridor. He crumbled under the heavy weight. Pain slicing through his body as more debris continued to fall, crushing the air out of him.

He pushed against the floor, hoping to move the dead weight off his body. They had to get out of the ship or they would surely die from the ship's impact. There was no way to maneuver their ship into a safe landing.

Orla tried to shout Arian's name, but it only came out as a croak. His levering turned out to be fruitless. He couldn't budge the heavy weight off his body. He knew he had to shift in order to get out from under the debris under which he was buried.

Closing his eyes, he prepared himself for the change, knowing that his injuries would make the shift very painful. He relaxed as he felt the subtle shimmering infuse his body. As his mass started to change the debris shifted as well.

He didn't hear his groan as a large piece of the bulkhead pulled away from the wall and landed in the middle of his back, but Arian must have. Her scream was the last thing he heard before he blacked out.

CHAPTER TWENTY

Arian stood, staring at the bulkhead crushing Orla as her screams died in the small ship. Looking at the blocked corridor, she knew she couldn't get out that way now, not that she'd even think about leaving Orla. She turned back toward the cockpit.

Fear quaked through her. What if she couldn't land this ship safely? Arian slipped into Orla's seat and pulled the console toward her.

First, she relaxed herself, just as she had seen Orla do many times. It wouldn't do her any good to try to steer the ship if she was so frightened that she couldn't think straight.

Once she felt like she had her fear under control, she pressed the buttons she needed to so she could see how much damage had been done to the ship. Oh Gods, it was extensive. Next, she checked the navigation system. Most of it had been wiped out, but with luck she should be able to stop the ship from its deathly nosedive.

Pressing a few controls, she pulled the ship slightly up, slowing their descent. She checked the scanners; they were still being followed, but at a distance. The other ships must believe they were dead and had backed off to see what had happened.

Arian frowned. If she slowed the ship too much, the other ships would start firing again. She calculated their descent, and what it would take for the ship to crash without smashing it into a thousand pieces on impact. Using the sensors, she looked for something that would disguise any true navigating she would do to land.

A mountain loomed on the horizon.

"Perfect." She aimed the ship toward the mountain. If she could deflect the ship off the top, she would be able to slow the ship down without it looking like anyone controlled it.

Arian ran her calculations again. She counted off the microns as the ship drew closer to the mountain top. Just as the ship would have plowed into the side of the mountain, she turned the ship, bouncing off, and spiraling down at a slower pace. She maneuvered the ship toward another, lower peak and bounced the ship off the top of it.

The ship slowed down just a little more. Although the ship continued to spiral down toward the earth, she felt sure she could land the ship without killing her and Orla in the process. If he wasn't already dead, and if all went according to plan.

Arian checked her scanners again to see what the other ships were doing. She didn't want to think about Orla being dead. He had to be alive, he just had to.

The other ships still followed at a distance.

As the ship closed in on the earth below, Arian prayed her calculations were correct. She braced herself for impact.

The ship slammed into the earth, digging a deep crater, until the ship finally stopped its forward movement.

Her head whipped back and then forward, impacting against the console and knocking her out cold.

Two ships alighted on the ground close to wreckage. A small squad exited the ship and surrounded it.

"Two of you blow that door," said the leader. Then he turned to two others. "You two go inside and see if there are any survivors."

The explosion rocked the small ship. A loud rumbling made them back up in fear that the ship would implode on itself. Once the dust cleared, the two assigned the look for survivors entered the ship. They exited the ship only securs after they entered.

"Well?"

"The bulkhead collapsed, sir. There is no way anyone survived that. If they did, they are trapped inside."

The captain of the squad nodded. "Set more explosives. I don't want anything left."

Pain shot through her body as she came to. It hurt to lift her head. A groan escaped her as she tried to sit up. Her whole body ached in places she didn't know could ache. Gingerly, she touched the side of her head, feeling something sticky. When she drew her hand away, she found blood on her fingers.

Emergency lights lit the cockpit, but the rest of the ship was dead.

Arian eased herself out of the pilot's chair. She couldn't be too badly hurt since she could move, even if every part of her body screamed at her to just lie down.

She turned toward the spot where Orla was trapped. How was she going to free him? Although the debris shifted, the heaviest pieces were wedged on top. Even though Grenta taught her how to use her powers to manipulate things, like the doors she did earlier, there was no way she could move them on her own. Her training hadn't gotten that far. Without moving them, she couldn't dig Orla out.

Arian looked around for something to use as a wedge to move the heavy pieces. Maybe with some leverage, she would be able to move the heavier pieces off the pile that was once the bulkhead.

As she walked over to a pipe that had pulled away from the viewing screen, she stumbled over an uneven section of the floor. Arian landed hard on her hands and knees. The impact shot excruciating pain directly into her brain. She rolled up into a ball as she tried to fight it. Tears swelled up in her eyes.

She turned her head to one side, which allowed her to rest her cheek against the deck floor. That was when she noticed the crack in the floor. Whatever she had tripped on sat a few millimeters up from the rest of the deck. The edge was a seam, not a broken part of the fuselage.

Her pain forgotten, she gripped the loosened floor panel and pulled it up. At first it wouldn't budge, but just as she was about to give up, she heard a creak, a groan, and then the panel coming loose in her hands.

She stared at a crawl space the panel revealed. A smile spread across her lips. She had forgotten all about this. It ran the entire length of the ship and should go directly under where Orla was trapped.

Arian pulled off the jacket she wore and gathered what she could to take with her. Along with a few rations that they had stored in the cockpit, she also pulled out the emergency kit, the portable radio, and a small torch.

First she tied the jacket around her waist, then she turned on the torch and sat on the edge of the opened space. Taking a deep breath, she slid into the small area.

Crawling along the tight space, she started to shake. She felt like the walls were closing in on her. Arian stopped for a few microns, staring at the black void in front of her. A loud groan filled the small space she laid in. Her imagination ran wild, making her believe that the floor was starting to give.

Her heart started to beat rapidly, she couldn't move. The thought of being crushed down here in the small dark space filled her, spiking her fear to a fevered pitch.

She felt a soft whisper in her head. Arian feared that someone was in the crawl space with her.

Arian.

A whimper escaped her.

Mistress.

"Orla?" She could hear him.

Yes, Mistress. Are you all right?

"Yes, Orla. I'm fine. Are you?" She started to crawl a little further in when she didn't hear an answer. "I'm going to try to free you, but I don't know where you are. Can you tap on the floor? Or do something to let me know where you are."

At first, she heard nothing, but her ears started to pick up a soft vibration. She moved a little farther. The vibration turned into a soft tapping noise. Arian rolled over and crab-walked along the crawl space, placing her hands on the metal above her head. Using that touch she found Orla's location. Each time he tapped she could feel it against her palms.

"Orla. I'm here. I have to look around and see where the closest panel is." She aimed her torch up toward the ceiling, looking for the small seams that showed where she might be able to open that panel to let her get to Orla. Arian found one just a little past where Orla laid. But what if it was buried?

"Orla, can you see in front of you? I need to know if you can see the floor panel." She heard a soft scraping sound, then heard Orla's thoughts in her mind.

Yes. Part of it is buried, but there is some space to open the panel.

Arian braced herself under the panel and shoved. It didn't budge.

"I can't move it, Orla. Is there something blocking it?" There was silence for a few securs.

Try again.

Arian braced herself again, this time using her legs to push the panel up. Her muscles quaked under the pressure, but she pushed the door up into the first locked position. Pushing herself into a sitting position she stuck her head through the small opening. The torch in her hand lit up the small space, and blinded Orla.

Do you mind?

"Sorry, Orla." She aimed the beam of the light behind him, to see how badly he was buried. At least three-fourths of him was hidden under the rubble. Her fear of how badly he was hurt must have shown on her face because she heard his thoughts again.

It's okay, Mistress. I think most of the weight is off me now. When we landed, the weight shifted, and I know nothing is crushing me from the hips up.

"You think?"

I can't feel anything below my waist.

Arian wanted to cry for him, but now was not the time. They had to get out of the ship, and she knew time was of the essence. Grasping him around the shoulders, she pulled with all her might, sliding him forward a few millimeters. Once she pulled him close enough to the lip of the opening, she slid further down the crawl space, and helped him drag his broken body out from under the debris, and into the crawl space behind her. As she inched backward, she pulled him along with her, keeping a tight grip around his shoulders. Her back ran into a wall, warning her that they had hit the end of the crawl space.

Using her torch once again she found another panel and pushed it open. After pulling herself up onto the floor, she reached down and pulled Orla up with her. She bit back a cry when she noticed the odd angles his legs laid in.

Arian stood up and opened the door, only to have sand blast her in the face. Once the sand died down, she scanned the area to see what caused it. Looking up, she saw two ships taking off. If she tried to move him now, they could be spotted.

Orla's hand on her arm grabbed her attention. *We must get out of here.*

"But those ships aren't out of sight yet."

And they won't be until the explosives go off.

"What explosives?" She looked where Orla pointed and saw the small devise attached the bulkhead. That was all it took to make her scramble for safety. Dragging Orla out of the door she tried to put as much space between them and the ship as quickly as she could. Hopefully, the ship was only scanning for the explosion and not for survivors. She threw up shields to hide them, but not knowing what type of equipment they had made her worry that they'd see them anyway.

A deafening boom shook the ground, knocking her feet from under her as the ship blew into a thousand pieces. Shrapnel whizzed by them, coming perilously close to where they were.

Arian bit back a cry as a piece bit into her leg. The dust cleared, revealing a big hole where the ship used to be. If she had been unconscious just a little longer, they wouldn't have made it out alive.

She breathed a sigh of relief as the two ships sped up into the sky and disappeared from sight.

"We have to find shelter." Arian stood up and winced when she tried to put pressure on the leg the shrapnel hit. Sitting down she pulled her leg toward her, found the piece and pulled it out of her leg. Tears welled up from the pain that caused. But she couldn't think about that right now. Her first goal was to find them someplace to hide until they could contact Grinnell.

She spied a large piece of the fuselage that would work great as a travois to carry Orla. Now all she had to do was find something she could pull it with and she could move him without having to drag him, and possibly add to his injuries.

Arian looked around but didn't find anything to use. The explosion did a good job of destroying anything she might have salvaged to use. She decided to inventory what she had salvaged to see if there was something she could use there.

Untying the jacket from around her waist she sat down in the dirt and spread the items out. She added the torch to the collection.

The food packets she stuffed in her pockets. There wasn't a lot, but enough to feed them for a little while. Long enough to give her time to find food around the area.

Next, she opened the first aid kit. Inside was a small pharmacy. That could help Orla. Gauze, tape, scissors, a flare, and candy. Candy? Arian put everything back into the kit and sat back. The gauze was too thin, it would break before she got a few meters. The tape might be strong enough, but it wouldn't stick to the metal.

"Maybe I can tie it on." She stood up and examined the sheet of metal. She found several holes in it and, unraveling the tape, she rolled the end to make it thin enough to fit through one of the holes. Once she threaded it through, she tied it off and measured off a long strip and cut it with the scissors, then repeated the process.

Her next daunting project was to get Orla on the make-shift carrier. How was she going to do this? Orla out-weighed her three to one. A Miran was a lot denser than the average humanoid. A man from her planet who was the same size would weigh about a third of what Orla did.

She brought the carrier next to Orla and decided to roll him onto it. Sweat broke out on her forehead as she tried to move him.

"Did you have to be so heavy?" she murmured to herself as she got a little leverage and pushed him halfway on to the carrier. Arian moved his legs, and swung them over, and in the process managed to roll him all the way on to the metal sheet.

"You," she puffed. "Are going on a diet when we get home. That or else I start working out and build up my muscles."

Arian slipped the first aid kit into Orla's jacket, stuffed most of the food packets into various pockets in Orla's clothing, securing the seams to make sure they didn't lose anything, then stepped into the small circle of tape. She rolled her coat up and tied it around her waist, pulled the tape up to rest against the middle of the jacket, and started to trudge off.

Trying to move Orla sapped all the strength out of her.

"You are the biggest piece of dead weight I've ever had to move," she complained as she slowly dragged him behind her.

Arian had to stop a lot to rest, but she finally traversed the land to the mountains she used to stop their descent. "Thank the Gods, we didn't land too far away from these mountains, or I would have left you out there on your on."

Arian knew she wouldn't have really left him, but she ached all over and was saying things just to break the silence. She placed Orla in the shade of the mountain as she started to look for a cave to hide in. She didn't want to have anyone find them while Orla healed.

Stopping, she shuddered at the thought that entered her head. If he ever healed. The fact that he didn't shift to heal himself, frightened her. She knew he had to be very weak if he couldn't shift. Would he die on her? She didn't want to think about that.

CHAPTER TWENTY-ONE

The cave she found wasn't too far from where she left Orla, but it was several meters up. How was she going to move him up there without help?

She knelt down beside him. "Orla, I found a place for us to stay in, but you must help me. I can't carry you."

Arian saw no evidence that Orla heard her, yet when she pulled him up against her back, she didn't find him that heavy. As she scrambled up the side of the mountain, he moved with her, allowing her to scale the face of the mountain without any trouble.

She pulled him into the mouth of the cave, then rested against the wall face for a few microns. Undoing the jacket from her waist again, she fluffed it into a pillow of Orla.

"I'm going to find firewood, and hopefully something comfortable for you to lie on. Just rest until I get back." She stood on the lip of the cave and scanned the terrain. The land below her was basically barren, which meant she had to go up to find anything. She took a deep breath then started to make her way up the side of the mountain. She was very glad that there were natural hand and foot holds along the side of the mountain. Now all she had to do is find what she needed and then figure out how she was going to get back to the cave.

Several horas later, Arian had a small fire burning in the mouth of the cave. As much as she feared someone might spot it, she didn't want to build it any deeper into the cave, in fear that it wouldn't light, or else eat up all the oxygen in the small cave.

As she fed a few more branches to the fire she smiled at herself. She had found a fallen log on one of the plateaus above them. After pulling Orla around for most of the afternoon, she found pushing it off the ledge easy. The shattering impact against the base of the mountain broke the tree into manageable pieces she could carry up to the cave.

She also found leaves, moss, and tree needles that allowed her to make a comfortable bed for Orla. After using the emergency scanner and finding Orla stable, she headed for the mouth of the cave.

Arian turned her head toward Orla. The fact that he still slept and hadn't shifted to heal himself worried her. Not knowing what to do, she had placed her hand on his forehead when she scanned him. No fever. In fact, he felt a little cold. That couldn't be good.

As the sun dipped behind the horizon, she heard the calls of some of the local birds, and well as a few of the predators. Game would help keep them fed and might help Orla get his strength back. The portable radio sat near Orla, but right now it was useless. With Grinnell out of orbit the only people that would pick her broadcast would be the people on the planet, and she didn't want to let them know they were still alive, or where to find them.

She leaned against the rock face at the mouth of the cave and watched as the stars slowly winked into the darkening sky.

Arian awoke to a stiff neck and stabs of pain in her hip. When she fell asleep, she didn't know, but she did know it was the pain that woke her up. Standing up, she stretched, and winced. She never used the scanner to examine herself. Considering she fell asleep almost immediately after making sure Orla was comfortable, it wasn't surprising.

She walked deeper into the cave and retrieved the scanner. Her scan showed minor cuts and abrasions, but she made it through pretty much unscathed. A miracle in itself. Next, she scanned Orla. It showed no change, but she did notice his temperature had dropped a little.

Although he hadn't spoken to her mentally since she brought him into the cave, she continued to speak to him as if he were awake and well. "Orla, I'm going to look for food. I'll be gone a while, but hopefully, I'll be back with food for us."

She frowned when she received no sort of acknowledgment from Orla. Arian climbed up to the plateau above them. It wasn't very wide, but she did notice a few edible plants there the last time she had climbed up. She also knew this would be the best place to find a young sapling to make a bow out of. Then she would search for the right tree to make the arrows. This could take all dura, if she didn't find what she needed right away, and she didn't want to be away from Orla that long.

The young trees stood tall and proud, reaching up toward the sun, like a child would reach up to a parent. One of the younger saplings just to her right would be perfect for what she wanted. She pulled a small sharp rock she had found in the cave out of her pocket and started to saw it against the base of the young tree. "I'm really sorry about this, but you have to understand it is for a good cause."

Once she sawed more than half way through, she drew out the pair of scissors from another pocket. She could just stand on the tree and snap the rest of it off, but she didn't want to risk the chance of breaking it the wrong way.

Then she rid the sapling of branches, using her rock or the scissors to cut them off. Once the young tree was free of its branches, she measured off the length she needed and cut off the excess. After putting the cuts she needed in each end she searched the foliage for a young frumage plant that had a shoot that was the right length.

Arian also pulled the rest of the plant, to use later. Its raw sweetness will add to their meager menu. Too bad she couldn't make the delicious syrup she liked to pour over her desserts. But how good would the syrup be without a cake or tart to pour it over, anyway. Chewing on the stalks will give them an added treat without having to worry about syrup or desserts.

She tied the shoot from the plant on each end of the sapling, arching the tree to the tautness she needed to make it a strong bow.

"Now all I have to do is find arrows." She checked the branches she cut off the tree, first. Luckily, she found three she could use among the branches she had cut off. Another nine would give her enough to start hunting after dark. In her search she also found several more plants that could be eaten.

She pulled them, knowing that hunting game could be a hit or miss situation. And knowing how bad her aim must be right now she'd bet on the miss more than the hit.

Arian slung the bow over her shoulder and held the three arrows she made. What was she going to do with them? She spied another plant she could use as a carryall. Arian scooped out the plant, leaving its husk intact and slung it over her back, then placed the arrows in it before she started hunting for more.

She knelt beside Orla. He remained asleep. She feared he was in a coma, but she felt soft whispers against her mind to ease her fears. Yet, Orla didn't wake up. She ended up grinding up part of the frumage plant and feeding that to him to give Orla some nourishment. She sat next to him, brushing his hair away from his face, the simple contact making her feel a little better.

"I wish you'd wake up, Orla. Seeing you this way worries me. I don't know what to do to help you." She stood up and slung the bow over her shoulder again.

A soft whisper brushed against her thoughts. *Your love.*

"If only it were that simple." Arian smiled sadly. She picked up the satchel with the arrows in it. "I'll be back as soon as I can. I'm going to see if I can catch any fresh meat for us."

She slipped out the mouth of the cave and scaled up the rock face until she hit a place that she thought would be a great area to hunt.

Several horas later, she headed back to the cave empty-handed. She knew she was a bad shot, but she never thought she was pathetic. Either

her arrows went wide from their mark, or she frightened the game off before she could ever raise the bow.

"The worst excuse for a hunter than anyone has ever seen," she mumbled to herself.

Arian walked into the cave. Propping her bow up against the wall and resting the satchel that held the arrows next to it, she closed in on Orla. She checked his forehead and found no fever. In fact, she swore that his temperature had dropped a little more.

"Orla, this can't be good. Your temperature continues to drop." She pulled the emergency kit closer to her and opened it up. Removing the scanner, she ran a diagnostic on Orla. It still showed him as stable.

"This cannot be right. You have slept far too long." She glanced down at the scanner. Could there be a setting for a Miran, which most believe is a fictitious race? She hadn't even thought about looking because normally a Miran wasn't in the listing. But if Orla programed it, he might have loaded info on his race into the scanner.

Arian wanted to kick herself for not checking earlier. In trying to find food and shelter, she forgot to look. She checked the data base of the scanner.

"Stars, there is a setting for Mirans." She rubbed her forehead. How could she have been so stupid. Once she reprogrammed the scanner to the setting for his race, she scanned Orla. She wanted to cry as what it told her. Orla was dying. The drop in his temperature was deadly to him.

"Orla, I'm sorry," she whispered. "I didn't think. If I had, I would have realized something was wrong."

She knew that was wrong. She knew something wasn't right from the beginning, but she never thought about resetting the program until now.

"Orla, I don't know what to do. You're getting worse. Please help me."

She didn't feel any tickling against her mind. "Talk to me, Orla. I need your help."

Arian was close to tears at this point. She didn't know how to help him without knowing what was wrong. The scanner didn't give her any remedies.

"What do you want me to do, Orla? I'm scared. What would I do without you? You have become such a large part of my life." She picked up his hand. "Please don't die, Orla. You mean too much to me."

Not knowing how to proceed, she rested her head against his chest. "My life would be empty without you."

Arian sat up with the realization that she loved him. Her heart started to beat harder at the thought. He was everything she ever wanted in a mate. If it wasn't for Dresuer, she would declare her love for him easily.

She wiped her tears away. Dresuer proved what a piece of truggar dung he was when he tried to turn them over to the general. Why hold back her feelings now? If Orla did die and she didn't tell him how she felt she would never forgive herself.

Gently touching his face, she ran her fingers over his strong jaw.

"I need to tell you something that isn't easy for me. My heart." She pounded her hand against her chest, opening her heart to him. "It aches at the thought of you being so ill. If I could give you my strength I would. You hold a very tender place in my heart. I love you."

A tear slipped down her cheek and splashed on to his hand.

"Please don't leave me, Orla. I don't know if I can live without you."

Something brushed softly against her mind, tickling against her thoughts. The gentle caress continued, slowly becoming bolder as it started to enter her thoughts. The tickling turned into a burning sensation.

Arian tried to fight it, fearing what was happening to her. She shook her head, hoping to dislodge the strange sensation, but it continued to grow inside her head. She rubbed her hand against her forehead. What was happening to her?

Her head felt like it was on fire. She started to rock back and forth against the pain.

"Orla, help me." Arian's voice barely a whisper. She couldn't keep her eyes open, the pain was so intense. If she didn't know better, she'd swear someone was beating her head with a spike.

Then, like a blanket. Comfort wrapped itself around her thoughts. Not being able to handle the shock to her system, she felt her mind shut down.

Just as her mind started to black out, she heard a soft whisper inside her head.

I love you too.

CHAPTER TWENTY-TWO

Consciousness came back to her in small bits. Arian remembered opening her eyes several times, only to fall back into a deep slumber. Although the pain had disappeared, her head still felt funny. As if it was stuffed with cotton. She wiped the back of her hand against her forehead as if the gesture would remove the cobwebs she felt in her head. Opening her eyes, she stared up at the ceiling, trying to remember what had happened.

She sat up with a jerk. Orla. Oh Gods, she prayed nothing had happened to him while she was unconscious. What she saw when she looked at him took her breath away.

Orla had somehow found the energy to shift into his Miran form.

"Oh thank the Gods." Without thought she crawled over to his pallet and wrapped her arms around him. His warmth wrapped around her like a cocoon. She buried her face in his fur, rubbing her chin against the silkiness.

A smile stole across her lips when she heard a soft purr emanate from him.

"I have to go and try to scare up some food for us," she murmured against his neck. She stayed curled up next to him for a few microns more, not wanting to leave him, but she knew she needed to try her hand at hunting again. The sun had already started to set, and now would be the best time for her to find the right spot to wait before the sun completely disappeared. In the dark, she'd do more stumbling than hunting.

She stepped out on the ledge and took a deep breath. The fresh air felt good as it entered her lungs. As quickly as she could, she scaled the side of the mountain to the plateau above. The rest must have been good for her because she climbed it in record time. Several quick scans revealed a great spot to wait for game to come into sight. Arian hid herself deep in the brush she picked and waited.

She would have missed the animal if it hadn't made such a loud sound because she was wondering how she knew to hide in the brush the way she did. The last time she tried hunting, she hid behind a tree and probably made more noise than a small Bressar, a squirrel like creature that was a was well known for breaking a tranquil dura with its scream.

A young pumat stepped into the clearing. Arian felt her breath catch in her throat. It was magnificent, standing four meters tall and fifteen points on its antlers. That creature would feed them for at least a cycle. Too bad she was such a bad shot. She studied the pumat. Maybe it wasn't so bad. At least she got a chance to see one. She could always tell stories of the one that got away when she got older. As if anyone would ever believe this one in the first place.

She pulled the bow off her arm and garbed an arrow. Fitting the arrow against the string, she pulled it back and waited. When the pumat moved into the right spot, she let the arrow fly.

Her jaw dropped when it hit its mark. "Stars!"

Just as she started to move out of the brushes, she heard something move. Crouching back down, she waited to see what would come into view.

Arian found climbing back down the mountain difficult with her catch. She had already lowered the pumat, but the smaller game she had strapped to her back. Although she might have gotten more than they could possibly eat before it went bad, she couldn't stop herself. It was like they were waiting for her to catch them.

The fire was going when she returned, but she didn't remember lighting it.

She checked on Orla before she started to cook everything she caught. He seemed to be sleeping peacefully. Arian wanted to kick herself, she knew there was no way he would have been able to light the fire. He was too weak. Yet she couldn't stop herself from checking to be sure.

Once sure he couldn't have been the one to light the fire, she checked the perimeter to make sure no one discovered their hideout. The fire burned bright by the time she laid each strip of meat out, ready to be cooked by the fire.

Arian felt something tickle her mind, causing her to look over her shoulder. Could someone be hiding in the cave? A thorough investigation revealed nothing. She shook her head. It must have been her imagination.

After checking on Orla again, she checked the first group of meat to make sure it was cooked through before she started with the next batch. Skewering the meat, she propped the sticks against the stones that circled the fire, made sure they hung over the flames, and sat back. The sensation that she was being watched still haunted her.

"All right, who is out there? Show yourselves." Arian waited to see if anyone did show themselves. She feared she was losing her mind. A couple of deep breaths, and rechecking the cave, she could prove no one had found them. Then why did she feel she wasn't alone? Orla was still out like a light. He hadn't moved at all since the last time she checked on him. So why the strange sensation?

Soft as a kiss, she felt something whisper against her neck. Her hand slapped over the exposed area, then she jumped to her feet. Someone was in the cave. They had to be.

Arian scooted over to Orla's pallet and grabbed the torch. The bright beam sliced through the darkened cave, revealing nothing.

"I know you are there. Stop playing games with me and show yourself." Soft laughter filled her head.

Arian.

"Orla?" She turned to the pallet but didn't find Orla awake.

Thank you for helping me heal.

"How?" Arian didn't remember doing anything specific to help him. That massive headache had knocked her out, making her worthless to Orla.

By being here when I needed you.

"When are you going to wake up? I've been so worried about you." She sat down next to him and started to run her fingers through his thick fur. A smile worked its way across her lips when she felt the vibration of his purr against her hand.

Soon, I'm almost healed, but not quite. A little more rest and I'll be as good as new.

Arian nodded as she rested her head against one of his massive shoulders. She couldn't stop herself from curling up with him. Her smile turned into one of contentment as she listened to his heart beat out a steady rhythm.

They laid like that for most of the dura. The only time Arian moved was to check on her cooking.

Orla finally woke up just as the sun set. Stretching his paws out in front of him, he yawned and arched his back.

"I saved you some of the meat. You need to regain your strength now."

Thank you, Mistress.

Arian led him to the small cache she had dug in the back of the cave. "I wasn't sure how much you would need so I only cooked what I thought I could eat in a cycle. Eat as much as you need. I can go hunting for more if I need to."

I can hunt for my own food, Mistress.

The heat of a blush tinged her cheeks. "Only if you need me to of course."

Silky fur rubbed against any exposed skin as Orla's tail snaked its way up her body. Arian stiffened at the passionate tingling sensation she felt when Orla's tail slid up under her tunic to wrap seductively against her bare upper torso.

Don't be embarrassed. You didn't know how quickly a Miran recovers from an illness. Thank you for saving the food, it will be more than enough. Why don't you go on and watch the sun finish setting while I eat?

Arian headed for the mouth of the cave, still feeling the effect of

Orla's intimate caress. The feel of his tail against her skin had never felt so sensual before. Her whole body screamed for more. Lost in her thoughts she didn't notice when Orla joined her a little while later in his human form until his hand brushed a stray hair away from her face.

She looked at him, happy to see him healed.

"It is a beautiful night."

"Yes, it is." Arian looked out over the horizon. The stars had just started to wink into view, looking like diamonds against the black void.

"Not as beautiful as you."

She ducked her head at his compliment. His gentle caress against her cheek made her look back up at him.

"You know you saved me."

"But how?"

He pressed a soft kiss against her temple. "With your mind."

"You're not making any sense."

"When a Miran gets seriously hurt and can't shift it's normally deadly, unless they can draw power from another source."

"And you drew from me?"

Orla paused for a micron. "In a way. The sources we can use is very limited. Normally, it is family, parents, siblings, or our mate, once the melding has occurred." He clasped her hand in his. "Do you remember what happened when you realized that I was dying?"

"Besides having that headache and passing out on you when you needed me most?" she asked sarcastically.

He gave her a lop-sided grin. "You opened your heart to me, revealing how much you really cared. When you did that our minds melded into one. That's why you ended up passing out. The pain you felt was my pain. Your mind shut down from it and allowed me to use what I needed to heal. Our minds are one now. Your thoughts are my thoughts."

"I don't understand." She turned her body toward him.

"Didn't you find it strange that in one night you went from not being able to hunt to stalking and hitting everything you aimed for?"

She hadn't thought about that. There had been no time to practice between her two hunting forays and look at all the food she caught. All this time, she thought she had just been nervous the first night, but now she had second thoughts.

"You guided me?"

"We share all our thoughts now. You have my knowledge of hunting, where to hide and how to aim properly." Orla knew he had to tell her the truth now. He could feel her mind starting to search his to see if what he said was true. If she found out the truth about his identity before he was able to tell her she might never forgive him.

"What did your father tell you about the Miran cub when you first got it?" He already knew but needed her to voice the information.

"That you were a gift from Dresuer, and you would bond with me for life and never leave my side." She paused for a moment, deep in thought. "You'd protect me from all harm."

Orla traced the outside of her fingers, sending sparks throughout her body, he watched her eyes as the sensation pooled in the center of her being.

"Mirans normally meet their mates in infancy and are constantly in contact with them. In a village with Miran children, the parents can normally tell pretty quickly which ones should be mates, and pair them off. The two cubs will live together from that point on like siblings."

"In my case, my father knew once I was betrothed, I had to go live with the child chosen for me in order for the bond to take place, or the marriage would never come to be."

A frown creased her forehead. "I don't understand."

"I think you do."

"If you were sent to live with your betrothed, that means..." Her eyes narrowed at the realization of what Orla just told her.

Time seemed to stand still when she heard him utter. "I am Dresuer."

CHAPTER TWENTY-THREE

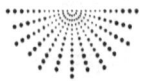

S he shot to her feet, glaring at him with a look that could kill.
Orla stood too. These next few microns weren't going to be easy, but their bond wouldn't allow either to keep secrets from the other now.

"How can you be Dresuer? You have been on this quest with me, you saw Dresuer for yourself." Her hands balled into fists.

"Dresuer is more of a title. That man you met is my twin brother."

"You don't look anything alike," she snapped at him.

Orla couldn't stop the grin from spreading across his face. "Not all twins look alike."

"I know that!" Anger rolled off her in waves.

Her thoughts told him what she wanted to do to him if this was true.

"Then why did you let me go on this quest? You knew I didn't want to go looking for Dresuer. And to know that he was with me all this time!" She slugged him in the arm.

"Because you needed to grow. And searching for Dresuer was the best way."

"Ha!"

"You wouldn't have learned how to use your Barou power. In fact, it might not have activated if we hadn't left your home world."

She shot him another hateful glare but nodded in agreement.

"You also wouldn't have learned to defend yourself." He watched her, waiting for her to bolt.

Another nod.

"Look at yourself, Arian. You are not the young innocent girl you were when you first went on this quest."

"But you lied to me."

"I didn't lie to you, I just kept some information from you to protect you."

"Humph." She crossed her arms over her chest. "I don't see any difference."

"What would have happened if General Varal had captured you at one of the times he could have? He would have forced you to tell him the truth about me if you knew, and he would do everything in his powers to hunt me down and kill me."

"You don't think your brother has told him the truth?"

"I was surprised when I found out he knew about me. My father and mother wanted to keep my existence a secret. Inheriting the miran blood is an honor but it can be a curse as well. I heard him talk about me, but he never mentioned my shifting ability. I don't think he knows about that. Right now, General Varal will treat him like a guest because he wants you and believes he has a bargaining chip with Dresuer. If he were to learn the truth, he'd kill my brother instantly. My brother knows this. He might be evil, but he's not stupid."

Arian looked at Orla. "So what do I do now? Start calling you Dresuer?"

"No." He smiled at her thunderous look. "My name is Orla. Dresuer is just the title I will have when it is time for me to rule my people."

"I can't believe you kept this from me and my father."

"Your father knew who I was."

Arian stared at him opened mouth. "That can't be true. The quest."

"He had his reasons. Your father wanted you safe, and the safest place for you was off your home world. Sending you on this quest was the only way."

"I need to be alone."

Orla just smiled wider and tapped the side of his head. No matter where she went, they would always share their thoughts now.

"I didn't ask for this."

"You gave yourself freely."

"I was under duress!" She threw her arms wide. "I couldn't let you die, Orla."

"Why?"

"Because..." her thoughts betrayed her. *I love you.*

I love you too, Arian.

She jumped when she heard his thoughts.

"There is one more step to make the bond complete. A ritual as old as time."

"And if I don't go along with it?"

"Then the bond will sever itself," said Orla.

Arian turned a pasty white color. "And you'll die?"

"Yes." That was the only problem with the bonding of minds. If they didn't complete the ritual he would die from the impact when the bond shattered in his mind, but he wasn't sure if Arian was ready for the next step. Just as their minds were one, so must their bodies be.

He knew the moment she read his thoughts because she blushed right down to her roots.

"Will we be able to read each other's thoughts all the time like this?"

"As we get adjusted to this, we'll learn how to control what we think to each other. Our mind sharing will be so natural we'll tune out the things we don't need to hear. Right now it's impossible for us to do. The bond is too new." He sensed her anger. She didn't ask for this when she went on her quest.

"I've been in love with you forever. Since the first time I saw you smile." He had to be honest in his feelings. She'd learn the truth sooner or later anyway.

"You've been my best friend as long as I've known you. I have confided things to you I wouldn't reveal to anyone else. But you never revealed the one thing you should have. How am I supposed to forgive you?"

"Because you love me?" He stepped up to her.

"That's beside the point." She wanted to stay angry at him. He could feel it through their connection, but his words affected her.

"Do you deny how you feel about me?" He brushed a strand of hair out of her face.

She glared at him. "No. I meant what I said."

"And everything I did was to protect you. General Veral would do anything to get you and I will do anything to keep you safe, including keeping information from you that could harm you if it fell into the wrong hands."

"So you were protecting me?"

"You know the general. What would he do if he suspected that you knew who the real Dresuer was?"

She sighed. "He would probably threaten to harm my people."

"And I couldn't allow him to have that kind of control."

She looked at him through her lashes. Desire for him spilled into his mind.

Orla took her hand and gestured for her to scale the mountain up to the plateau. Once they reached the wooded area, he took her hand once more and knelt.

"Since the duras of the ancients, when the Miran ruled the galaxy, the joining of mates is a glorious occasion." Orla looked up at Arian and waited for her to say the next part.

She knelt down facing him. "To show one's love," she started off hesitantly. "And to show the universe the joy they share as one."

He smiled at her as she repeated the words his mind fed to her.

"This night, Orla and Arian shall seal the bond forged between them. Their minds and bodies will become one."

The leaves on the trees rustled their agreement.

"This bonding is a deep and powerful commitment between two souls. Something not to be taken lightly," said Arian. "Love transcends everything, including time."

"If the two souls here have committed themselves to this joining, no one can tear it asunder." Orla looked deep in Arian's eyes. "My love for you gives me the strength to wake up each dura. I want this bond to be."

He watched as Arian swallowed hard. He squeezed her hand reassuringly.

"You are the stars and the moons of all the worlds to me. I want this bond to be."

With a gentle hand he caressed her cheek. Love shined in his eyes for her. He slid his hand down the column of her throat.

Arian tilted her head back. His touch excited her. She felt feather like kisses raining across her brow and cheek. Her hands started to mimic the path Orla forged with his own. The feel of his hard muscles beneath her hand thrilled her.

She felt the gentle kiss of the wind against her skin as Orla slowly undressed her. Kissing and caressing each piece of skin he revealed. Need started to build inside her, and only Orla could relieve the pressure. A quickening fluttered in her stomach. She had never felt so sensitive.

Desire, quick and sure raced through his blood with each reaction she gave to his love-making. Now devoid of her tunic, he pressed her down into the sweet grasses that would be their bed. Capturing her lips with his, he led the dance their tongues would do as he removed the rest of her clothing.

The soft caress of the wind against his bare back alerted him that she had done the same to him, yet he didn't even notice this.

She whimpered when he moved his lips to her throat, but the whimper turned into a gasp when he captured a rosy pink nipple in his mouth.

"Gods, you taste so sweet. I must taste all of you." Orla continued to pay homage to her breast, feeling it swell under his ministrations. After a quick kiss against the valley between the two peaks he turned his attention to her other breast. That one tasted just as sweet to him. Blooming under his tongue.

He moved his lips downward, nipping and licking against her sensitive skin. He quickly dipped his tongue into her belly-button, only to find it too sweet to leave alone, especially when she giggled each time his tongue swirled around the edge.

He slid down her body, using his hands to heat the path his lips wanted to take. After abandoning her belly button, he nipped at her hip. His hands worked their magic on her thighs, silently asking her to open for him.

Orla gently laved her moist center and felt her stiffen against him.
"Orla."

"Shh, my love. My only desire is to bring you pleasure." His tongue caressed her again. She wanted more from him, but he wanted to be sure she was ready.

She moaned. "It feels wonderful."

He buried his face against her, loving her, bringing her to heights she never knew existed. Her body convulsed with the power of her orgasm.

Orla rose above her. He captured a breast in his mouth once again and suckled her as he started to enter her sweet core. He wanted to go slowly, but passion urged him to go fast. Entering her, he gave her body a chance to adjust to his size before he pushed a little deeper.

"Arian, you feel so good." His breathing coarse and ragged. He must sound like he had just ran a marathon.

She wrapped her ankles around his thighs, urging him deeper.

"I don't want to hurt you," he murmured against her neck as he slid in just a little more.

"I want you inside me, Orla. All of you, now. Please." She urged him once more with her legs.

He buried himself completely inside her, tearing the fragile membrane that proved her innocence.

She gasped against him. The pain quickly faded to pleasure.

He started to move against her, slowly at first, but picking up momentum as the sensations took over.

They moved together perfectly, sensing what the other enjoyed and concentrating on increasing that pleasure.

Orla could feel her muscles start to tighten around him, then they would back off. Together, they raced for something their bodies instinctively knew waited for them.

He wanted to slow things down, extend their pleasure, but Arian would have none of that, she touched just the right spots on his body to make him keep up his fevered pitch.

Just as they reached the pentacle, they felt the bond solidify, forging their bodies and their souls together forever.

He purred and nipped her shoulder as he found his release. Arian practically keened when her body had hit the highest heights.

They lay in each other's arms, exhausted, but sated.

"I never knew," said Arian.

"Neither did I," Orla rumbled, still embedded inside her. His head buried against the side of her neck.

"Will it always be that wonderful?"

Orla pulled back to look at her and noticed a wicked gleam in her eye. "I don't know. We'll have to do it again to find out."

She circled one of his nipples with the tip a finger.

He felt his body react.

"We really should be sure, don't you think?" She tightened against him and felt him grow inside her.

He nuzzled her neck as his fingers worked a little magic of their own.

She arched against the hand he rested against one of her breasts and tilted her hips under him.

He closed his eyes against the sensations her body caused in his. Levering himself up on his arms he looked down at her.

She used the opportunity to suckle one of his flat nipples.

That was all it took for him to show her that each time they made love it would be spectacular.

Grinnell sat in the captain's chair, wondering what he should do about Arian and Orla. They had been gone a little under a cycle now. He had promised Orla one cycle before he went back to search for them. Even though they hadn't hit the time limit, Grinnell was ready to go after them now. The Gods knew what could have happened to them in this time.

He jumped at the popping sound that came out of his radio.

"Grinnell."

He quickly turned on the radio. "Orla? Is that you?"

Orla verified his identity by using a password he had given to Grinnell that no one else would have been able to figure out.

"Do you need us to come and get you?"

"Yes. Our ship was destroyed when we tried to evade the general's troops."

"Evade? What happened."

"We'll tell you later."

"All right. We're about three horas from orbit."

"Use the cloaking devise when you enter orbit. Contact me on this signal when you get here, and we'll give you our coordinates. Orla out."

The communication line went dead, and Grinnell flew into action. He called everyone onto the bridge and explained the situation.

"I need everyone helping right now. Browlman, you are on communications. Grenta, you're now on scanners. Tymin, you will work the transporters when I tell you to. Let's bring Orla and Arian home."

CHAPTER TWENTY-FOUR

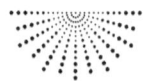

The ship hid behind one of the planet's moons when Grinnell contacted Orla. They put themselves in a synchronous orbit with the moon, hoping that if the ship could be detected for the few securs it had to de-cloak to beam Arian and Orla up, it would read as an echo from the moon.

"Timing must be perfect people. When I say drop the shields, those shields must go down and the beaming must start. We have a very small window. The quicker we can get this done the better off we are. If we're lucky, they won't detect us at all."

Grenta scanned the surface and located Orla and Arian close to where they should have been. Feeding the info to Tymin, she checked to see if any of the normal patrols were heading in their direction.

"Everything is normal," said Grenta.

"I have coordinates," said Tymin.

Grinnell nodded. They maneuvered the ship as close as they could before he gave the word.

"Now."

Tymin hit the locking mechanism and started the beaming process.

"Three ships are headed this way," reported Grenta.

"We have them!" Tymin practically jumped up and down in his seat when he told everyone.

"Leabo, get that cloaking devise back up." Grinnell nodded to the Browlman.

She let the ship coast back in to the shadow of the moon.

"All engines stop."

Cloaked, and silent they hung in space and held their breath, hoping the ships would think they had just detected some sort of glitch in their systems.

Orla and Arian stepped on the bridge just before they heard the pilots of the ships speaking to each other.

"There is nothing here."

"One more sweep of the area and we'll head back to base."

"Yes, sir."

They all let out a relieved sigh when the ships turned and headed back to the planet.

The Browlman was the first to move toward them. "I am so glad to see you two unharmed. We had feared the worst." She hugged Arian.

"It got a little scary, but we survived," said Arian as she returned the woman's hug.

Grenta stepped up to them, first looking Arian over, then making eye contact with Orla.

Orla met her gaze.

Grenta smiled at him and shook his hand. "It is good to have you back."

"So where to now?" asked Grinnell.

"Home," said Arian.

Everyone started talking at once, giving Arian a slight headache. She was still dealing with sharing every thought with Orla, handling a barrage of questions on top of that made her cringe.

Orla came to her rescue. "Arian has been through an ordeal and needs to rest."

"Then let's meet in the mess hall in three horas," said Grinnell. "Everybody in agreement?"

Although everyone was bursting with questions, they all agreed to wait.

Orla placed his hand against the small of her back and escorted her to their room. The moment the door closed he stepped close and enveloped her in a hug. "Are you all right? I could feel the distress you felt."

She nodded against his chest. A sigh escaping her at the comfort a simple hug could give her.

"They just started all at once, and I wasn't prepared for that. I just felt overwhelmed." Arian buried her face against him, taking a deep breath. "I love the way you smell. Like a forest after the rain."

"You are changing the subject." He nuzzled her hair.

"It was just the two of us on that planet. I didn't have to remember what my position was, or that stupid quest. I could just be your mate."

His arms tightened around her. "We are alone now."

"Are you trying to distract me?" She moaned when she felt his lips on her throat.

"I only wish to relax you," he murmured between kisses.

"You mean turn my bones to fumage." He knew just where to touch her because of their mental connection. Even if she wanted to focus on what she would say to their friends in a few horas he knew how to make her thoughts fly away.

"I like fumage." He had opened the front of her tunic, releasing her breasts to his hands. His hands caressed one as his mouth closed over the tip of another.

Her body felt like it was melting. Orla maneuvered her to their small bed and eased her down. No words were needed as they removed each other's clothing, caressing or kissing the skin they exposed.

The heat of his mouth on her throat made her moan. She brushed her fingers against his chest. He had a soft dusting of hair all over his body. She assumed it was because he was Miran. It felt silky against her hands, tickling her palms as she traced his muscles. Her fingers dipped into the plains and valleys his muscles created, working her way down to his erection.

Orla growled when she wrapped her hand around the velvet smooth flesh.

"Gods Arian, that feels good."

"How about this?" she stroked him.

"Yes." He shook as she slid her hand from the tip to the base. "Please don't stop."

His words gave her power. As she continued to bring him pleasure, she felt his fingers slip into her folds, stroking her softly and making her body shake as well. Her body tightened as he brought her closer and closer to an orgasm.

Just as she reached her climax, he stopped what he was doing and grabbed her hands. He then centered himself and slid in deep. That sent her over the edge, causing her body to tighten against him in a vice like grip. Both groaned at the sensation. Orla set a pace that she met thrust for thrust. All her nerve endings were on fire. They raced toward their orgasms together.

She felt each caress against her walls. Need flooded her. All she wanted was the release she found in his arms. She felt her body squeeze against him as he stroked a sensitive spot that left her wanting to beg for more. Orla knew to move the same way to bring her the same pleasure. A few more strokes had her grabbing the sheets beneath her. Now she wasn't sure if she could take much more. Then it started. Heat pooled in her groin before spreading through her body. Everything tightened inside her and she felt like she was freefalling with Orla at her side.

Orla brushed her hair away from her face. "I love you."

She smiled up at him. "I love you too. I think I have for a long time, I just didn't know it."

He rolled over and brought her with him, wrapping her in his embrace while she rested her head against his chest.

"You know I must take care of General Varal." She lifted her head up. "Going to the planet is the one thing the general wouldn't expect, if he realizes we're still alive."

"General Varal is too smart to believe he got rid of us that easily." He brushed his finger along her collar bone.

Arian had to agree. She rested her head back on his chest. Her thoughts focused on the best way to reclaim her planet.

"How do you plan on stopping the general?"

"The only thing I can come up with is I walk into General Varal's stronghold, he'll think he has won and that will give my people the chance they need to take over."

"Arian."

"Orla, I know what I am thinking is risky, but it is the only option I can think of right now. Once we explain what I want to do, maybe someone else will come up with a better plan."

Three horas later, everyone sat in the mess hall.

"It is time to stop General Varal," Arian said. "The only plan I have come up with so far is to contact my people and let them know my plan."

"What is your plan?" asked Grinnell.

"To turn myself over to General Varal."

"What?" Grinnell exclaimed. "Do you want to get yourself killed?"

"No." She looked over at Orla, who sat at her side. "I have too much too live for, but I must stop him. If we can get in and talk to the leaders of the different villages, we might be able to get them to help."

Orla took her hand in his in silent support. His gesture didn't go unnoticed.

"The easiest way to contact everyone would be to use the communications system in the palace. If we can get that far I can get to the communications center without being detected."

"We can't let you do this. You're the queen. Risking your life shouldn't be an option."

"Can you come up with a better plan?" she countered.

Silence greeted her.

"Then we shall move forward with Arian's plan," said Orla. "First, we must figure out a way to get into the palace undetected."

"The cloaking devise should get the ship on the planet safely," said Grinnell.

"And I can get us into the palace," said Arian. "As a child my parents showed me all the secret passages in and out of the palace. I'm sure the general hasn't learned them all yet. My father only showed him the most obvious ones."

"But you don't know if he's stumbled across any of the others."

"No, but I also don't think he'll have those guarded. Knowing

General Varal, he has kept those secret passages to himself, just in case he needs them to escape."

"But he could have set up surveillance cameras to keep an eye on those passages just in case you'd try to slip into the palace undetected," Grinnell countered.

"True, but he doesn't know about my Barou blood. He'd never expect me to create a false image for his cameras."

"Wouldn't he be suspicious after your attempted rescue?"

Arian blanched. She hadn't thought about that. But there was no way the general knew about her talent. During the time she had while waiting for Orla to heal she realized that Dresuer must have told them she was there and that was what sounded the alarm. If there had been a Barou master there she never would have been able to get the doors to move. "He doesn't know that I am Barou. Knowing him, he will probably suspect an advanced technology more than a powerful mind. General Varal would have no reason to suspect me of that. When we tried to rescue Dresuer I didn't create an illusion that could make him suspicious. This time I will hide our presence completely."

"But what if you are wrong?" asked Grinnell

"Then I'll have to rely on you to contact the villages for me and hope you can convenience them to act quickly."

"I don't like this."

"I don't like this either, Grinnell," said Orla. "But she's right. If Arian's people hear and see her, they will back her. We must try to get into the communication center so she can give them a message."

"And what will that message be? You can't possibly tell them to meet with you, General Varal will be the first to show up and arrest you."

Arian smiled. "I only want to broadcast four words. Don't trust General Varal. Those four words will let them know I have a plan."

Arian sat on their bunk later that evening, brushing out her hair.

"And what is that plan?" asked Orla. He leaned against one of the bulkheads and watched the brush caress her hair as it slid through the white tresses.

"I need to get the people to storm the palace, but that plan could change once I see how the general has set up his command." Arian sat down her brush. "This is very risky, but I can't make any other decisions until I see the palace again. Knowing how the general has taken over the planet will be the key in how my plans will work. If he has blockaded the villages, we can slip in and out without anyone knowing, but if he has guards posted in every village, then we'll have to figure out another way to reach them."

Orla pushed himself off the wall and walked toward her. "Your life can't be jeopardized."

"I know that." She stood up and met him half way. "When we first started this quest, I was very naive, but I have learned. The only way to defeat the general is to play his game."

"My love." Orla touched her soft cheek. "Why can't you let me take care of this?"

"Because." She closed her eyes as his fingers stroked her jaw and neck. "I am the one responsible for all these people. They need to know that I have a stake in it too."

"By handing yourself over to General Varal? They might refuse you because they think your plan is foolhardy."

"These people barely know who I am. My father was their leader, I was only the princess. I have to prove to them that I am a queen worthy of following, because if they don't follow me, all is lost." She snuggled in close to him, reveling in his heat. A smile spread across her lips as his arms wrapped around her.

"A good queen would also share the weight of her responsibilities with those who love her." His words vibrated through her.

"And I do share those responsibilities. If I didn't, you wouldn't know about my plans."

"And the moment you tried to sneak away to implement them, I would be right there by your side."

"That thought sharing thing, huh?"

"No." He touched one finger to her lips. "My heart would know you were in jeopardy, and fight to keep you safe."

She buried her face against his chest as his words surrounded her heart. This was the support she needed from him, and without asking, he gave it to her. She didn't think she could love him more.

"You didn't finish brushing your hair."

"You're right." Arian ran her fingers through it, hitting several snags. She didn't feel like completing her ritual, but she knew if she didn't tomorrow her hair would take on a life of its own and she wouldn't be able to control it again for several duras. A sigh escaped her as she picked up the brush again.

Orla took the brush from her. "May I?"

She wondered what he was up to. Orla kept his mind blank as he looked back at her.

The thought of someone else brushing her hair sounded heavenly, so she nodded her consent, then followed him to the small bunk she had sat on earlier.

He sat behind her, brush in hand.

As the brush slid through her hair, Arian didn't think. She allowed the sensations to flow through her. Closing her eyes, she tilted her head back, wondering why this brushing felt better than any other she had ever had. It felt so sensual. Each stroke relaxed her a little bit more, to a point where she felt like she was melting.

If Orla hit any snags in her hair, she didn't notice. Arian was too caught up in the desire that filtered through her from a simple hair brushing.

She almost whimpered when Orla set the brush down on the bed but sighed when his fingers replaced the brush. His fingers cupped her scalp, then slid through her hair, looking for any snags he might have missed with the brush. Each time his fingers caressed her scalp, she felt the flames of desire leap a little higher.

Orla's hand cupped her scalp again, but instead of sliding through her hair, this time they gently tugged her head backwards. Another sigh slipped out of her as she felt his lips slide across her neck.

"Can I assume you liked that?" he whispered in her ear.

"Oh, the Gods, yes. You can brush my hair anytime." She turned her face toward his. Their lips only a few inches away from each other.

Arian wasn't sure who closed the distance between them, but as long as she felt the pressure of Orla's lips against hers, she didn't care. His tongue traced the outside of her lips before delving into the depths of her mouth. Fire raced through her veins.

She pressed herself against him, wanting to feel his body against hers. Frustration filled her when she felt the barriers of their clothing, but she couldn't help but smile when she felt the proof of his desire through those same constricting clothes. At least she knew he was as affected as her.

His tongue slid down the outside of her throat, branding her.

"Love me, Orla."

He smiled against the hollow of her throat. "I already do."

"No." Arian shook her head. "Make love to me. I want to feel you inside of me."

Orla rested his head against hers. She felt the shutter that racked his body. He wanted her just as bad as she wanted him but was hesitant. Arian realized he was worried about hurting her. Her body wasn't used to sexual activity and she could become sore if they weren't careful.

"If I don't feel your love fill me soon, I will die."

Orla didn't need any more encouragement. He grabbed the bottom of her tunic, lifted it above her head, then eased her down on their bed. He pulled his tunic off as well. The feel of her flesh against his made him sigh in contentment.

Arian's hands caressed the down like hairs on his chest, drawing little circles against his skin. The soft brushes had him shaking to his core. Even though they had just mated they had already become comfortable with each other. Arian never tried to shield her thoughts from him. Now that she knew the truth about him he had nothing to hide from her.

"You are so beautiful." He pressed his lips to her stomach. "And your skin tastes so sweet."

She shifted beneath him as he kissed his way up to one breast, alerting him to what she wanted. Her soft skin called to him. He felt her hand close around his shaft, sliding her fingers up and down the tight flesh. Each gentle touch had him holding his breath. Gods, that felt good. With their mental connection she knew just how to grasp him and where to apply pressure to give him the most pleasure.

"You aren't fighting fair."

She smiled at him. "Is there a problem?"

"Nothing I can't fix." He used his mouth to blaze a trail up her body until he could reach her mouth. He tugged her hands away from his member so he could center himself and drive home. Arian moaned when he entered her. He paused, wanting to be sure that her moan was from pleasure and not pain.

"Orla, I'm fine. Your touch calms and heals. I haven't had any discomfort. All you have given me is pleasure."

He rose above her. "I'm very happy to hear that, Mistress." A slight frown creased her forehead. "Are you alright?"

"Yes." She smiled up at him. "But I am your mate, why are you still calling me mistress."

"That has been my endearment for you since we were children." He brushed a few strands of hair out of her face. "Does it bother you?"

"No, but it seems so formal." She traced the outline of one of his pictorial muscle. "Like Tymin calling you master."

"True but he uses it as a form of respect." He loved the feel of her hands on his chest.

"How about you limit when you use it? Here in our bed doesn't seem like the right place."

"What do you want me to call you here? My vixen?" He bent his head to nibble on her ear.

"Vixen?"

"You did initiate this." He then pressed kisses along her jaw line.

"True." She sighed. "But I know what you think, and you will treat me like a fragile piece of glass if I let you."

"I want to keep you safe." Orla planted a quick kiss to her lips. "You are my world."

"And I feel the same way." She brushed her fingers across his ribs. "I just found you, I can't lose you this fast."

"Arian, I have waited for this all my life. I'm not going anywhere."

"Especially right now." She rubbed a leg against his hip. "I need you."

"Thank the Gods." He pulled out and surged back in again, making Arian arch against him.

"Yes, please."

Orla set a slow but deep pace that had both of them gasping. She sent him silent signals that showed him what she wanted. The more he gave her the more intense the sensations became.

"Gods, Orla, that feels so good." She shifted her hips, allowing him to slide in deeper. They groaned in unison. "If you keep this up, I'll never want to leave this bed."

"As you wish." He picked up the pace and she met him thrust for thrust. They raced toward their orgasms. Orla captured her lips with his just as they each reached their pentacle. Arian arched into him as hers took over. His started securs later.

They were breathing hard when they felt the last little fingers of their release leave them.

"Now as you were saying?" He nuzzled her throat.

She laughed as she traced the muscles on his arms. "I would love to do nothing more than stay here with you, but we have a job to do."

"And nothing I could do would change your mind?" He pulsed inside her.

"Well…"

CHAPTER TWENTY-FIVE

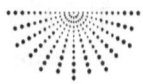

A rian held her breath as they entered her planet's atmosphere. If General Varal detected them this early, everything she hoped to accomplish would die a sad and hopeless death.

The ship touched down close to the palace, with no sign of pursuit. Her heart leaped. So far so good.

Grinnell walked up to her, his stance showed his skepticism. "Are you sure you want us to abandon ship?"

"Yes. It's safer that way."

Grinnell might not agree with her, but he obeyed her.

Under the cloak of darkness they snuck away from the ship. Grinnell led Tymin, The Browlman, Grenta and Leabo toward the nearest village to wait for Arian and Orla, while the other two headed for the palace.

"Are you sure?"

"Yes." She looked up at Orla, seeing his silhouette against the starlit sky. By the Gods, he was beautiful standing in front of her, hands on hips, the stars winking and blinking behind him. The moment etched itself in her memory.

Centering herself, she created a shield of invisibility for them.

He gestured for her to go first, since she knew a way into the palace.

Arian headed to the left side of the palace, searching for the hidden door her father had shown her yepas ago. The darkness made it difficult. Arian had tried to cloak a torch as well, but found it still beyond her powers, and she refused to do anything that could alert the guards they were there. If the general found out they were trying to gain entrance to the palace all her plans would crumble around her.

The door, hidden in the night shadows, blended into the rock face the palace was built on. She felt around the edge of the seam, found the spring mechanism and sprung it. The door slid open soundlessly.

Arian glanced up at Orla before entering the opening. Fear that the general knew what she was up to had her heart pounding in her ears. If he knew... She shook her head. She had to keep her wits about her. Now wasn't the time to second guess her decision.

They worked their way through the maze of corridors, heading deeper into the center. Arian led then through one hidden corridor then another. After walking for what seemed like forever, she finally paused in front of a seamed wall.

"This will put us in the corridor outside the communication center. There should be two guards. I'll shield us from their eyes until you are ready." She reached for his hand, entwining their fingers. "Ready?"

Orla nodded.

Arian cleared her thoughts. She called to her talent, allowing it to envelop her and Orla. Opening her eyes once again, she touched the hinge and opened the door.

They slipped out into the brightly lit corridor.

Luck was with them. There was only one guard to contend with. They inched their way next to the guard. Orla took him out without letting go of Arian. All the camera saw was the guard suddenly slumping over as if he fell asleep.

Arian was surprised to find the communication center empty. Her father always kept three people manning the equipment. But it made their job that much easier.

Adrian created an image of an empty room, so she and Orla could separate as they worked.

Working quickly, they set up the equipment they brought with them and placed them were they needed them. Once they finished and made sure everything worked the way they wanted it to, they slipped back out and escaped the confines of the palace.

They raced through the gardens, to hide in the abandoned grotto some ancestor had built eons ago. Now overgrown with vines, other than Arian and Orla, no one knew about the place.

It was perfect for the next step of their mission.

Laying on her belly, Arian wiggled through the small opening, finding it a lot narrower than when she was a child.

"You have grown quite a bit since your last visit."

She didn't comment but did manage to turn around and glare at him, before pulling herself into the tiny area.

Orla shifted into his Miran shape, then slid through the opening effortlessly. He shifted back, then gave Arian an innocent smile.

"Don't even think it," she grumbled.

The satchel that held their equipment still sat outside. Before Arian could move Orla reached up and pulled it into the grotto with them.

"First things first." Orla pointed at her necklace. "The shield."

Within securs she had the small ball activated and the shield up. Then she sat on the packed dirt floor and set to work on assembling the communication equipment.

"I just hope this works." She plugged in the touch pad keyboard into the back of the small black communication box.

"The system?"

"No. This whole idea." She snapped a few more sections together, creating a small satellite dish. "What if no one responds to my message? Maybe they think I have abandoned them. I have been gone a long time."

He hunkered down in front of her. "You worry too much."

"But they don't know me as anything other than the princess. The moment I became queen I ran away."

"You didn't run away."

"You and I know that, but how would they know it? The news files?" She tried to attach a cable to the satellite but couldn't get the plug into the hole. Arian groaned her frustration.

Orla took it away from her and finished the task that eluded her.

"Thanks."

"You sell yourself short, Mistress. Those news files told the galaxy that you were searching for your betrothed. Your people would understand that you were looking for a champion."

She shrugged. "You mean the one who has been right under my nose the entire time?"

"Of course." He continued to assemble the pieces, until it was done. "There. It's ready to be tested."

Arian slipped a small disc from her necklace and placed it in the receptacle on the left side of the devise. Flipping a switch, it hummed to life. She tuned in the palace frequency.

The general's voice filled the grotto.

"People of Emorai. Taxes are due tomorrow. Those of you who can't meet the money due will be able to waive your tax by having one able bodied male conscripted into my army."

Arian looked at Orla. "What taxes?"

He shook his head.

"Anyone else not able to pay will be able to waive the tax by turning their land over to me."

"That Frewmas!" One flip of a switch, and she overrode the general's signal. "My people, don't listen to General Varal. His vile rule is coming to an end. I have returned to take back what he has stolen from us."

Varal sat in the throne room, a smile on his face. If everything goes according to plan, he'll own most of the planet before Arian returned. Then, even if she returned with a whole army, the League of Planets board would still side with him. And he'd own the controlling power.

He opened all communication frequencies and spoke to the people. Varal had already taken most of the young men away from the farms, as the families scrambled to pay the taxes. Most were left with turning their farms and businesses over to him or risk the dungeon.

He had barely gotten through the beginning of his speech when he heard her voice. He knew it was Arian the moment she spoke one syllable, her melodious voice angered him.

"Block the transmission!"

He smiled as his guards scurried around like moruse, furry little rodents that made their homes in trash heaps and caves.

"Sir." The one speaking quaked in front of him. "We can't, they are using the palace system."

"What?" He rose out of his chair in anger. How did she get into the palace? "You mean she is in the communications center and you're still standing here? I want her captured! Now!"

Men poured out the door, racing down the hallway toward the com center.

Varal smiled. He loved the effect he had on people. He took a leisurely stroll down to the center. Now that he had Arian in custody, all his worries would disappear. The people would do anything he wanted if they hoped to keep their queen safe.

He could kill her, but he wouldn't. Instead he planned on forcing her to marry him. That way their sons would be legal heirs to the monarchy. If they carried the royal blood in their vines they could rule.

He walked up to the com center and found his men standing at attention. Good, they had already gained control of the room. Moving past his men he entered the room, already feeling a gloating smile spread across his face. What he did find astounded him.

"Where is she?"

"We don't know, sir," said the lieutenant in charge. "When we entered the room there was no trace of her."

General Varal could feel his blood pressure start to rise. He pushed past the lieutenant to see for himself. His men dashed out of the room when he entered.

She had to be here somewhere. He snatched open the doors to a closet. Nothing. Varal ripped the spare uniforms out. Throwing them about the floor as he dug through. Arian was small enough to still be hiding in the closet. Replacement parts stored on the shelves inside blocked his view. He grabbed each of them and threw them onto the floor as well. Each one hitting the floor with a little more force than the one before.

By the time he had reached the bottom of the closet, and had to admit she was not in there, he had been throwing the parts across the room, listening to them shatter as they smashed into the wall.

Continuing his search, he ripped open every cabinet, over turned any table or chair he could to vent his rising anger.

"Where the hell is she?" he bellowed.

His rhetorical question was met with silence.

When he stepped out of the room every man stood at attention. "Lieutenant."

The lieutenant stepped forward.

Varal watched his Adam's apple bob. Seeing his fear helped calm him down, just a little. "Who was on watch when that broadcast went across?"

"Private Zoram."

"Bring him to me."

The lieutenant gestured to the man in question.

Wide eyed and sweating, the young man took a tentative step forward.

"How did this happen?"

"I—I don't know, sir." Zoram stood at attention. His eyes straight ahead, his face three shades whiter than normal.

"Unacceptable." Varal rubbed his chin. "This can't go unpunished. Lieutenant, kill him."

"Sir?"

Varal pulled out his blaster and shot the private, evaporating him. He then aimed his gun at the lieutenant. "Are you hard of hearing, Lieutenant?"

"No, sir."

Varal noticed a trickle of sweat slid down the man's face. "If you won't follow out my orders without question, I have no use for you."

"Yes, sir."

"Where is the man who first told me about the transmission coming from inside the palace."

The man stepped forward.

Varal could smell his fear. Lifting his blaster out of his holster, Varal pointed it at the young man before swinging it toward the lieutenant. Pulling the trigger, he fired his blaster. The lieutenant disappeared.

"You are now lieutenant," he said to the young man. "Remember your lesson."

Yes, sir." He gave Varal a smart salute then set the rest of the guards on duty to search the palace and grounds for Arian.

Varal smiled as he headed back to the throne room. Now that he had showed how he didn't tolerate any insubordination, he knew his men would search for her until they found her. Fearing for their lives would give them the incentive to search longer and harder. Not bad for a duras work.

Arian turned off the equipment. "We have to go now."

She looked up at Orla. Her anger overrode her common sense.

If she had just waited and followed their plan, she wouldn't have jeopardized their lives like she had done. General Varal would not stop looking for her until he caught her now. She had basically slapped him in the face.

"How much time do you think we have?" She stood up and followed Orla out of the grotto.

"Just a few microns. Once Varal realizes we're not in the palace he'll widen his search."

Leaving the equipment behind, they skirted around the large statues in the garden, praying they would clear the palace grounds undetected.

Before they got halfway across the grounds the exterior lights snapped on along with the spotlights.

They flattened themselves down behind the huge water fountain in the center of the garden.

"I can't hide us from the spotlights."

Orla turned his head toward her and touched her temple. *Why?*

I can't hide our shadows.

CHAPTER TWENTY-SIX

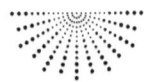

*A*s long as they don't see any movement, we should be okay.

Orla grabbed her arm and pulled her to her feet. Just as the light swept past the fountain they started to run toward the massive gate wall that surrounded the palace grounds.

And what if they are using heat seeking scanners?

Orla hadn't thought of that. *Just how do I get you to stop thinking about everything that can go wrong?*

I don't know. She looked up at him. Her fear shined in her eyes.

He wanted to kiss her. That would make her forget all her fears, but this was neither the time nor the place. Instead he steered her toward the wall they still had to get over. *Remind me to kiss you later.*

I have to remind you? She heard Orla's chuckle in her mind as they drew closer to their freedom.

The spotlights scanning the grounds illuminated an area directly in front of them and revealed a squad of soldiers searching the wall for them.

Orla changed their direction to avoid them but making their goal a little further away.

Shouts behind them made Arian jump, but Orla's grip urged her on.

I think they found the grotto. We must hurry.

They reached the wall.

Knowing General Varal, the security is at maximum. Can we get over this wall without setting off any alarms? Arian knew the palace had the best security system in case of attack.

Orla thought for a moment. *Yes. There was a breach in the security grid just a few kilometers west of that brace.*

Arian looked at him in shock. *How did you know that?*

I liked to explore. No one ever thought about stopping a Miran going out into the gardens at night. Still holding her hand, he led her to the spot he remembered. Orla picked up a small rock and threw it against the wall. If the breach had been fixed, they would have been witness to a light show and captured in securs, but the area remained dark.

Orla cupped his hands, giving Arian a foothold to boost her up over the wall. Then he scrambled up after her. He saw her jump down the other side before pressing herself against the wall to wait for him. He landed next to her gracefully.

Guards scoured the area, as the spotlights moved across the front lawn. All they had to do was make the small copse of trees at the edge of the perimeter and they would be free.

Just as the spotlight slid past where they were hiding, they broke into a run.

Orla could hear Arian's ragged breathing as they dashed into the wooded area. She fell to her knees, dragging air into her lungs. "That was fun."

Orla couldn't fight the smile that started to spread across his face. Her dry wit hit at the strangest times. "Glad you enjoyed it. Would you like to try it again?"

She looked at him like he was crazy.

"That's what I thought. Let's go find someplace safe to spend the night."

Orla climbed into the hayloft of a barn behind Arian. Neither wanted to ask anyone to take them in. He didn't know what the bounty on their heads could be, but he bet it would pay the taxes for at least one luna.

When faced with that type of motivation, he knew someone would turn them in to save their home, and he couldn't blame them.

Arian's exhaustion showed on her face. She curled up on the closest bale of hay and fell sound asleep.

He left her where she was and made a soft bed out of the loose hay toward the back of the loft. Once he finished, he scooped Arian up in his arms and carried her to the makeshift bed.

He watched as she snuggled deeper into the hay, sighing contentedly as she drifted deeper into sleep. Orla lay down beside her and pulled more loose hay on top of them so they wouldn't be easily discovered, then he pulled Arian into his arms and drifted off.

Orla opened his eyes just before the sun would start to rise and wake the small farm. He kissed Arian's brow.

"Time to wake up."

She mumbled something incoherent.

He nuzzled her neck, letting his tongue stroke a leisurely path up and down the column of her throat.

A moan escaped her as she opened her eyes.

"Good morning."

"It is when you wake me like that." She stretched out and yawned.

"We must get going. The people here should be moving about soon, and we need to leave before they spot us."

She nodded as she stood up. They climbed down the wooden ladder, leaving a trail of hay in their wake.

Arian started to pull hay from inside her tunic.

Orla stopped her. "I know it itches, but they'll know someone slept in the loft if they find handfuls of hay where it shouldn't be. Once we're far enough away you can rid yourself of the hay, and we'll look for a stream soon where we can bathe ourselves and our clothes."

The look she gave him was not a happy one, but she did as he asked. But even after she had pulled most of the bits of hay from her clothing, Arian found herself scratching and twitching from some that eluded her.

Flat pastures gave way to woods. The majestic purple mountain range that surrounded the valley the palace sat in loomed into view.

Orla noticed the sound first. He knew Arian heard the roar of a waterfall when she shot him a hopeful look. Since he had denied her a bath two times before, he couldn't do it again. Of course, the first one was no more than a mud hole, and the second was too close to one farmer's grazing pasture.

"Are you sure?"

"Yes. We are far enough away from the farm lands now. Once we get over the mountains, we should be able to catch up with Grinnell and Leabo."

"We have to climb those mountains? I don't remember you mentioning that."

"That is where the farm we are to meet up with everyone is."

"I do believe you left out that bit of information."

"Did you think we would meet someplace the general could find us?"

She didn't answer his question. Instead she said, "I'm going to bathe."

He loved watching the sway of her hips, even when accented with a slight awkward twitch when a trapped piece of hay pricked her. His heart started to pound as she peeled off her tunic and pants. She stood in all her glory, hay riddled clothing in one hand when she dove into the water.

He thought she was going to leap out of the water as quickly as she dove in when she came up gasping.

"C-c-c-cold."

"The mountain rivers feed this waterfall."

She shot him a scathing look.

"There are also warm springs that feed this lake. If you'd like I can show you where they are."

She just glared at him harder.

Orla stripped off his clothing and plunged into the icy waters. Swimming to the center of the lake, he gestured for her to join him.

She sighed as warmer water swirled around her body.

"Better?"

"Much." She laid her head back in the water, floating along in the warmed water.

His mouth went dry as her breasts broke through the surface, the sun glimmering in the water still clinging to her skin. How he would like to lick those drops off her body.

Orla swam into the frigid waters to cool his ardor. As much as he wanted her, he knew they needed to focus. They had to catch up with their friends before the general did. He finished bathing quickly, rinsed his clothes free of the hay, then climbed up on the bank to let the sun dry his skin.

Arian still scrubbed her clothes when he put on his semi-wet ones. Thank the Gods the fabric was made to dry quickly, or they could be detained for quite a while. Orla wasn't sure if he could handle that, being alone with Arian made him forget the danger they were in. All he wanted to do was take her into his arms and kiss her until she melted in his hands, make love to her until she screamed her pleasure.

"Arian, we must be going."

"I'm just making sure I have gotten all of it out of my clothes."

"I'm sure you have. You've been scrubbing your clothing for a good twenty microns."

She trudged out of the water, spread her dripping clothing out, and sat beside him.

"How are we to go over those mountains?"

"We won't. In one of my excursions I found a series of caves that will take us through the mountain to the other side." Orla pitched a rock into the lake. "You need to get dressed. The sooner we are inside the caves the safer I will feel."

"Do you sense the general's men?"

"No. But I know they are widening their search for us. The general wants you found at all costs."

"I can't believe I'm wanted like a criminal on my own planet." Arian pulled on her pants, mumbling when the wetness of the material hampered her desire to pull them up her legs. "This is not dry enough."

"Arian."

"I know, I know. We don't have time to waste." She shrugged on her shirt, plucking at the sleeves and the bodice where it decided to cling. "At least I don't itch anymore."

"But I'll miss the little jigs you did when a stray stalk stuck you in the wrong spot."

"You weren't supposed to notice that."

Orla started off toward the mountain. "When it comes you, I notice everything."

Arian stared at the mouth of the cave with trepidation. Her old fears came back to her.

Orla reached for her hand, but she pulled it out of his grasp.

"I'm not sure I can do this, Orla."

"You have to, my love." He took both of her hands in his. "You are much stronger than you realize."

"But..."

"Don't look at it. Look at me." He grasped her chin, tilting her head so that she could only see his face. "You faced this fear once before, inside the shuttle. Instead of cowering in the control seats, you overcame your fear to rescue me. If you hadn't, we'd both be dead now."

"I did that because one fear overrode another." She dipped her head down in embarrassment.

"What fear was that?"

"That I'd never see you again. I couldn't live with that thought." Orla lifted her chin once more, the heat of his hand seeped deep into her being.

"If you don't go through those caves, then the general will find us and take over the planet forever. Can you live with that? Knowing your people would be left to the mercy of General Varal because you were too afraid to go inside a cave?"

She glanced away again. Her fear for Orla's safety was an all-consuming thing. It overrode everything. Why didn't her desire to help her people do the same thing? The thought of going inside those caves had her quaking at her knees.

Just as she was about to turn away in shame, Orla's thoughts mingled with hers. *Let me help you. Make your fears my fears, and I'll make my strengths your strengths.*

She shook her head no. They had both learned to shield their thoughts from one another a little over the last few cycles. If she let him into her mind completely, he would know that her love for her people wasn't strong enough to overcome her fear. She wasn't sure she could face him again if he knew that.

CHAPTER TWENTY-SEVEN

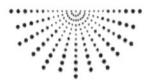

She looked up at him, finding an expectant look on his face. He had a faith in her she didn't possess. Her fear melted away a little with that knowledge.

How could he believe in her so strongly when she didn't believe in herself? The determination to save her people was still there, but all the naivetés she had when she first started this quest had been burned away as she faced one crucible after another. She didn't know if she would succeed. That was her real fear now. But how could she make Orla understand that?

"Win or lose, Arian. I will always be by your side."

Her heart swelled. She loved him so much. And she knew then that she would follow him to the ends of the galaxy if he asked her to.

Arian opened her mind to him and felt the gentle caress of his mind as it entered hers. Her fears and hesitations had been pushed to the back of her mind, and she knew Orla had found them easily, yet he didn't speak about them.

"Hold my hand."

Her fingers clasped around his, locking them in a death grip.

He drew her forward, closer to the black yawning abyss. Her grip tightened, and her feet dragged, but she didn't halt their process.

As the coolness of the interior of the cave covered them, Arian's heart rate sped up. She felt the heat of Orla's hand on her chest after they had taken several steps inside. He must have felt it too.

"Do not fear, Mistress. I will protect you."

"It's so dark in here." Warmth surrounded her when Orla stepped closer. One of his hands slid up the back of her neck into her hairline. The gentle pressure of his lips against hers made her sigh. When his tongue dipped into her mouth, she forgot all her fears. All she could do was hang on to Orla like a lifeline and savor the sensations his kisses caused.

The kiss ended too quickly for her. Nibbles and gentle kisses rained on her throat.

"Are your eyes closed?" He nipped at the delicate shell of her earlobe.

"Yes," she moaned.

"Are you afraid now?" he murmured against her ear.

"Not when you kiss me that way."

"Even though your eyes are closed and all you see is darkness?"

Arian opened her eyes. She wasn't afraid as long as he held her this way, like a precious gem.

"Now look around. Can you see anything?"

At first glance everything was black. She couldn't see Orla's face, just inches from her own, but then she noticed that she could make out a few things, including Orla's reassuring smile. "How?"

"We're sharing my night vision. I don't know how well this will work, so stay close to me just in case." His warm hand incased her own.

"I'll be so close you'll probably trip over me." Arian swallowed the lump in her throat as Orla started to walk deeper in the cave. She glanced up, then wished she hadn't. Not knowing what was up there made her imagination run wild.

"Most of the inhabitants of these caves are more afraid of us than we are of them. As long as you don't make any loud noises, they will leave us alone." Orla pulled her closer and wrapped one arm around her shoulders.

The first cave seemed to go on forever, but Arian finally noticed that the interior seemed a little brighter. Then she saw it. The opening of the other end of the cave. A soft squeal escaped her before Orla clamped a hand over her mouth.

Not a sound.

She nodded. Tugging on Orla's hand she moved quickly toward the cave's opening. A fresh cool breeze ruffled her hair. Her eyes closed as she dragged the sweet fresh air into her lungs.

"The next cave is close."

Arian fell into step next to him. As much as she wanted to ask him to let them rest, she remained quiet. The sooner she got this over with, the better she would be. Then she would ask what type of creatures they had passed without her knowledge.

The second cave was much shorter than the first one. Arian didn't really have a chance to feel frightened before they reemerged out in the open once again.

Only one more to go.

This cave had a lot of twists and turns in it. Arian knew if it wasn't for Orla, she would be so turned around she'd never find her way out of the cave. She shivered at the thought.

Orla patted her hand.

They moved quickly through the twisting cave.

Arian ran into the back of Orla when he stopped suddenly. What did he sense? She prayed it wasn't Varal's troops. That would mean they figured out their plans too soon, and there was only one way that could have happened. Someone told Varal of those plans.

"How did they find us?" whispered Arian.

That was what Orla wanted to know. How did the general's men find them so fast? They never revealed this part of their plan to the others. Arian didn't even know they would be traveling through the caves until they reached them. No one knew about these caves, since most just flew over them, and they were too far away from any of the villages for any children to find and explore. So how did they find them?

Orla looked at Arian. Her necklace winked in the slight light from the opening. A tracking device. It probably only worked on this planet, which is why Varal never found them before. But why didn't he try to capture them last night, while they slept in that barn? He'd try to work though this puzzle when he had more time.

Give me your necklace.

Why? She gripped the item in question in her hand.

There's no time for questions, just give it to me. He leaned and grabbed her necklace from her. With one yank he broke the chain.

Pulling her to him he shoved her to the ground and shifted into his Miran form. *No matter what happens stay here.*

Necklace clamped tightly in his jaw he bounded toward the entrance.

Several guards screamed when they saw his eyes glowing in the darkness. He growled in response.

The sound vibrated throughout the cave, startling its inhabitants and forcing the thousands of creatures clinging to the walls to take flight. As they flew past him toward the guards he threw the pendant with his mouth and smiled when one of the creatures grabbed it with its small taloned feet. Now they wouldn't be able to track Arian.

He slunk back into the cave and laid down next to Arian, who shook with fear. The sound of all the winged creatures above them had her frightened to the core.

The guards out front weren't doing much better. They tried to fire at the nocturnal animals as they flew out the entrance, causing the creatures to get angry and attack. At least half of the men fell down the sharp ravine trying to avoid the talons aimed at them.

Another shout sounded, telling the men to retreat.

Silence settled around them once again.

Using his muzzle, he nudged her. Arian scrambled to her feet and ran to the mouth of the cave. She clung to the outside of the mountain, dragging air into her lungs and trying desperately to stop the pounding in her heart.

Orla, still in his Miran shape, sauntered out and sat at her feet. He watched a myriad of emotions flicker across her face.

"There was some sort of tracking device in that necklace, wasn't there?"

I think so.

"Orla, ever since he found us on that ship when we left here, I have wondered how. A tracking device never crossed my mind." She slid down the mountain wall and sat in the dirt next to him. "But if I have had that tracking device on me all this time, why didn't he use it to find me before this, and why didn't they know where we were last night?"

I don't know, Mistress. I have wondered the same thing.

"Let's go join our friends."

Orla padded down the side of the mountain next to her.

"Aren't you going to shift back?"

Once we get close enough to the farm I will. With the general's men so close right now I need my extra senses to let me know what they are up to. We won't be caught like that again.

Arian breathed a sigh of relief when she saw the farm house come into view. As long as the general hadn't already arrested their friends, they should still be able to pull this off.

"Always so cynical?" asked Orla.

"I learned from the best," she responded as she took his hand. They needed to talk, but first they had to tell their friends what they had learned while in the palace.

Arian's face crinkled when she caught a whiff of Tymin.

"At least we know they are here," said Orla.

"As long as Tymin is with them we will always know."

Orla grinned. He placed his hand on the small of her back and ushered her toward the house. Silence greeted them. Was the silence because the troopers had already captured their friends?

One of the curtains swayed gently against the window just before the door burst open. The rush of noise startled their senses.

Orla felt the wind get knocked out of him before his head hit the ground. A loud oof escaped him. Blinking, he looked up to find the Browlman sitting on top of him.

"Is this how you will always greet me?"

She smiled at him sheepishly. "When I worry, yes."

"There was no reason to worry."

"The troops have been crawling all over this area for horas. What were we to think?" she asked from her perch.

"We feared they had already captured all of you and we were walking into a trap," said Arian.

The Browlman glanced up at Arian. "Then we have all lived with the same thoughts the last few horas." She climbed off Orla. "I am glad to see you safe."

Grenta clasped Arian's arm in silent communication.

"I think we should all get inside before those troopers come back," said Grinnell.

Quickly, everyone slipped back inside the safety of the house.

"Have you contacted everyone I asked you to?" asked Arian.

"Yes," said Grinnell. "About half of them agreed to come tonight to listen to what you have to say."

"Only half?"

"The other half will be here tomorrow before dawn."

Arian smiled. Her people haven't forgotten her.

Arian sat on the back porch of the small farm house and watched the sun set behind the mountains. A shudder ran through her body at the thought of the caves she knew were there. If it hadn't been for Orla, she would have never been able to make it through them. Her fear of them was just as strong but knowing she had been able to face that fear and overcome it changed her in ways she was just beginning to understand.

Just before the back door opened, Arian slid over to make room for Orla. She sensed his approach a few sccurs before.

Orla sat beside her without speaking. She already knew his thoughts. He felt it was dangerous for her to be out here, but he also understood why she needed the time alone.

"I have to convince them, Orla."

"You will find that they already know what must be done."

"But will they want to? They will risk their lives to try to stop the general. What if they don't want to?" She inhaled the deep heady scent of the flowers planted around the small house.

"We'll face that when we have to. First, you need to eat. Grenta wants you to work with her for a few horas too. You haven't exercised your talent in a while and she fears that you'll lose control."

"No, she doesn't. She just wants to keep me busy so I won't think about what must be done." Arian sighed. "But it might be the best thing for me right now. This waiting is awful."

Orla stood before offering her his hand. "Then let's go eat."

"I'm really not hungry right now." She accepted his hand and pushed herself to her feet. "I'll go find Grenta."

"She's in the barn."

"Thank you, Orla." She leaned in and planted a soft kiss on his cheek. She hopped over the two steps that separated her from the ground and headed toward the free-standing barn.

A soft glow of several lamps filled the interior, making her hurry for the warmth and protection of the light.

"Finally," said Grenta.

"Been waiting long then?"

"Since you left the ship." Grenta crossed her arms across her bosom. "Unless you practiced while you were gone."

"I did have a chance or two to use my talent while I was away."

"Don't get snippy with me, young lady. You only used it when you had to. That can be deadly for a Barou. You must practice every dura without fail."

A sigh escaped her lips, but she remained silent as she nodded her agreement. It would do no good arguing with Grenta, but perhaps she could conjure up a scary enough image to make her think twice. She smiled at the prospect.

CHAPTER TWENTY-EIGHT

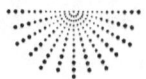

"You can't!" thundered one of the fifty men who surrounded her in the small barn she had been practicing in earlier. Grumbles of agreement followed his words.

"I must," Arian said quietly. "General Varal wants me. If I turn myself over to him, then he just might leave the rest of you alone."

"My Queen, you honestly can't believe that," said another. "He would use you against us."

"The moment the general believes he has captured me he'll think he won, and he'd never suspect an insurrection with me under control." She stood up. "I have a plan, one I need your help to pull off. But you must agree to all of the plan in order for it to work."

Grumbling from her guests grew in volume while they spoke amongst themselves. She could tell by the snippets of conversation that they didn't want her to jeopardize her life to make this plan work. They felt their queen should be protected at all costs.

Arian clasped her hands behind her back, waiting for them to come to some sort of decision. As much as her friends wanted to be there for moral support, she refused them, knowing she had to face her people by herself. She needed their support and wanted to have it before they knew who all would be involved. Besides, if any of her visitors were spies,

General Varal would still believe that she was doing this by herself. It would be a moot point if the General attacked at this moment, but at least they would have a few securs of surprise before everyone was captured.

Tension in her body grew with every micron she waited. Her fear that her people would refuse to stand behind her took over her mind. How would she be able to stop the General if she didn't have their help?

Soothing thoughts filled her mind. *You worry too much.*

I can't help it, what if they don't want to help. Arian looked about. The men still sat in small groups discussing her fate.

Give them a chance, Mistress. This isn't an easy decision for them to make.

She knew Orla was right. Concentrating on a calming exercise Grenta had taught her, she forced herself to relax. Working herself into an anxiety attack wouldn't do anyone any good.

Just when she thought she couldn't wait any longer one of her guests stood up.

"My Queen, you must understand that we love you and because of that we can't agree to your proposal. Your life can't be jeopardized at all. There must be another way."

"I was asked that same question once before." Arian sat down on a bale of hay next to her. "And this is the answer I gave them. Can you come up with a better plan? If so I will gladly use it."

A murmur rose from amongst the crowd.

"What about a straight-out attack?"

"The general has turned the palace into a fortress. There is no way we can overtake it without sabotaging it from the inside." She paused for a few securs as her friends entered the barn to join the rest. "I was able to sneak into the palace one time without his knowledge, but I doubt if we could pull that off again. The general doesn't like to be made a fool of, and that is exactly what I did when I snuck into the palace the last time."

"Well, cutting off his speech probably didn't sit real well with him. He hates being interrupted," said Orla.

Laughter filled the room.

"He also would never suspect that your young naive queen would ever come up with a plan to try to defeat him. Especially if he thinks he's caught me before I can put my plans in motion." Arian gestured for Orla to join her. She watched as he sauntered up to her. A soft smile spread across her face as she took his hand in hers. "My goal is to get inside and right under the General's nose, shut down his security system so we can take back what is rightfully ours."

"But first I want to introduce you to Orla, my betrothed."

The volume rose quickly as everyone reacted to her words.

"For those of you who know why I left the planet, I went in search of my betrothed."

"General Varal says your betrothed is his guest and waiting for you to return."

"The man under the General's care is a fake. This is my true betrothed and the man I love." Her words must have stunned the crowd. Their silence was so thick she could have cut it with a laser sword.

She heard a soft shuffle of feet as each of the men stood. Arian placed her hand on her heart, fearing they didn't approve of her choice and were standing to leave.

Instead, they each honored her by bowing and extending their hands out, palm up, the same way they greeted her father whenever he went to visit their small villages in person.

She blinked, fighting back the tears of joy she felt at their gesture. Squeezing Orla's hand, she glanced up at his face. Did she see tears shimmering in his eyes?

Moving as one Orla and Arian showed their gratitude by returning the gesture.

When Arian stood up once again, she found every man down on one knee.

"You honor me." Her heart had leaped up into her throat, making the words hard for her. Their kneeling in honor proved they pledged their life to her. "I hope I can live up to your loyalty."

"How can we help you with your plan, My Queen?" asked one man.

Arian smiled and proceeded to tell them of her plans.

The sun just started to peek up over the horizon when she had answered the last question about her plan. The first group were still there when the second group of village leaders had arrived. They had all worked through the night, honing the plan she had laid out until they had thought of just about every contingency. She hoped it would be enough.

Arian stood at the doors of the barn and watched the last man step out of sight. Orla's presence right behind her. The sun's first rays washed over her as she stood there, filling her with its warmth and energy.

"They love you very much."

She nodded before she headed back in the barn. Arian didn't feel like she deserved their love. What had she done to deserve it?

"You question their loyalty?" asked Orla after he had followed her into the barn.

"No. That isn't the question." Arian sat down on the bale of hay she had used as a seat most of the night. "I don't know what I did to deserve their loyalty."

Orla knelt beside her. He lifted her chin with a gentle hand. "You left everything you knew to go in search of a man you had never met to fulfill a promise to your father, and you fulfilled that promise. Arian, you could have left here and never looked back, but you didn't. You came back to them and for them. Your people know that."

"Our people."

"Our people. How could they not be loyal to someone who showed their loyalty the way you did."

"And what did I do to deserve someone like you?" She cupped her hand against his cheek.

"Fell in love with me."

"It was that simple?"

"It was for me." His tongue darted out and licked her palm. "Show me how much you love me, Arian."

"Here? Now?" A slight blush crept into her cheeks at the thought. "What if we get caught?"

"Some find the thought of getting caught to be an aphrodisiac."

"Not me." Her blush deepened. "I'd be too nervous."

"This isn't the same woman I guided through the cave. She had no inhibitions." He leaned forward, forcing her to lean back toward the bale of hay she sat on so she could look at him.

"She also knew no one would walk in on her at any moment." Arian found her upper torso bracketed by Orla's arms.

"I want to feel you against me. I need your heat to surround me." He brushed his face against hers.

His words melted her fear away and caused a fire to start to burn deep inside her. Arian found she couldn't support her arms any more. Her back pressed itself into the hay, she looked up into his darkened eyes.

"I love the taste of you." Orla pressed a soft kiss against her cheek, before nibbling on her earlobe.

Her hands skimmed across his shirt. Aching to feel his skin against her hands she started to undo the shirt that blocked her way.

"I love the way your scent envelopes me. Blocking any thought but the desire to touch you." He buried his nose into the crook of her neck, inhaling deeply.

Arian spread her hands over his chest, feeling his heart beating rapidly beneath her fingertips. "I do this to you?"

"And this." He guided her hands to the proof of his desire.

She smiled at the hard length of him.

"You do this to me just by being near me. All it takes is a smile, or a laugh and I want you so bad I don't care who knows."

"A smile?" she asked, sliding her hands back up to the warmth of his chest.

"Yes." He watched her lips twitch with mirth. "A smile just like that one." He pressed a kiss to the corner of her mouth, then nibbled on her lips before pressing a kiss to the other corner.

She sighed his name as he continued to follow a path down her throat to the hollow of her neck. His tongue darted against her skin, the unexpected warmth of it pulled a gasp out of her.

"I love the feel of your skin against my tongue. Soft as silk and as sweet as milk." He pushed the collar of her shirt out of his way, branding every inch of her exposed skin with his mouth. His fingers made short work of her top, opening it to his questing lips. He feasted on her. Teasing and nipping her sensitive skin, making her moan with pleasure. She arched against him when his lips closed around the tip of her breast.

He felt her hands on him, knowing she was too caught up in the sensations to worry about who might find them. His plans on seducing her worked. When he felt her legs wrap around his naked hips, he realized they worked a little too well. He didn't remember her divesting him of his clothes.

"You have been busy, my love."

"Thought I'd save you the time." Arian rubbed herself against him.

"You mean you didn't want to have to wait."

"There's that too," she murmured while she stroked the tight muscles along his stomach.

"Keep that up, and you won't have to," he growled. Orla claimed her lips with his as he positioned himself over her. Just as he entered her, he opened his mind so that their minds and bodies would be one.

Her body enveloped him, surrounding him with her heat. When he started to move, Arian mimicked him. As their bodies moved together, one sensation after another washed over him. He felt his desire increase with each stroke. Arian's muscles tightened against him, forcing him to fight to maintain control.

Arian convulsed against him when the first wave of her orgasm took her over the brink. He buried his face against her neck as he felt the sensations she did, rocking against her as she continued to climax. Her whole body tensed and drew him in deeper as she hit the pinnacle. Her muscles tightening around him started his spiral toward release. Penetrating deeper and quicker, he swept her along with him, sharing the emotions roaring through him.

Orla felt the scream rising in Arian as he drew closer to the abyss. Covering her mouth with his, he swallowed her scream before she could give it a voice. He gave one last final thrust and felt his body shatter into a million pieces.

CHAPTER TWENTY-NINE

Arian tried not to blush when they exited the barn a little while later. She knew the physical union was a very natural thing but wondering what everyone thought had her a little nervous. Orla squeezed her hand.

"I know I'm being silly, but I just can't help it," she whispered to him as she glanced around. At least no one would see them leaving the barn.

"I promise they won't point and whisper behind your back."

Arian grimaced when she caught a whiff of Tymin. The little man stepped into their paths just as she schooled her features back to normal.

"Master, the other men have arrived and are waiting to speak to you."

"Thank you, Tymin." Orla smiled at Arian before he kissed her on the forehead and took his leave. "I'll catch up with you as soon as I can."

Arian nodded and looked at the farm house, wondering what she should do. She felt a little awkward going into the house alone. A trapped feeling overcame her when she watched the door open.

The Browlman stepped out onto the small porch. She stretched her tiny frame before walking down the stairs.

"Ah, Arian, it's such a glorious dura is it not? I was thinking of going to the pond for a bath. Would you care to join me?"

Arian could only nod. A blush crept into her cheeks when she thought about the last time she bathed in a pond.

"Good. Let's go."

"But I'll need to gather a few things."

"I have an extra cloth you can wrap around yourself and I understand that this pond has a rare soap root that grows at its banks. Its fragrance can't be rivaled by any expensive scent."

Arian wanted to get a change of clothes, and possibly give the Browlman enough time to bath by herself so Arian could have some privacy herself, but it didn't look like she would get her way.

The Browlman linked arms with her and led her to the pond that was down the hill from the farm. "This is the perfect place. No one can see us from the house, yet we are still within hearing distance."

Arian glanced about the small pond, smiling despite her discomfort. It was a beautiful spot. The early morning rays danced across the surface of the pond, winking at her as the golden hued water dipped and bowed in front of her. A small leaf floated down and landed on the glass like surface, making small ripples in its wake. A soft splash drew her attention to the Browlman, who had already undressed and jumped into the lake.

"I'm going to get some of those roots, but they are a little further out. If you stay right here, I'll bring back enough for both of us."

Arian nodded and waited for the Browlman to swim off. Quickly, she shed her clothing, putting it next to the Browlman's pile of clothes and then entered the water. It's cool kiss against her skin felt heavenly. Dipping her head back into the water, she ran her fingers through her hair, releasing several pieces of hay as she combed it out. No wonder her head itched.

The Browlman swam back toward her a few microns later with several stalks of the plant clutched in her hand. She handed a couple to Arian, then proceeded to wash herself.

Arian had soaped up her hair when Tymin came within smelling distance. She couldn't hide the wince that skittered across her brow.

"You are not welcomed here, Tymin."

He ducked his head. "I just wish to speak to you."

"Not now," said the Browlman.

He nodded and started to shuffle off, then he stopped and

backtracked a few steps. Placing a crumpled bouquet on a small rock outcropping he mumbled. "Thems for you."

His simple gesture made Arian smile. "He has a good heart you know."

"I know he does," said the Browlman.

"But you're going to punish him a little more," Arian finished for her.

"You don't understand."

"Yes I do. He left you without a word." Arian dunked her head under the water to rinse the soap from her hair. "Have you ever asked him why he left?"

"No. She hasn't," said Tymin. His voice floating over the small rise to them.

"You're not supposed to eavesdrop either."

"Why don't you ask him, Browlman? Are you afraid of the answer you might get?"

The Browlman didn't respond. Instead she lathered her hair and scrubbed it with a vengeance.

"Well, Tymin. I would like to know why you would leave someone like the Browlman. You must have had a good reason." Arian spread the soap root across her shoulders. The sweet fragrance surrounded her.

"I did. I get her a gift."

"A gift? I don't understand."

"You're not the only one," grumbled the Browlman.

"A gift, very special. Me had to go long distance to get the gift. It take long time."

"What happened to the gift?"

"Here."

So Tymin had the gift with him now.

"Then why didn't you go home and give it to the Browlman when you first got it?" asked Arian. She wished she could get him to give her a straight answer, but there were times when she had to talk in circles to get the information from him.

"Master."

"Orla?"

"Yes." Tymin paused for a moment. "Master found me then. He freed me."

"You were a prisoner?" This was getting more confusing by the microns. Arian wished she knew how the two of them met.

"They said I cheated a man."

"But you didn't."

"No. Tymin never cheat. They wanted the gift, but they didn't get it. Tymin hid it."

"So Orla help you escape?"

"Yes."

Arian washed one arm as she thought about what Tymin said. Orla gave her the impression that Tymin wasn't that trustworthy. If Tymin was telling the truth, then what did he do to make Orla think otherwise?

"Master said I owed him. And I was afraid."

"Afraid of what?"

"Her anger."

She looked over at the Browlman, who had turned her back on them. Arian guessed the Browlman thought if she ignored them, she could pretend she didn't hear them.

It was time to leave. Arian slipped out of the water and wrapped the long sheet around her body before the Browlman realized what she had done. She walked up to Tymin.

"Speak to her. Give her the gift that cost you so much."

Tymin nodded and looked over his shoulder. Arian wasn't sure if he would do what she told him, but she hoped he would. They needed to work out their differences.

She returned to the farm house and got dressed. Hoping she would get a chance to speak to Orla. Even with their mental connection she liked speaking out loud when she wanted his opinion.

Tymin walked slowly toward the house.

Arian frowned as she watched. Opening the back door, she stepped out on the porch and called his name. "Is she still angry with you?"

He nodded. "She won't take the gift."

"Would you like me to give it to her?"

He stopped and stared at Arian. "You would do that for me?"

"Of course, Tymin."

"Thank you." He dug into his shirt pocket and handed her a small bauble.

She didn't know what it was, but she handled it as if it was priceless. Carrying it carefully in her hand, she headed back to the pond. The Browlman sat on the bank of the water, combing out her hair.

Arian sat down next to the Browlman and stared out over the water.

"He asked me to give you this." Arian sat the small gift on the ground between them. The sunlight glimmered off its smooth surface, splashing a rainbow of colors across the two of them.

"This is the gift he had?" The Browlman gingerly reached for the small sphere. "This belonged to my mother. I thought it lost to me forever."

They sat in silence for a few moments, while the Browlman turned it over in her hands.

"Will you excuse me?" Without waiting for a response from Arian the Browlman stood up and headed in the direction of the house.

"She seemed to be in a hurry," said Orla as he crouched down beside her.

"I believe she needs to speak to Tymin." Arian looked up at him. "You never told me how you met him anyway."

"He was dangling in the grip of a very large and angry man. From what I heard, the man accused Tymin of stealing something that was his. Tymin, of course, denied it." Orla offered her his hand. "The man had a reputation of being cruel."

Arian accepted his help and pulled herself to her feet.

"Since he couldn't produce the stolen object, I couldn't leave Tymin in his grip, so to speak."

She smirked at his words.

"And he owed you?" she asked.

"That was the strangest part. I never expected Tymin to want to stay with me. I figured once he realized he was free he'd disappear, but instead he followed me like a shadow. Telling everyone that I was his master."

"For some reason he felt like he owed me. I am hoping forcing him on this quest will fulfill any obligation he feels toward me."

"And the Browlman?" Arian slipped her hand around his arm. The warmth of his muscles flowed from her fingertips to her heart.

"An added bonus. Tymin never spoke about her. Believe me, if I had known I would have made the two of them face each other a long time ago."

Arian just smiled. That bauble seemed to be the crux of their relationship. If she could trust her instincts, all should be well between the two of them now. Of course, with Tymin and the Browlman, nothing ever went the way she would expect.

"Is everything in place now?" Arian asked.

"Yes. We'll head for the palace this evening. If all goes well, the general will have us inside the gate in just a few horas."

Arian could only nod. She really didn't want to go through with this but knew there was no other way. If the general believed that she had been stopped before she could implement some plan to overthrow him then he wouldn't expect the real overthrow when it happened. She just hoped she could go through with it.

"You can do this."

She rested her head against his shoulder. "By the Gods, I hope so. What if General Varal sees through it? What will we do?"

"Why do you always expect the worse?"

"I don't know. I guess because this it. This is where we win or lose."

"Mistress, you must believe that you will win. You can't give the general that edge. If you fear failure you will fail automatically."

"I can't lose. Too much is at stake."

"Then just think about winning."

Arian dressed in her royal robes. Donning the garment felt strange to her after shedding it so long ago. Stepping in front of the small mirror that was nailed to the wall of her room she studied herself. Although she looked the same on the outside, she knew she was different on the inside. She didn't feel like a queen.

Before she started her journey, she had always thought along the lines of being a queen and how she should react. It was all she knew. But once she left, she started to realize that being a queen was nothing more than a job, just like the soldiers that work for General Varal, and just because she was a queen didn't mean she should be treated any differently than a candle maker. She realized her title didn't mean a lot away from her planet. She was just another person. She kinda liked that.

Those thoughts led her down another road that frightened her. What if she didn't want to be queen anymore? What would her people do? Would they think she was abandoning them? Or would they understand?

Would she be able to continue as queen if her people wanted her to remain?

A soft knock on the door interrupted her thoughts.

Arian crossed to the door and opened it. The Browlman stood on the other side. She watched in shock as the Browlman gave her a respectful bow.

"What are you doing?" asked Arian.

"Acting on instinct." The Browlman looked up at her and smiled. "I'm sorry, but the moment I saw you in your royal robes it was automatic."

"But they are only clothes."

"True, but on you they enhance the leader you are." The Browlman escorted her to the barn, where a small contingent of men waited for her.

Each man showed their respect by bowing in her presence. "Gentlemen, thank you, but I should be the one bowing. You are giving up your lives for me. You know the general will fight to the death to capture me."

"It is you who is risking her life to save an entire planet, my Queen. Giving my life so many can be saved is one of the reasons I joined the military in the first place. I have a wife and three children, and they deserve to live and grow secure in knowing that they are safe from people like General Varal. I give my life freely for them, and you."

Arian dashed a few tears from her eyes.

Orla cupped her elbow. "It is time."

She nodded and allowed him to steer her toward a small hover craft outside the barn. Her mouth dropped open when she saw the royal symbol etched on the side of it.

"Isn't that the one we left at the mountain retreat?"

"Yes, Mistress. Can you think of a better way for the queen to travel?"

"But we'll be an obvious target."

"Yes we will." Orla smiled. "And the General wouldn't expect you to travel in anything less."

Arian wasn't sure if she agreed with Orla. The general might smell a trap if they are too obvious.

"The general would never stoop so low to ride in any vehicle that didn't reflect his position. And he would expect you to be the same way. As strange as it may seem, the general would be more suspicious if you were captured in something else. He'd know you had help planning this takeover and would expect more."

"And this way he'll believe that I had planned it all on my own? Why?"

"Because a queen shouldn't know the first thing about trying to overthrow someone else's government. She would leave that to her army." Orla helped her to her seat. "If she is calling all the moves, then she wouldn't think about the fact that the general would stop a vehicle with the royal seal, she would probably just want the fastest vehicle."

"I hope you know what you are doing, Orla."

"I would never jeopardize your life." Orla lifted her hand from her lap and kissed it.

"I know that, but what if you are wrong."

"I have studied the general too long not to know how his mind works. This will be exactly what he will expect."

CHAPTER THIRTY

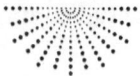

"Sir, we're picking up a small craft on radar."

Varal leaned over the guard to peer at the radar screen. "Hmmm. Everyone knows about the curfew, correct."

"Yes, sir."

"Send out a squad. Shoot them down."

The young man nodded. He scrambled a squad, giving them the general's orders.

Arian sat rigidly in her seat. She wanted to get this over with, but it seemed the general had other plans. "Anything?"

"The sky is still clear." The young man turned to smiled at her. A loud beep filled the air, making him turn back toward the screen quickly. "Wait, we have company. And they are firing."

"Evasive maneuvers," shouted Orla. "Everything will be over if they shoot us down."

"General? You need to see this."

"What?" he groused. "Haven't they destroyed that ship yet."

"No sir. They wanted you to see this before they moved forward with your order."

"Perhaps we should just eliminate both ships and be done with it." He stepped up to the main monitor to see why his men disobeyed a direct order. "No one disobeys me."

A picture flashed on the screen that almost made his heart stop. He punched several buttons so he could communicate with his ship.

"The royal crest?"

"Yes, sir. You ordered everyone to contact you the moment we saw the Queen or anything that could be affiliated with her." The line crackled. "That is the official symbol, sir. We checked."

"Force that ship down, but do not kill the Queen, if she is on that ship. I want her alive at all costs."

"Yes, sir."

Varal closed the comlink and rubbed his chin. A smile slowly crept onto his face. It was almost too good to be true, but if Arian was on that ship, he was close to having everything he wanted.

"Check for other ships or any ground movement. Be thorough. If you can't find anything then you'd better be able to tell me which insects are where. I want proof that all is quiet out there."

Arian released her safety harness and knelt next to the pilot's seat.

"Get back to your seat, Mistress," said Orla.

"No. If I'm going to die, it won't be sitting in that seat doing nothing."

"There is nothing you can do." The ship dipped down quickly, causing Orla to grab Arian so she wouldn't slide into the pilot consol.

A blast crossed over their bow.

"My Queen, they are trying to contact us," said the co-pilot.

"Let's hear it," answered Arian.

"You are in Palace space, and breaking curfew. Land now, or your ship will be blown out of the sky."

Arian looked at Orla.

"Don't answer them. Continue to try to outmaneuver them. We must make this look good." Arian touched Orla's face. "If we give in too easily, they will be suspicious."

Arian made her way back to her seat.

"They are firing on us again," said the co-pilot.

The ship vibrated from a blast that hit its mark.

"They've taken out our main engine. Prepare for a crash landing."

The ship shook as it started to plummet to the ground.

Arian gripped her safety harness as the ground grew closer. Everyone inside the ship stared out the view screen, hoping they would survive the impact.

"Impact in 30 securs," shouted the co-pilot.

The ship groaned just before it plowed into the dirt. Arian felt herself being jerked forward before the ship started its long slide against the earth. It finally stopped when it hit a large rock formation. The ship rocked from the impact.

"Is everyone okay?" asked Orla as he released his harness and went back to check on Arian.

"I'm fine, Orla." She glanced at the men who traveled with them. "Are you sure you want to go through with this? You don't have to do this."

"If I want to remain with you, I do. The general will allow you to keep your pet."

"But..."

"My secret will not go past these men. They have already been briefed."

He sat at her feet. A soft shimmer surrounded his body. Within securs, her pet sat where Orla had been.

If any of the guards had a reaction to seeing this, they didn't show it.

Banging against the hull of the ship filled the interior.

"They are coming, My Queen," said one of the guards. "We will defend you as long as possible."

"Remember your instructions," said Arian. Closing her eyes, she cloaked the men from view.

The hatch door groaned as it was pried open from the outside.

"Remain where you are," they were ordered. Several palace guards entered the ship. They hesitated for a few securs when they saw their Queen before they followed their orders.

Arian wondered if they would have sided with her if she had asked for their help. She was ushered out of the ship flanked by palace guards and guided to the other ship.

"Wait! My pet! I can't leave without Orla."

A loud growl came from the damaged ship. Arian fought a smile when several guards backed off as Orla exited the ship. He paused at the bottom of the ramp and roared.

"Orla. Here." As long as they gave Orla a wide berth, they shouldn't realize they had uninvited guests on their ship.

The Miran looked over to where Arian stood, surrounded by guards. He growled again then sauntered over to her side.

Arian brushed her fingers over his fur.

"The General wants to speak to you, my Queen. He has been worried for your safety."

Arian didn't respond. She just followed them onto the ship. Orla sat at her feet and rested his massive head on her lap.

"Don't get any funny ideas," she whispered.

Like what?

The blush that spread across her cheeks told him what she was thinking.

Why, mistress, how very naughty. Orla rubbed his face in her lap.

Arian grabbed his head and lifted it.

"Is there a problem, my Queen? We could put your pet in one of the holds." One of the two pilots turned to look at her.

"Oh, no. Orla just doesn't like to be confined. All ships bother him. He'll be fine as long as he stays with me." Arian held onto Orla's fur in fear that they would be separated. "You said the general has been worried about me?"

"Yes."

"Why? Everyone knew I'd be mourning my father's death for six lunas. Has something happened that I wasn't aware of?" She glanced back to the bulkheads, making sure she still shielded the men from her ship.

He turned back toward the screen at her words. "No, my Queen."

Arian wanted to ask him more. Was he lying to her, or did he not really know what was going on? A mental thought against that idea from Orla kept her mouth closed. So she waited.

The palace loomed in the horizon. She knew she'd get her information first hand very soon.

The engines roared as it made its descent. Arian felt her heart hammering in her chest as the doors opened. Flanked once again by several guards, she exited the ship.

"There you are, Arian. I'm so glad you made it back all right." Varal stepped up to her to take her hand.

"General." Arian pulled her hand out of reach. She watched a frown flicker across his face.

"You look tired. Why don't you go to your chambers and freshen up? Meet me in the throne room in a half hora. We have a lot to discuss."

"Yes, we do."

"Oh and leave that miran behind."

"Orla goes where he pleases. You know that." Arian placed her hand on the top of Orla's head.

Varal stepped close. "If that animal shows up in the throne room, I'll have it shot."

"Threatening me already, Varal? What will your men think? I am still Queen." Arian had spoken softly, so that only Varal would hear her.

"I never threaten." He stepped back and smiled at her. "One half hora. If you're not there I'll send someone after you."

"Oh, I'll be there, Varal. Of that you could be sure of." She stood and watched Varal walk away. He seemed so sure of himself, if only he knew what was in store for him.

She continued to shield the men from detection as long as she could. Just as they made their way to the barracks door, she noticed they came into view. They had stepped out of range. She hoped they could accomplish what needed to be done without losing their lives.

"My Queen?" one of Varal's guards asked.

Arian nodded and allowed them to escort her. She found herself being ushered to her quarters. Two guards started to enter her rooms, but she would have none of that. "Out."

"My Queen, the general–"

"Is in my employ. I will not tolerate any men in my quarters. If you persist, I will contact the general and have you ordered out."

Both guards bowed and exited the room.

She studied her room, seeing it differently than she did before she left. The opulence never bothered her before, but now it was too much.

"Things will have to change, Orla."

That's what we are here to do.

I'm not talking about removing the general from power. I'm talking about the way of life here. Arian glanced around her room. *Why did we live like this when the people outside the palace had to live dura to dura for their existence?*

Orla shifted back to human form.

"One thing at a time, Arian." He pulled her into his arms and gave her one quick, but powerful kiss. "You be safe. I'll try to join you as quickly as I can."

She nodded and watched as he shifted back. Walking to the doors to her rooms, she opened them and looked about for her guards.

Orla slipped past her and bounded down the hall.

"I am ready to speak to the general now."

"Of course, my Queen." The guard speaking bowed. "Please allow us to escort you."

"I know my way."

The guards looked at each other. "We must insist."

"In other words, the general has commanded it."

They didn't respond as they led her to the throne room.

Arian didn't know exactly what to expect, but it wasn't finding the general sitting on her father's throne.

"That is not your throne, Varal. It is mine." She started up the stairs to her father's throne.

"So you want it back, Arian? You can have it back. Under one condition."

"And what condition is that?"

"Marry me."

CHAPTER THIRTY-ONE

"Marry you?" Arian laughed. "Why should I marry you? I am the ruler, not you."

Varal stood up. "Because I control this planet now. Your guards listen to me. No one will help you if you try to defy me."

"I have already defied you at every turn."

"True. You have been a worthy adversary, but you are now in my custody. Those that helped you will be found out and executed."

"There will always be more to help me."

"And who exactly do you think will help you? My guards?"

"The people of this planet." Arian climbed up one more step to the throne. "Do you think they will allow you to continue to destroy their planet? Many are starving to death now that you have taken their land and their children to be in your army. Don't you realize that those children will rebel when they find out how you have treated their families? That you went back on your word?"

"They will obey me!"

"No one obeys a tyrant for long, Varal."

In two strides Varal stood beside her, gripping her throat and lifting her off the floor.

"What's the matter, General? Did I hit a nerve?" she asked with a strangled voice.

Varal released her and watched in satisfaction as Arian crumpled at his feet. He turned and climbed up the last few steps to the throne. Once he made a big show of seating himself, he started to question her. "So my Queen, how did you infiltrate the palace the last time?"

Arian didn't like hearing her title coming off his tongue. It sounded almost like a sneer when he said it.

"I asked you a question."

"I know you did." Arian watched a deep red flush work its way up Varal's neck, then creep up across his face to the roots of his hair.

"And I expect an answer."

"Or what? You'll kill me?"

"I will make you wish you have answered me." Varal spoke in a soft voice. His knuckles white from gripping the throne tightly.

"You threaten me? Do you think these people will listen to you if any harm comes to me? I am their queen. If they believe you have done something to me, they will rebel. Then where would you be? How will you maintain your army if you have to kill the very people you use to fill those ranks?"

"Silence!" With lightning speed, Varal lashed out and slapped Arian hard enough across the face to knock her down.

Sitting half on one step, Arian pressed a palm to her cheek. She didn't even see Varal move out of the seat before she felt the blow against her face. A quick opening and closing of her mouth let her know that her jaw wasn't broken, but she knew she'd have a nasty bruise from this.

She glanced up when the lights flickered a little. Was it her imagination or had Orla reached his destination? A smile creased her bruised cheek when she saw a distinct pattern to the blinking lights. Orla had gotten to the control center and turned off the security grid. He also had trapped a lot of Varal's guards in different sections of the palace by turning off the power or locking them in and changing the security codes. Her smile deepened, knowing Orla's old virus would lock up the system so no one would be able to access any of the security grids.

Straightening her shoulders, Arian rose regally and faced Varal.

"Your time is numbered now, Varal. The palace is surrounded."

"You threaten me, Arian?" Varal laughed. "You honestly want me to believe this? We've been watching the roads and air. There has been no movement. Your people aren't there. This coup you've planned won't happen."

"Then it wouldn't hurt for you to check and prove me wrong, would it?" Arian crossed her arms in front of her, hoping her nervousness didn't show.

Varal studied her for a few moments. She assumed he was deciding whether to humor her, because finally he did issue a command to one of the guards to turn on the view screen.

The image of the palace gates shimmered into view. Gates that stood wide open without a sentry in sight.

"Contact the head guard on that gate. Find out where those men are."

Several securs ticked by before the communications officer spoke. "There is no answer, sir."

"No answer? That's impossible." Varal practically leaped down the steps from the throne to get to where the communications officer sat. He flipped from one camera to another, looking for some sign that everything was fine. Each camera revealed the lack of guards where he knew they should be. Varal turned to glare at Arian.

"So, my Queen, what exactly did you do?"

"Why Varal, what could I do? I have been here with you the whole time." She smiled, knowing the guards she had hidden from view had done their job.

A loud crash vibrated through the air.

"It sounds like they are getting closer. Surrender, Varal, and you just might live through this."

"Never." Varal jerked the young man out of the chair and opened all the com links. "This is an emergency, all troops to the throne room on the double."

Varal turned and gave Arian a wicked grin. "My guards will be here any secur. Your puny attempt to regain your throne will be crushed."

They stared at each other. Arian trying to give him a haute look instead of a frightened one. If guards did pour through the door, then part of their plan didn't work, but if they didn't, then...

Several microns ticked by, neither breaking eye contact. A flush started to creep up the general's face once again. He finally looked away to scream at the communication officer. "Where are they?"

"They're not coming." Arian's voice rang loud and clear. "My puny attempt to take over as you so elegantly worded it included locking out most of your guards. They're not going to help you, General. Most are either trapped in rooms where their codes won't work or passed out from gases that have been pumped throughout the palace. This is the only room those fumes didn't touch."

Varal angrily punched a few buttons and found Arian had told the truth. Everywhere he looked his men where either trapped inside a room or passed out on the floor. As he stood there watching several men slipping to the floor in the last room he punched up on the screen, he growled deep in his throat.

"In a few microns every one of your men outside this room will be asleep. Those helping me will have no trouble reaching this room. You've been defeated, Varal. It's time to give up."

"If you don't stop your men, I'll kill your fiancé."

"That man you have in your custody isn't my fiancé. The real Dresuer has been the one helping me reclaim my planet."

"And what about the father?" asked Varal. "Should I kill him instead?"

Don't give in, Arian. My father will be freed momentarily. Several men have already gone down to the dudgeons to free my brother. I will let them know my father is there as well."

"You no longer have control, Varal." Arian walked up the steps to the throne. "How did you plan on killing him? I won't let you near him."

"With this." Varal showed her a small remote. "I have planted a bomb under the throne. All I have to do is press this button and the whole place will go up in a big explosion."

"So you would kill us all?"

"No." He moved quickly, grabbing Arian by the waist, and hauling her body up against his. "You and I will survive."

"Let go of me," she demanded as she fought against the hold he had on her. The cold press of steel against her throat stopped her. She swallowed hard and felt the blade bite into her neck.

"You have lost, Varal. Face that fact." Arian hoped she could convince him to let her go. One wrong move and he'd slit her throat.

"You will still be mine, Arian." His hot breath fanned across her skin.

"But this planet won't be yours. The people will now have control. I have abolished the monarchy, Varal. There will be nothing for you to conquer."

"If you come with me quietly. I won't kill you, Arian, and I won't detonate the bomb." He pulled her along with him as he headed toward one wall.

She felt the blood drain from her face. The wall they headed for held an old escape route to the roof. Somehow, she had to stall him.

"If I go with you, you promise you won't detonate the bomb?"

"You aren't in the position to bargain with me."

"If you kill me, they will kill you." Arian slowed their pace. "All I am asking is you leave that remote behind. Just put it on the throne and I'll go with you peaceably."

The general smiled.

Arian knew he figured he could detonate it from his ship, but she planned on destroying his ship if he tried to do that. It might be the last thing she ever did, but at least she'd know she didn't die in vain. He'd die with her.

Varal crossed to the throne and haphazardly dropped the remote on the cushion of the chair. He stared at the entrances into the throne room. Pulling another remote out of a pocket he pressed a series of buttons. The throne room doors closed with an ominous bang.

"That should keep them busy for a while." Grabbing Arian's wrist, Varal pulled her along behind him, heading toward the wall once again and the passage to freedom.

Arian glanced back at the doors that separated her from Orla. Her heart screamed for his protection. Her body longed for his touch. In her mind she felt him surround her. His thoughts gave her the strength to go through with this unexpected twist in their plan. She just hoped Orla would be able to rescue her before the general could leave the planet.

They climbed the steep steps to the roof. Varal force the exit door open with a groan of metal and of man.

Fresh air bathed Arian. She looked across the roof to see what she feared. One of Varal's fastest ships waiting for them.

Varal started to pull her quickly across the tarmac, closing the distance between them and the ship. He slowed down when the doors of the ship didn't open.

"Where are my guards?" he muttered.

Arian assumed he didn't realize he had said the words out loud. But it eased the fear gripping her, hearing that things weren't going the way Varal had hoped. She found herself being pulled backward, up against Varal's body.

A slight movement in the corner of her eye caught her attention. Her heart leaped when one by one, ten of her people climb up on the roof, surrounding them. Closing her eyes, Arian drew on her power, creating more images to look like they were completely surrounded.

General Varal grabbed a fistful of her hair, yanking her head back. She felt the wicked looking blade against her throat once again.

"One step closer and I'll slice her throat."

"You harm one hair on her head and I'll hunt you down." Came a voice to their left, just behind Varal's ship.

Varal tightened his grip on her. "Show yourself."

One man stepped forward. His face shadowed by the ship, but Arian knew who singled himself out.

"Who are you?"

"My name is Orla."

"Ha. Orla is the name of Arian's pet."

Orla bowed.

General Varal started to laugh. Then he remembered the myth about the first born of the Priesat. Could it be true? This man was both man and beast? His grip tightened on Arian at the thought.

CHAPTER THIRTY-TWO

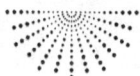

"R elease Arian."

　　"Or what?" asked Varal.

"I will kill you with my bare hands." Orla stepped closer, so that Varal could finally see his face.

Arian felt the general suck air into his lungs when he saw him.

"You."

"Yes. I have been told that I look like my father," said Orla. He took a few steps closer. "And you have a death grip on my mate. Release her."

He tightened his grip as an answer.

Arian found breathing hard. She tugged on his arm, hoping to loosen his grip.

"I see." Orla smiled as he crossed his arms over his massive chest. "You're afraid."

"I fear no one," growled Varal.

"Then why are you hiding behind her? She can't protect you from a sniper who aims at your head."

Varal jerked her around with him as he scanned the area.

"If you are a man, then prove it. Fight me. If you can kill me then you can leave here."

"And if I don't?"

Arian felt the death grip the general had on her lessen. Allowing sweet fresh air to fill her lungs again.

"Then you're mine."

"I want more." Varal paused. "If I win, I get you both. Arian as my wife and you as my slave. You will do everything I ask, without hesitation."

"No." Arian fought against Varal, causing the knife to draw blood. She knew what he meant. He would force Orla to watch as Varal took her.

"Arian, you lack the faith that I'll win?"

She closed her eyes for a few securs. He was right, her faith was what he needed, and she would give him more. Arian looked up into his eyes. "I love you, and have complete faith that you will win, but I can't stop my heart from wanting to keep you from harm."

"Oh, how sweet." Sarcasm dripping from Varal's words. "What weapons will we use."

"No weapons." Arian pulled on the general's arm and found herself free of his grip. She turned to face him. "This battle will be based on brute strength."

"A battle to the death?" Varal glared at Orla, totally ignoring Arian.

"Yes." Orla gave the general a feral smile.

This wasn't what Arian wanted. She hoped keeping them from using weapons would keep them both alive. The general must come to trial, and Orla must live.

The fire in Orla's eyes frightened her. He wanted to exact vengeance on this man from the beginning, but never said a word. Their bond let her know exactly what his thoughts were. Weapons would remove the joy of watching the general fight for his life and lose.

They started circling each other, trying to maneuver for control.

Arian's heart climbed up in her throat. The wild look in Varal's eyes let her know he wanted to do bodily harm to Orla. He wanted to kill her mate with his bare hands. She felt her heart stop when General Varal attacked first, griping Orla in a Draman neck hold, designed to block the breathing passage of any species.

She breathed a sigh of relief when Orla shook him off easily. But felt the air in her lungs freeze when he grabbed the general in a bear hug.

Varal tried to reach behind him to get a grip on Orla. Although he didn't get a good hold on Orla, Varal did manage to slice his face up with his finger nails. A loud growl filled the air and Orla crushed his ribs, forcing air out of Varal's lungs. General Varal slipped through his hold, knocking Orla off his feet.

"I'm going to enjoy killing you, Orla. If it hadn't been for you, Arian would have been mine long ago." Varal dropped one knee into Orla's stomach.

Arian felt the pain that shot through Orla's body.

Varal tried to move in for the kill, but Orla was too fast, quickly rolling out of harm's way.

"You're wrong, Varal. Arian did all of this on her own. I only supported her decisions. You remember the attack to free my brother?"

Varal's face showed his shock at Orla's words.

"Come now. You had all the pieces of the puzzle. Are you telling me that you never put it together?" Orla gave him a superior smile. "I am the oldest of twins. My brother is not the true heir to my father's throne. I am."

"How? No one spoke of you." Varal started to move around Orla.

"You didn't ask the right questions." Orla moved with Varal, never letting out of his sight. "But we digress. Arian has been the force behind everything we have done. She is the one who planned to free my brother. She is also the one who told us how to infiltrate the palace, take over the communication device, and disrupt your transmission. And she is the one who planned this coup. She is the one who has defeated you, not me."

"This is only a minor setback. Once you're dead everything will go forward as I have originally planned." Varal started to circle around again.

"You think you can control Arian?" Orla laughed. He continued to move with Varal, facing him at all times.

Arian kept her gaze on the general, watching his every move. She knew, sooner or later Varal would try to cheat. When he did, she would be ready for him.

Varal growled and lunged at Orla, only to find himself flat on his face.

"Is that all you know, General? Brute strength? Where's your cunning?"

In a crouching position, he spun on his heel to face Orla, and glaring at him with such hatred that Arian shuddered. She almost missed the general slipping his hand into his boot, but a glimmer of light on metal caught her eye. Damn, he had a concealed weapon.

She wanted to kick herself. Why didn't she demand that he be checked for weapons before they started to fight? This poor judgement could cost Orla his life.

Not if Arian had anything to do with it. She closed her eyes and focused her mind and her powers. She'd make sure Varal wouldn't use the weapon as he planned. Now what was it Varal was afraid of?

Varal grinned as he grasped the warm metal resting in his boot. Tired of the games, he wanted to show this alien who was in control. Ever so slowly, he slid the small blaster up his pant leg. Alerting this Orla, if that was his real name, to what he planned could ruin everything. As he slid it up over his hip he smiled. In just a few microns Arian would be his. He swung the weapon up over his head, preparing to point it directly at Orla's heart. He glanced up and screamed.

One look was all it took.

Instead of the blaster he found his hand encased by a deadly vermarian worm.

"Get it off me," he screamed as he struggled with the creature. Varal tried prying it off, to no avail. The worm just tightened its hold. He dropped to the roof. Laying there, paralyzed as the worm slid up his arm to wrap itself around his throat. Its tiny mouth opened to reveal the large retractable fangs it hid in its head.

Varal knew if it bit him, he would be dead. His heart started to beat harder. Blood rushed through his ears. He felt white hot pinpricks of pain shooting up his arm to his heart.

The warmth of the fangs sinking into his neck was the last thing he felt before he fell into oblivion.

CHAPTER THIRTY-THREE

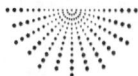

A rian watched with a satisfied smile as the general crumpled to the floor. Her flow of energy started to weaken as she relaxed her concentration on her creation. Slowly, it started to dissipate. The moment she felt the last bit of energy release itself she ran to Orla's side.

"Are you all right? I was so afraid that he'd hurt you." They latched onto each other as the rest of her men surround the general. Her hands couldn't keep still. She had to be sure that Orla was all right. Running them over his chest, arms and back she breathed a sigh of relief.

"I'm fine, Mistress. A little bruised, and sore, but unharmed." Orla ran his fingers through her hair. "And you? Did he hurt you?"

"No. Only frightened me." She buried her face in his shirt, allowing his scent to fill her, spreading a calm throughout her body.

"And what did you do to the general?" Orla nodded toward the men as they tried to wake the general.

"I knew he would cheat so I kept an eye on him. He pulled a blaster out of his boot, planning to shoot you with it. I altered it to look like a vermarian worm." She looked up at him, drinking in his presence, so happy that he was safe and alive.

"Your power was a sight to see. It looked so real. I truly thought that worm had snuck into Varal's boot and attacked him." Orla's forehead creased as he looked over her head toward where the general lay.

One of the men walked over to where they stood.

"He deserved it, trying to cheat like that. I remembered that he was afraid of anything that slithered. Hoping he would stop fighting to rid himself of the creature, and in the process, he'd throw away the blaster, I created the one thing that would scare him." Arian didn't pay attention to the man walking up to them. "I didn't expect him to faint, but he has a real strong fear of them."

"My Queen?"

Arian turned in Orla's arms and looked up. "Yes?"

"He's dead."

"Dead?" She felt her blood turn to ice. He couldn't be dead, because if he was dead that meant she killed him, and if she killed him, then she wasn't worthy of leading these people any more.

"Yes, Ma'am. We're going to take him to the med lab to find out what caused it."

She felt the color drain out of her face. The first time she had been proud of her ability and she ended up killing. She came close to telling them not to bother but held her tongue. She didn't know how to handle this and didn't want Orla to realize how much this bothered her until she could come to terms with it.

Her skills at keeping him out of her mind were still weak, but each dura they grew stronger. Arian hoped this time she'd block him out completely.

Silently, and continuing to keep her thoughts to herself, she followed everyone to the med lab. Even if their lives would be easier with the general's death, a tiny part of her hoped he still lived. She didn't want to be responsible for killing Varal, no matter how evil he was.

Time seemed to move slowly while she waited for her men to hook the general up to the monitors. She wished they would hurry up and tell her what she feared had happened.

Orla placed a quick kiss on her forehead, then stepped up to the medical bed. Not wanting to be noticed that much, she stood close to the door, away from everyone, as the men worked on Varal. If he died from fear, then she would know that she was the reason his heart stopped.

It didn't take very long for her to hear what she expected. General Varal died from heart failure.

Arian backed out of the room while everyone still hovered around Varal's body. She started walking down the corridor, her steps quickening until she was practically running. On the verge of tears, Arian wanted to reach her room as quickly as possible. The moment she closed the doors, she sagged against them in relief. Having a few securs alone should help clear her head, but it didn't.

All she could think of was the power she felt flow through her as she created that image. She felt proud of her creation. It was the best one she had ever made.

Obviously too well. It killed the man.

Rubbing her forehead, she started to pace. How did her power get so out of hand? Arian thought she had learned to control it. Grenta even commented on her ability to control and focus her power. Obviously, her pride got in the way and had her believing something that wasn't true.

One thing was for certain. She couldn't remain at the palace until she could control her power better, with true control would come humility. Something she must be missing to make such a grave error. Perhaps an isolated cave up in the mountains would work for her.

That was what she would do. Find some place away from everyone to practice and not come back until she could control it without fear of this happening again. Pulling a bag from her closet she started to fill it. Her mind wandering, she didn't pay attention to what she put in it but loaded it with whatever her hand happened to fall on.

She grabbed pillows, blankets, clothing, even a few toiletries, replaying the scene over and over in her head. Each time she remembered the moment she created the worm she knew she had to. Orla meant everything to her. There was nothing else her mind could come up with that she could have done without Orla coming to harm. Even if she had a chance to change history, she wouldn't be able to change anything. Her mind was so occupied, she didn't sense company until she felt someone's hand on her shoulders.

"Where are you going?"

Turning quickly, she moved backwards. She just about jumped out of her skin when she felt the hand on her shoulder. For a secur, she feared that Varal had just grabbed her shoulder. She didn't know if it was guilt that drove her, but somehow, she thought Varal had somehow cheated death and had come after her.

Short-lived relief washed over her. She turned and stared at Orla, knowing that now she'd have to explain to him that she was leaving.

Alone.

"You have packed your bags. Can I ask why?"

"Oh." Rubbing the shoulder Orla had touched, Arian glanced at her bag, as if she saw it for the first time. "I need more time to learn to control my powers. My plan is to go away for a while and work on that knowledge."

"But why are you doing this now?"

"What better time?" Arian couldn't look at Orla. "Varal has been stopped, and I'm not needed now."

"What are you talking about? Your people love you and will always need you."

"After all that has happened, how can they want and need me?" Arian still refused to look at Orla.

"You didn't kill him." He wanted to take her into his arms and give her the comfort she needed right now, but he maintained his distance. This was something Arian had to do on her own. "Mistress, he had a weak heart. According the information we found in his records the royal physician only gave him a luna to live. When Varal found out the truth, he had the doctor killed. He refused to believe his doctor."

"And it was my image that cause his weak heart to stop. If he hadn't been afraid, he might not have felt the stress that killed him."

"How do you know he wouldn't have had that heart attack anyway?" Orla placed his hands on her shoulders again. "You are blaming yourself for something you had no control over."

"It doesn't matter."

"Yes it does."

Arian turned from him, hoping he would leave her with her thoughts like he had done many times in the past. She'd use that time to escape.

"Come with me." Orla stepped close and took her hand.

"Why?" She tried to pull her hand away, but Orla's grip couldn't be broken.

"Have I ever led you down the wrong path?"

She shook her head and followed him mutely down the corridor. Curiosity got the best of her when she realized that they were headed for the palace doors.

Just before they reached them, the doors swung open. A loud cheer filled the air.

Orla turned and motioned for her to follow him out the massive doors.

What she found shocked her when she walked out on the steps. There before her stood a sea of people. So many, it went on forever. Arian glanced up at Orla.

"They've been arriving for the last hora or so." Orla spoke softly in her ear. "The moment the word went out that Varal was dead they started coming here."

Why?" Arian asked.

"To see their queen. The woman who single handedly stopped Varal. They love you, Mistress."

She looked out again. Seeing all her people with different eyes. No longer was she the innocent queen. Now she had a taste of what it was like to be in their shoes. Awe filled her as she looked at so many faces.

"Now, remember. One man died so all these people could live," Orla whispered in her ear.

She raised her hand, signaling that she wanted to speak. The people hushed quickly.

Taking a deep breath, she steadied her thoughts. "My people, I'm very happy to be standing here today on this joyous occasion. With your help, we have wrested the control back from General Varal."

A loud shout drowned her out.

Once again, she raised her arm, silencing the throng. "Varal taught us all a very important lesson. Having one leader can be very dangerous if that leader isn't thinking about the good of the people." She paused to let her words sink in. "So, as your queen I wish to make a decree that from this dura forth. There will be no more monarchy."

A loud murmur rushed through the ranks, reaching her ears quickly.

"Hear me out. As long as one person controls all of this planet we will always run the risk of this happening over and over again. As your queen

I can't allow that. I must think about what is best for you, and the best is to allow you to govern yourselves." She felt Orla's pride enter her mind.

"Tomorrow, I want the leaders of each village to come to the palace. We will begin to create a new government then." She stopped speaking, fighting the tears that threatened to spill down her cheeks.

"Once the new government is in place I will be stepping down as your queen." Without waiting for their response, she turned and headed toward the doors.

Like a whisper against her neck, she heard her name being lifted on the wind. Slowly, the chant grew in intensity, becoming so loud that she couldn't hear herself think. She turned back toward her people. Humbled by their love.

Orla stepped up behind her and wrapped his arms around her. "I love you."

She turned in his arms. "I love you too."

"Do you truly want to give up all of this?" Orla cupped her chin and lifted her head until she looked him in the eye. "You have everything you could want here."

"I only want you. I want to go wherever you are, here, or at your home planet."

"You did this for me?"

"For the both of us. You are my destiny."

Orla hugged her close, so proud of how much she had grown as a person during this quest. She might be giving up the monarchy, but she'd always be his queen.

EPILOGUE

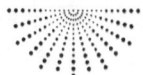

Once again, they stood on the platform waiting for a hovercraft, but this time Orla stood beside her in his human form. His arm wrapped tightly around her.

Grinnell stepped on to the platform to greet them. "The ship is ready when you are, My Queen."

"Grinnell, please don't use that title any more. I am no longer queen."

"Old habits die hard." He gave her a carefree smile.

"Are you sure you want to go with us?" asked Arian. "You are giving up an awful lot to go with us."

"Not that much."

"The new government offered you the leadership of the planet army," said Orla.

"I'm not ready to settle in one place. I like the other job they offered me instead." He gestured for them to walk with him. "I found out while I was on the run that I liked being out there. The thought of deep space exploration excites me. My new quest, once I take you and your family back home."

"Where is my father and brother?"

"Your brother has already been put in a holding cell, as you requested. Your father should be arriving momentarily."

"And Tymin, the Browlman, and Grenta, have they arrived yet?"

"No. But I have heard from all three. They are on their way." Grinnell pressed several buttons on a wrist ban.

Arian smiled as the doors of the ship opened. Once she set foot on that ship her life would change again, but this time she was in charge of her destiny. Her quest for freedom turned into a quest for love, something she found when she wasn't even looking for it.

She noticed the crowd parting quickly, like ripples from a small rock after it dropped below the surface of a lake. It only took a few moments before she knew what caused the people to move so quickly.

Actually, it was her nose that knew.

Orla chuckled when he saw her face crinkle up.

"I've tried very hard to get used to his smell. But there are still times then I just can't prepare myself quick enough." Arian looked up at the man she loved.

"If he and the Browlman are to stay with us. You will have to learn to live with the smell."

She looked out to where Tymin and the Browlman stood. "I promise to control my dislike better. Sooner or later I should become used to it, right?"

"Doubt it. I've known him a long time and have never gotten used to it. Just admit that, and you'll learn to ignore it."

Arian made a face. She didn't think she could ever get used to his smell.

Tymin and the Browlman walked up the steps. The Browlman hugged Orla then Arian.

"Being invited to serve you on your wedding dura brings joy to my heart."

Arian blushed. They decided to wait until they returned Orla's family back to his planet to marry. The Browlman and Grenta were the closest friends she had, and Arian asked them to stand in their wedding. The Browlman had been so touched by her gesture she spoke about it constantly.

Tymin must have sensed her unease because he hurried his wife inside.

Arian smiled. She looked out once again, looking for Grenta. It didn't take very long before she saw her. Her quiet unobtrusive style allowed her to slip through the crowd. Very few noticed her, but Arian found she could spot her easily. Grenta had explained to her that it was her Barou talent that recognized her. One master could always detect another.

"Have you spotted Grenta yet?" asked Orla.

"Yes." She pointed. "She's right over there."

Orla leaned against her as he strained to see her.

A few microns later Grenta stood before them.

"You saw me?"

"Yes."

She smiled. "It will be nice to see my husband again."

"I'm glad we will get to see him soon," said Arian.

"He will be very happy to see you two marry."

"And you? Will you go back to the Barou world and confront them? You have proved that you are a good trainer."

Grenta patted Arian's shoulder. "With you behind me, how can I fail?"

"You won't."

Grinnell stepped forward. "It is time to go."

They nodded as they entered the ship. For some, the quest was finished, but for others, it had just started.

Don't miss out on your next favorite book!

Join the Satin Romance mailing list
www.satinromance.com/mail.html

THANK YOU FOR READING

Did you enjoy this book?

We invite you to leave a review at your favorite book site, such as Goodreads, Amazon, Barnes & Noble, etc.

DID YOU KNOW THAT LEAVING A REVIEW...

- Helps other readers find books they may enjoy.
- Gives you a chance to let your voice be heard.
- Gives authors recognition for their hard work.
- Doesn't have to be long. A sentence or two about why you liked the book will do.

ABOUT THE AUTHOR

Writing for Barbara Donlon Bradley started innocently enough, like most she kept diaries, journals, and wrote an occasional letter but she also had a vivid imagination and wrote scenes and short stories adding characters to her favorite shows and comic books. As time went on she found the passion for writing to be a strong drive for her. Humor is also very strong in her life. No matter how hard she tries to write something deep and dark, it will never happen. That humor bleeds into her writing. Since she can't beat it she has learned to use it to her advantage.

www.barbaradonlonbradley.com

Also Available

Love Is…
A Portrait in Time
Love on the Run
A Quest For Love

www.ingramcontent.com/pod-product-compliance
Lightning Source LLC
Chambersburg PA
CBHW050459260626
47157CB00004B/1111